I0632877

Home At Last

Judith Keim

BOOKS BY JUDITH KEIM

THE HARTWELL WOMEN SERIES:

The Talking Tree – 1
Sweet Talk – 2
Straight Talk – 3
Baby Talk – 4
The Hartwell Women – Boxed Set

THE BEACH HOUSE HOTEL SERIES:

Breakfast at The Beach House Hotel – 1
Lunch at The Beach House Hotel – 2
Dinner at The Beach House Hotel – 3
Christmas at The Beach House Hotel – 4
Margaritas at The Beach House Hotel – 5 (2021)
Dessert at The Beach House Hotel – 6 (2022)

THE FAT FRIDAYS GROUP:

Fat Fridays – 1
Sassy Saturdays – 2
Secret Sundays – 3

SALTY KEY INN BOOKS:

Finding Me – 1
Finding My Way – 2
Finding Love – 3
Finding Family – 4

CHANDLER HILL INN BOOKS:

Going Home – 1
Coming Home – 2
Home at Last – 3

SEASHELL COTTAGE BOOKS:

    A Christmas Star
    Change of Heart
    A Summer of Surprises
    A Road Trip to Remember
    The Beach Babes – (2022)

DESERT SAGE INN BOOKS:

    The Desert Flowers – Rose – 1
    The Desert Flowers – Lily – 2 (Fall 2021)
    The Desert Flowers – Willow – 3 (2022)
    The Desert Flowers – Mistletoe & Holly – 4 (2022)

Winning BIG – a little love story for all ages

For more information: **http://amzn.to/2jamIaF**

PRAISE FOR JUDITH KEIM'S NOVELS

THE BEACH HOUSE HOTEL SERIES

"Love the characters in this series. This series was my first introduction to Judith Keim. She is now one of my favorites. Looking forward to reading more of her books."

BREAKFAST AT THE BEACH HOUSE HOTEL is an easy, delightful read that offers romance, family relationships, and strong women learning to be stronger. Real life situations filter through the pages. Enjoy!"

LUNCH AT THE BEACH HOUSE HOTEL – "This series is such a joy to read. You feel you are actually living with them. Can't wait to read the latest one."

DINNER AT THE BEACH HOUSE HOTEL – "A Terrific Read! As usual, Judith Keim did it again. Enjoyed immensely. Continue writing such pleasantly reading books for all of us readers."

CHRISTMAS AT THE BEACH HOUSE HOTEL – "Not Just Another Christmas Novel. This is book number four in the series and my introduction to Judith Keim's writing. I wasn't disappointed. The characters are dimensional and engaging. The plot is well crafted and advances at a pleasing pace. The Florida location is interesting and warming. It was a delight to read a romance novel with mature female protagonists. Ann and Rhoda have life experiences that enrich the story. It's a clever book about friends and extended family. Buy copies for your book group pals and enjoy this seasonal read."

THE HARTWELL WOMEN SERIES – Books 1 – 4
"This was an EXCELLENT series. When I discovered Judith Keim, I read all of her books back to back. I thoroughly enjoyed the women Keim has written about. They are believable and you want to just jump into their lives and be their friends! I can't wait for any upcoming books!"

"I fell into Judith Keim's Hartwell Women series and have read & enjoyed all of her books in every series. Each centers around a strong & interesting woman character and their family interaction. Good reads that leave you wanting more."

THE FAT FRIDAYS GROUP – Books 1 – 3
"Excellent story line for each character, and an insightful representation of situations which deal with some of the contemporary issues women are faced with today."

"I love this author's books. Her characters and their lives are realistic. The power of women's friendships is a common and beautiful theme that is threaded throughout this story."

THE SALTY KEY INN SERIES
FINDING ME – *"I thoroughly enjoyed the first book in this series and cannot wait for the others! The characters are endearing with the same struggles we all encounter. The setting makes me feel like I am a guest at The Salty Key Inn...relaxed, happy & light-hearted! The men are yummy and the women strong. You can't get better than that! Happy Reading!"*

FINDING MY WAY- *"Loved the family dynamics as well as uncertain emotions of dating and falling in love.*

Appreciated the morals and strength of parenting throughout. Just couldn't put this book down."

FINDING LOVE – *"I waited for this book because the first two was such good reads. This one didn't disappoint.... Judith Keim always puts substance into her books. This book was no different, I learned about PTSD, accepting oneself, there is always going to be problems but stick it out and make it work. Just the way life is. In some ways a lot like my life. Judith is right, it needs another book and I will definitely be reading it. Hope you choose to read this series, you will get so much out of it."*

FINDING FAMILY – *"Completing this series is like eating the last chip. Love Judith's writing, and her female characters are always smart, strong, vulnerable to life and love experiences."*

"This was a refreshing book. Bringing the heart and soul of the family to us."

CHANDLER HILL INN SERIES

GOING HOME – *"I absolutely could not put this book down. Started at night and read late into the middle of the night. As a child of the '60s, the Vietnam war was front and center so this resonated with me. All the characters in the book were so well developed that the reader felt like they were friends of the family."*

"I was completely immersed in this book, with the beautiful descriptive writing, and the authors' way of bringing her characters to life. I felt like I was right inside her story."

<u>COMING HOME</u> – "*Coming Home is a winner. The characters are well-developed, nuanced and likable. Enjoyed the vineyard setting, learning about wine growing and seeing the challenges Cami faces in running and growing a business. I look forward to the next book in this series!*"

"*Coming Home was such a wonderful story. The author has a gift for getting the reader right to the heart of things.*"

<u>HOME AT LAST</u> – "*In this wonderful conclusion, to a heartfelt and emotional trilogy set in Oregon's stunning wine country, Judith Keim has tied up the Chandler Hill series with the perfect bow.*"

"*Overall, this is truly a wonderful addition to the Chandler Hill Inn series. Judith Keim definitely knows how to perfectly weave together a beautiful and heartfelt story.*"

"*The storyline has some beautiful scenes along with family drama. Judith Keim has created characters with interactions that are believable and some of the subjects the story deals with are poignant.*"

SEASHELL COTTAGE BOOKS
<u>A CHRISTMAS STAR</u> – "*Love, laughter, sadness, great food, and hope for the future, all in one book. It doesn't get any better than this stunning read.*"

"*A Christmas Star is a heartwarming Christmas story featuring endearing characters. So many Christmas books are set in snowbound places...it was a nice change to read a Christmas story that takes place on a warm sandy beach!*" Susan Peterson

CHANGE OF HEART – *"CHANGE OF HEART is the summer read we've all been waiting for. Judith Keim is a master at creating fascinating characters that are simply irresistible. Her stories leave you with a big smile on your face and a heart bursting with love."*
~Kellie Coates Gilbert, author of the popular Sun Valley Series

A SUMMER OF SURPRISES – *"The story is filled with a roller coaster of emotions and self-discovery. Finding love again and rebuilding family relationships."*

"Ms. Keim uses this book as an amazing platform to show that with hard emotional work, belief in yourself and love, the scars of abuse can be conquered. It in no way preaches, it's a lovely story with a happy ending."

"The character development was excellent. I felt I knew these people my whole life. The story development was very well thought out I was drawn [in] from the beginning."

DESERT SAGE INN BOOKS
THE DESERT FLOWERS – ROSE – *"The Desert Flowers - Rose, is the first book in the new series by Judith Keim. I always look forward to new books by Judith Keim, and this one is definitely a wonderful way to begin The Desert Sage Inn Series!"*

"In this first of a series, we see each woman come into her own and view new beginnings even as they must take this tearful journey as they slowly lose a dear friend. This is a very well written book with well-developed and likable main characters. It was interesting and enlightening as the first

portion of this saga unfolded. I very much enjoyed this book and I do recommend it"

"Judith Keim is one of those authors that you can always depend on to give you a great story with fantastic characters. I'm excited to know that she is writing a new series and after reading book 1 in the series, I can't wait to read the rest of the books."!

Home At Last

A Chandler Hill Inn Book - 3

Judith Keim

Wild Quail Publishing

Home at Last is a work of fiction. Names, characters, places, public or private institutions, corporations, towns, and incidents are the product of the author's imagination or are used fictitiously. Any resemblance to actual events, locales, or persons, living or dead, is coincidental.

No part of this book may be reproduced or transmitted in any form or by any electronic or mechanical means, including information storage and retrieval systems, without permission in writing from the author, except by a reviewer who may quote brief passages in a review. This book may not be resold or uploaded for distribution to others. For permissions contact the author directly via electronic mail:

wildquail.pub@gmail.com

www.judithkeim.com,

Published in the United States of America by:

Wild Quail Publishing
PO Box 171332
Boise, ID 83717-1332

ISBN# 978-1-7327494-0-5
Copyright ©2020 Judith Keim
All rights reserved

Dedication

This book is dedicated to friends and family who give me a home of my heart.

CHAPTER ONE

Louise "Lulu" Kingsley sat on the deck of Camilla Chandler's home and wondered how she could be so lucky to live in a place like the Willamette Valley, Oregon. The journey to reach this point had been more than painful—it had almost destroyed her. But, here at Chandler Hill, she felt she might have found her true home at last.

Staring out at the rolling hills and the rows of grapevines devoid of their fruit after the harvest, she saw the goodness of the land, its beauty, and, most of all, the comforting prospect of more harvests to come. She thought of this continuity of life as a renewal of her own.

If Cami hadn't offered her a place to stay and a job in a new location, Lulu wasn't sure she could have survived the last year of family scandal and misfortune. For anyone who didn't know much about her, they'd think her life was a privileged, easy one as the daughter of a rich, powerful man who'd one day wanted to run for president of the United States. But the man who tied her to her newly discovered half-sister was a man of too many appetites, and his actions had hurt others, including her fragile mother and her.

The understanding shown by the half-sister she'd never known growing up meant the world to her. Cami came from a long line of kind, generous Chandler and Lopez families. Living and working at the Chandler Hill Inn and Winery was more than an ordinary existence. For Lulu, it meant finding a loving place in the world, one she'd desperately needed.

"I thought I'd find you here," said Cami, stepping onto the

deck and standing behind her. "I love to sit here and gaze out at the land. It's very peaceful toward the end of the day and, as always, I think of Nonnee. My grandmother's love of the land was the foundation for everything that's been done here with both the inn and the winery."

Lulu turned around in her rocking chair and smiled up at Cami. Not much older than she, Cami's big heart matched her usual smile. Though Cami wasn't as tall as Lulu and had totally opposite coloring, their facial features were astonishingly alike. Among other things, they shared a tiny quirk—misshapen earlobes, a genetic inheritance from their father. Lulu wished she had strawberry-blond curls like Cami and her grandmother, Lettie Chandler, but Lulu's hair was straight and dark.

Cami took a seat in a chair next to her. "Gwen is very pleased to have you assist her at The Barn. I explained it was only temporary, that you'd agreed to handle our marketing program. But with the holiday season not that far away, I understand both she and I will need your help until after the New Year."

"I love being part of the staff," said Lulu, meaning it.

Cami gave her a tender smile. "Sweetie, you're much more than one of the staff; you're family. We intend to use your marketing and sales skills here at the inn and the other two wineries now associated with Chandler Hill."

A warmth filled Lulu. Being part of a real, healthy family was such a gift. An only child after the death of her younger brother, Teddy, at the age of ten, she'd always longed for siblings. Cami's grandfather, Rafe, was a wonderful man who'd been very kind to her. They'd formed a bond over the fact that her father and Autumn Chandler, Lettie and Rafe's daughter, had met and fallen in love, producing Cami. The rest of Cami's family consisted of people who weren't related by blood, but were still a close-knit group.

Cami nudged Lulu's arm playfully. "By the way, I think Miguel was disappointed you weren't at the strategy meeting today."

Heat flooded Lulu's cheeks. Miguel Lopez was one of the most handsome men she'd ever seen. Like his great-uncle, Rafe, he had hair so dark and shiny it resembled the wings of a blackbird or the smooth coat of a panther. She couldn't decide which. His straight nose, dark, intelligent eyes, and full, kissable lips had every young woman in the valley swooning in the wake of his sexy butt. Those were the very reasons Lulu had no intention of ever getting involved with him. His easy ability to attract others reminded her too much of her father.

"How did the meeting go?" Lulu asked. "Are the three different vineyards able to establish a joint purchasing program for supplies, advertising, and other services?" Chandler Hill, Taunton Estates, and Lone Creek Winery were all part of a group set up under one umbrella for financial purposes. Cami's fiancé, Drew Farley, along with Dan Thurston, Adam Kurey, and Miguel, had formed a partnership to buy the Lone Creek Winery after a fire had destroyed sections of vines in its acreage.

"We're ironing out details to combine some of the operations, but yes, it's moving forward. With you about to begin handling the marketing for all three, it simplifies those matters." Cami grinned at her. "So glad you're here."

The sound of someone approaching sent Sophie, Cami's black-and-tan miniature dachshund into motion. She barked and ran to greet Rafe.

"Hi, come join us," said Cami. She rose and pulled a chair over for Rafe. "The sun will be setting soon, but it's still pleasant outside for this time of year. In fact, I was thinking of staying here for a while and tasting a new pinot noir release from Taunton Estates." Her eyes sparkled as she teased him. "You, as owner, might want to judge it for yourself."

Rafe laughed. "I think I should, especially if it means I get to spend time with my two favorite women." His gaze swept over them, bringing a smile to all three.

It was this kind of banter that Lulu loved most. Rafe was such a decent person. In his seventies, he was a quiet man who lived and loved and worked hard. He still mourned Lettie Chandler, who'd passed away over a year and a half ago. She had been and still was the love of Rafe's life. Lulu was grateful to have this wonderful man part of her life, especially after the scandal involving her father.

Cami went to get the wine and glasses, leaving Lulu and Rafe alone.

Rafe said, "It used to be that things got quiet after the harvest and all the hoopla that went with it. But the Chandler Hill Inn with its spa and special vacation and bridal packages have kept business going throughout these months. Christmas, the New Year, and Valentine's Day are big deals here now."

"I can't wait for the Christmas celebration," Lulu said, giving him a smile. "I hope to convince my mother to make the trip here. I think it would be good for her."

Cami overheard them as she stepped onto the deck, set the tray down, and poured the wine into the three glasses. "How's your mother doing?"

Lulu couldn't hide the sadness in her voice. "With her, I never know for certain. Her depression comes and goes, becoming more of a merry-go-round when she sneaks drugs or alcohol. I've talked to the doctors about it. They try to discuss newer options, medicines, and therapies. Heaven knows, she's tried a lot of programs, but nothing seems to work. My counselor has advised me that aside from encouragement, there's not much I can do."

"That's sad," said Cami, setting the wine bottle down on the table and handing the glasses of wine to Lulu and Rafe.

"I'm learning that it's not my job to keep her spirits up and help her stay sober," Lulu continued. "My father used to tell me, 'Take care of your mother.' when he went away. Our lives changed dramatically when my brother drowned, and she became suicidal. Nothing's been the same since." She hated the tremor in her voice.

Cami rose and wrapped her arms around Lulu. "I'm sorry. That's too much for a young girl to handle."

Lulu paused a moment to pull herself together. It felt unfamiliar to accept this sign of acknowledgement. *If I'd only been there when Teddy decided to go swimming alone at the beach.*

Rafe broke into her musing about the guilt she carried and always would. "Okay, ladies! Let's taste this wine. I hope it's as good as my new marketing director says." His words brought a smile to Lulu. She'd put a good spin on the product.

They'd just proclaimed the wine excellent when Drew arrived. Drew Farley was as nice a guy as he looked. His tawny-colored eyes matched his hair, which was what she would call the color of butterscotch. He kissed Cami hello and sank into one of the chairs on the deck with a soft groan. "Ah, it's good to be home. I've been working with Dan on the last bit of cleanup and updating of the house at Lone Creek. He and Becca expect to move in next week."

"I'm happy for them," said Lulu. "I know how excited Becca is to have a house of her own. After having her for my assistant, I'm glad she'll be settled here and can continue to work for me."

"Yes, it's a fair deal all around," Drew said. "We're lucky the fire at the vineyard didn't do any significant damage to the house, and they have a place to live on the property for free in exchange for taking care of it." He accepted the glass Cami handed him, swirled it in the glass, sniffed it, and then took a sip. "What do you think? Is this as good as I thought it might be as one of Taunton Estates' best?"

"It's a lovely wine with a nice, fruity bouquet and a smooth finish." Cami grinned at him. "I can't wait to get more involved in Chandler Hill wines. Then I'll really test your work."

Rafe laughed. "I knew it was a good idea to put these two up against one another. Both Taunton Estates and Chandler Hill wines are already great, but I suspect they'll be even better with Cami and Drew competing."

Lulu laughed with the others.

Drew turned to her. "We're going to have a big party to celebrate Becca and Dan's move into Rod Mitchell's old house. Miguel told me to tell you to be sure to come."

Lulu rolled her eyes. "I'll be there. Becca already invited me. She has a teacher friend she wants me to meet."

"You mean Ross Coughlin?" said Cami. "He seems very nice. He's easy on the eyes too." She laughed when Drew arched his eyebrows at her. "Don't worry. You're very easy on my eyes."

"Is this Ross Coughlin the young man who started the after-school program at the elementary school?" asked Rafe.

"Yes, that's what I've been told," said Cami.

"In the spring, I'd like to be able to volunteer there on my time off," said Lulu. "I enjoy being with the kids."

"You're great with the kids who come to the inn," said Cami. "I admire that."

"Thanks." Lulu hadn't told anyone this, but working with the kids at her old job at a school had made her feel as if she was making amends for the time she hadn't been there to prevent her brother's drowning. She'd talked to a psychologist about it and knew it wasn't her fault, but she always felt better after being with other kids who needed her attention.

As for herself, she wasn't sure she wanted children of her own, not when it required making sure they were safe from all the dangers of the world.

Lulu was sitting in her office at the inn going over additions to the website when Becca knocked on her door.

Short and round, bubbly, and with no pretensions, Becca had green eyes that sparkled with a sense of fun that was contagious. She was someone with whom Lulu had easily made friends. They both understood how lucky they were to be a part of Chandler Hill Inn's executive staff.

The inn, started in the late seventies by Lettie, had grown into an exclusive, upscale, full-service inn with thirty guest rooms, a well-known dining room, a spa, a swimming pool, an all-purpose functions building called Chandler Hall, and a gift shop, The Barn. Not as simple as the name sounded, The Barn contained a busy retail area full of unique gifts and a wine-tasting room on the second floor, where people could sit and taste a variety of Chandler Hill wines and sample appetizers served throughout the day. Members of the Chandler Hill Wine Club often arrived toward the end of the day to sip wine and catch up with one another.

"How's it going?" Becca asked Lulu. "Has the wedding information online been updated to showcase our holiday themes?"

Lulu nodded and grinned. "It almost makes me want to get married."

"I can hardly wait for my wedding. We've been thinking of a winter wedding, but now we're not sure, with Dan buying into the Lone Creek Winery and working hard to make it profitable. I've picked out a few wedding dresses that will be suitable any time of year. I've narrowed it down to two, but when the time gets closer, you and Cami will have to help me decide."

"I'd be honored to help," said Lulu sincerely. There'd been a time when she had been too busy dealing with her father's upcoming run for president to think about meeting with friends to discuss such things as wedding dresses. Now that her world had fallen apart with his sudden death, she realized how self-centered she'd been. She hoped her welcome into the Chandler-Lopez family would change all that.

"Dan just called. He and Drew are taking Cami and me to Nick's. Want to come along?"

"No, thanks. That would make it an odd number for dinner."

Becca shook her head and sighed. "We knew you'd say that, so we already invited Miguel too. What do you say?"

Lulu groaned at their attempt to pair her up with Miguel. "You know I don't have any interest in him."

"Exactly," said Becca. "It'll be good for him to be with someone like you. I swear all he does is smile at a woman, and she falls in love with him. Now that he's a part owner of Lone Creek Winery, women think he's rich, and the situation has gotten worse. It's ridiculous, of course, because what money any of us has is being put back into the winery, and we don't expect any significant profit from it for a couple of years."

Lulu laughed at the mental picture Becca had drawn for her. She'd skipped lunch, and going out to dinner sounded easy. "Okay, I'm in, but it's nothing more than a dinner date. At this stage of my life, I have to concentrate on healing myself and helping my mother. I don't have the time or energy to fuss over a guy who's too popular for his own good."

"Sounds like a plan to me," said Becca beaming at her. "When I met you last spring at Justine Devon's wedding, I had no idea we'd become this close. You seemed so sure of yourself and very sophisticated. I'm beginning to see the real person you are underneath all that notoriety."

"And?" Lulu held her breath. Becca's answer was so important to her. Back then, she'd been scared that the rumors circulating about her father were true.

"And I like what I see," said Becca. "Cami does too. That means a lot to me."

"Who could ask for a better sister? Everyone says Cami's like her grandmother. Knowing how much Rafe still loves her, I have to believe Lettie must have been a fabulous woman."

"Oh, yes, and Rafe is a wonderful man." Becca got to her feet. "See you around seven o'clock. We're all meeting at Nick's."

Lulu decided to drive herself to Nick's. Italian food was her favorite, and in this area, Nick's was the place to go for it. She liked being independent. If things didn't go well at the restaurant, she'd have no problem leaving.

Nick's small storefront belied the space behind it. Even on a weekday in the fall, delicious aromas, customers, and pleasant conversation filled the restaurant as she stepped through the entrance.

From the back of the restaurant, Becca waved to her. Lulu hurried over to the table, relieved Miguel hadn't arrived yet. Cami had told her he'd be a little late. Drew got to his feet as she approached and helped her into a chair next to him. It appeared Miguel would be seated on the other side of her.

Dan greeted her and asked, "What would you like to drink?"

"Whatever you all are having. In this crowd, I know it's going to be something good."

Drew signaled the waitress. "Cami tells me you're developing quite a palate for wine. Maybe I'll put it to good use on the grapes I want to use for Lettie's Creek Wine. By the way, have you seen the label Cami designed for it?"

When she shook her head, he picked up his phone, scrolled through photos, and turned the phone over to her.

Lulu studied the photograph of a mockup for a label and grinned. "Hummingbirds. I love it."

Cami beamed at her. "I thought it was appropriate. Nonnee loved hummingbirds. And they seemed to love her too. In fact, I thought the design would be good to use on T-shirts to sell at The Barn. What do you think?"

"Great idea, huh?" said Becca.

"Yes. I like it a lot," Lulu replied. "Maybe we could use it for our website too."

"Okay, okay. Enough 'shop talk.' This is a date night, remember?" said Dan growling playfully. A teddy bear of a man with brown, curly hair, blue eyes, and an easy disposition, he was someone Lulu thought was perfect for Becca.

Smiling, Miguel approached them. "Hi, everyone," he said and slid into the empty chair next to Lulu. "Sorry I'm late. I had to fix another leak at the farmhouse."

Drew frowned at Miguel. "Now that Rod's old house at Lone Creek is ready, maybe the group can help Rafe fix up the farmhouse at Taunton Estates. You'll want to live there with a family someday."

Miguel held up his hands. "I don't know about that, but it would be a good investment to fix it up because the bones of that house are nice. It just needs to be updated."

Rafe's youngest sister, Rose, came over to the table. "Are

you ready to order?"

"Hi, Aunt Rose," said Cami. 'I'm going to go with the special. I love cod and the way you fix it here."

Rose looked at Lulu. "And you?"

"The same. I'm hungry for seafood."

Becca chose the game hen, and all three men chose the steak.

As they waited for their meal, they dipped fresh, hard-crusted bread into seasoned olive oil and continued their conversation about the happenings at all three wineries. Listening to them, Lulu envied the opportunity each of them had to do something meaningful with their lives. After being forced abruptly to abandon her plans, she was still wondering about her future, even as she'd agreed to help them with the marketing of their properties.

Lulu was startled out of her thoughts by seeing a male figure stomping across the room toward them, his face red, his eyes narrowed. It took a moment before she realized he was heading right to her.

"Hey, aren't you that daughter of Congressman Kingsley? He's what's wrong with America today, that lying piece of scum."

Lulu felt the blood leave her face and gripped the table, searching for words. "I don't know what you're talking about." She gave Cami a helpless look.

"This woman is not who you're looking for," said Cami firmly.

The man narrowed his eyes and studied Cami. "Yeah? What's her name?"

"Weezie Lopez," Cami answered smoothly, bringing looks of surprise to the others sitting with her.

Miguel got to his feet. Drew and Dan followed suit.

"You'd better leave now," said Miguel, signaling Rose. As

she approached, Miguel said, "This man is leaving. I'm walking him out now. I'll take care of his bill."

Rose gave the man a wary look and turned back to Miguel. "No need. He's already paid."

As Miguel walked away with the stranger, Lulu got out of her seat and rushed into the ladies' room.

In the privacy of the room, she burst into tears. She heard the door open and knew who it was before she turned to face Cami.

"Are you all right?" Cami asked, looking worried.

Lulu shook her head. "I'm so tired of being blamed for things my father may or may not have done. Why can't everyone leave me alone?"

Cami's arms came around her. "Some people love to hang onto angry, no matter how false something might be. They're frustrated with their lives, unhappy about many things, and love to lash out at people they don't even know."

"Well, I'm sick and tired of it," said Lulu, wanting to throw herself down on the floor kicking and screaming like a two-year-old. She took a wet paper towel and dabbed at her eyes. "I'll be fine. Go ahead and get back to the others. I don't want to disturb our dinner. The entrées must be ready."

Lulu made sure her mascara hadn't run, planted a smile on her face, and headed out to the others. She'd had a lot of practice acting as if she was all right when she wasn't at all.

As Lulu found her seat at the table, Becca winked at her. "Hi, Weezie Lopez! I love your name!"

Lulu couldn't help laughing.

"It just popped out of my mouth," said Cami amid their laughter.

Miguel turned to her. "Are you all right?"

His look of concern was touching. Trying to be upbeat, she said, "I will be."

"Fair enough," said Dan. "Let's enjoy our meal. Here it comes!"

As Lulu sat with the others she thought of her father. At the time of his death, he had been accused by several women of sexual assault, and he was attempting to defend himself against these allegations. Theirs had never been a happy family, especially after the death of her brother. Now, she and Cami knew that her father had always loved Cami's mother, not Lulu's mother—the woman he'd married for political gain.

"Let's go down to the Green Grape for dancing and a little fun," said Becca as they finished their meal. "It's been a while since we've all been there."

Cami glanced at Lulu. "Okay?"

"Yes," she answered, eager to put the bad incident behind her.

CHAPTER TWO

The Green Grape was a bar in a quiet spot one block away from the main street. It was a favorite of the locals because the stream of visitors from elsewhere often didn't know it was there. The inside walls of an old brick building once used for storage had been ripped out, opening a space large enough to hold a bar at one end, a small stage, and plenty of room for tables, booths, and a dance floor. When local bands weren't playing, karaoke was offered.

When they arrived at the bar, they discovered a jazz group performing. Lulu was glad it wasn't a karaoke night. She couldn't sing worth a darn.

They found a table for six, and the guys went to the bar to get beers. Left alone, Cami and Becca turned to her.

"Are you okay?" Becca asked.

"Thanks, I'm feeling better. You understand why it's so upsetting. Right?"

Cami grinned, reached across the table, and squeezed her hand. "Yes, Weezie. We get it."

Lulu laughed. "Weezie Lopez does have a certain local ring to it, doesn't it?" She glanced at Miguel who was bringing a beer to her.

Miguel handed her a bottle and slid into the chair next to hers.

The soft music gave Lulu a sense of intimacy as he turned to her. "I know you and Cami are related, but what's the deal with your father?" he asked. "Why was that man so angry? Do you face this kind of crap all the time?"

"I try to stay out of the limelight as much as I can. Especially with my mother being so vulnerable. But sometimes a jerk will come along and try to harass me for being who I am. I'm not proud of what my father was accused of doing, but he did some good things to help people. I keep reminding myself of that."

Miguel sent her a thoughtful look. "I know what you mean. My father wasn't exactly the pride of the Lopez clan. Maybe that's why I work so hard to make sure I don't get into the same kind of trouble."

"What kind of trouble was that?"

A flush of embarrassment colored his cheeks. "Gambling. He used to take off for the old Indian Head Casino every chance he got. One night the people he owed money to found him and killed him. That was enough for me to vow never to be as reckless, as stupid as he was." Miguel stopped talking and gazed at her with widened eyes. "*Ay! Dio mio!* I don't tell that to many people."

"I don't think you can say anything that will shock me," said Lulu. "Between Hollywood and politics, it's all been done before."

"Wow!" Miguel said gazing into her eyes. "I'm sorry you've been so hurt." He held out his hand. "C'mon. They're playing a slow number. Let's join Cami and Drew on the dance floor."

Lulu hesitated a moment and then told herself to let go of the past and enjoy the present. Being in this funky bar in this small town was a long way from the kind of evening she used to spend attending large social affairs and mixing with wealthy donors.

When Miguel's arms came around her, she relaxed and swayed to the music with him. As she leaned against his solid chest, she told herself it was the adrenaline fading away, but she knew it was more than that. She felt ... safe with him. He'd protected her when she was frozen with fear.

Her mood was shattered by a high-pitched shriek in her ear.

"Miguel Lopez! How dare you leave me hanging? I called and called you. You were supposed to meet up with me tonight." The redhead who was scolding Miguel shoved Lulu aside and stood glaring at Miguel.

Miguel gave Lulu an apologetic look and turned to the irate woman. "I told you I might see you around sometime. I did not mention hooking up with you tonight."

"But I thought ..."

Lulu interrupted the conversation. "Look, Miguel, I've got to get back home anyway. You stay, and I'll see you around sometime." It wasn't a mistake that she was using his own words to the redhead. She'd hoped Miguel was different from what she'd initially thought, but he'd turned out to be a player, after all.

She heard him calling her name as she made her way through the crowd toward the exit. She waved to Cami and kept on going, glad she'd thought to drive her own car.

He caught up to her. "Hey, look! Don't leave. We're just getting to know one another and I like you."

Lulu shook her head. Bad memories of women flocking after her father tore at her insides. She didn't want to endure that kind of circumstance again. "Thanks. But I really do have to go." She told herself it was best if she just walked away, though she regretted the need to do so.

As Thanksgiving approached, Lulu found herself even busier helping out at The Barn. She was glad for it. Miguel had tried to call her, but she'd ignored each attempt.

Her workload grew. Online sales had grown tremendously,

and stock needed to be photographed for The Barn website featuring things for sale for Christmas. Even though the process was tedious, making sure the lighting was right to showcase each item was work Lulu liked. She was comfortable behind a camera. It was fun to make each creation look unique with just the perfect amount of light, the right angle.

While staff members worked to stock things for the catalog inventory and prepare for the onslaught of sales to come, she photographed and wrote sales copy for each. As she described the attractive set of red-wine glasses engraved with the Chandler Hill logo, Lulu thought of her father, who had always admired her ability to create slogans and news copy for his campaigns.

Her father had loved her the best he could. She knew that. But after meeting Rafe and becoming part of Chandler Hill, she now understood what honest, unselfish affection felt like. Rafe's attention to her, an "outlaw granddaughter," was genuine in a way that made her feel secure with him. There were no conditions, just acceptance.

"How are you coming?" Cami asked, swinging into her office.

Lulu looked up from her computer. "Just doing the last three gifts. Good idea to pair these glasses with printed cocktail napkins to match. It's the little touches that make it special."

"That, and the chocolate I've ordered from San Francisco to accompany the wine." Cami put a hand on Lulu's shoulder and bent over to read the blurb.

"Distinctive quality ready for you to enjoy."

"You're so good at this," Cami exclaimed. "Who knew I'd end up with such a talented sister."

Lulu and Cami exchanged smiles.

"Are you going to be ready to handle your first wedding this weekend as our candid photographer?" asked Cami. "Fall weddings here are so lovely."

Lulu nodded emphatically. "I'll be ready. I didn't realize when I signed up for the photography elective in college I'd end up using my skill like this. I love taking pictures of people. Maybe because I grew up meeting so many surrounding my father. They always fascinated me."

"I'm very grateful you'll give this a try. I think it's a great service to offer our brides. Photographing couples on their special occasions is another added feature to events here at the inn. We do so by offering links to videographers and professional portrait photographers. But this more informal approach is something we wanted to test with you. We can't always hire professional help for the brides, and sometimes they don't want it."

"Not a problem. I'm happy to help you any way I can." At first, Lulu hadn't understood that being an integral part of the inn and vineyard meant working 24/7, but she soon discovered that's what it meant for everyone, including Cami. The Chandler Hill crew was a good one.

"Laurel is planning on meeting with you tomorrow to go over the details of the wedding. I'll leave you two to handle it for a sweet, young couple from Idaho." Cami saluted her and left.

Lulu turned back to the screen for a last edit of the verbiage she'd put together.

Later, she was preparing to go back to Cami's house when her cell phone chimed. She checked caller ID. *Miguel Lopez.* Again. She let the call go into voice mail. She'd decided to have nothing to do with him.

Two days later, Lulu stood with Laurel Nelson in the lobby

waiting for the arrival of Sarah Pendleton and Lee Wing. She wanted to get a candid photograph of them arriving at the inn. Her forte was capturing spontaneous moments. A videographer had been hired to film the actual wedding ceremony.

A shiny black Range Rover promptly pulled up to the front of the inn as scheduled. Lulu adjusted her camera for a close-up of the couple as Sarah and Lee emerged from his SUV. A small woman with blond hair, Sarah stood beside a thin, handsome Asian man. Their eyes lit and smiles crossed their faces as they stared up at the inn crowning the hill like a tiara on a royal head.

Click! Click! Lulu stood at the entrance and captured the moment and then followed Laurel out the front door to greet them.

Laurel was the perfect person to oversee weddings. Attractive and refined, she exuded enthusiasm for each of her wedding projects. She'd been known to bring a smile to even a disgruntled bride's face.

"Welcome to the Chandler Hill Inn," Laurel said with a practiced smile. "I'm Laurel Nelson. I'll be handling your wedding details. And this is Louise Kingsley, your candid photographer. We're so happy you're here to celebrate your big day."

After handshakes all around, Laurel said, "We have your room ready."

"Thanks. The other two couples are coming directly from Boise and will arrive later today," said Sarah. "We came from Portland. We really appreciate your help with our last-minute plans for this evening."

"You have followed through with everything as we asked?" Lee asked. His dark eyes focused on Laurel, and Lulu had the impression he was used to having people do his bidding.

"Oh, yes," said Laurel. "It took us a while to find the proper music, but I think you'll be pleased."

Lee made a little bow. "Many thanks. I want this ceremony to be perfect for Sarah."

Sarah's face lit with pleasure. As she turned to him, *Click!* There was no mistaking their love for one another.

"We'll send someone out for your luggage," Laurel said. "Why don't you come in and register. Then, if you like, I can give you a quick tour. It isn't often that weddings are planned with no prior visits to the property. But nowadays, with online videos and reviews of the property, people have a pretty good idea what Chandler Hill Inn can offer."

Sarah smiled and, with a sweep of her arm, indicated their surroundings. "The minute I saw photos of it, I knew it would be perfect for us."

Laurel and Lulu led the bridal couple inside. After she snapped a few more photos, Lulu left them and went to Chandler Hall, the functions building. The main room was being sectioned off, and decorations were already being assembled in the small area by the fireplace for both the wedding ceremony and reception that would take place a little later.

Cynthia, from Fabulous Florals, was decorating with yellow and red chrysanthemums and lilies Sarah and Lee had requested. A red-linen tablecloth covered the round of six for the wedding party. A miniature bouquet sat at each place next to a crystal tea-light holder. The effect was stunning.

Lulu knew from reading information in the wedding folder that this was a small, private wedding to counter the disapproval of Lee's family. His father had picked out a bride for Lee among the families of his wealthy business associates. Bright and capable, Lee was willing to go against his family's old-fashioned wishes. And with money apparently no problem, he'd arranged a very lovely ceremony for the woman he loved.

The thought of such devotion to his bride drew a sigh from Lulu. She and one of her father's young supporters, Wilson Chambers, had enjoyed a mild flirtation, but that's as far as it had gone.

"What do you think?" said Cynthia, standing back to admire the effect of her work.

"It's gorgeous. Red and gold are important colors for this culture, and with the dull colors outside at this time of year, it's refreshing to see them."

"I can't wait to see what the bride will wear," said Cynthia. "Her online photo makes her seem like a tiny angel with blond hair and big blue eyes. You'll take plenty of photos, won't you?"

"Yes, I promise," Lulu said. With the way Sarah and Lee had gazed at one another, she was sure to get a lot of romantic shots.

As Lulu was leaving Chandler Hall, Laurel approached with Sarah and Lee. "You're going to love what's been done! See you later."

Lulu hurried off. One of the requirements of her job as a wedding photographer was to dress appropriately for each ceremony. She wanted to compliment the couple by wearing something extra nice. And she needed to make sure the photo albums she'd ordered had arrived at The Barn. In addition to photos on a disk, this couple had ordered actual photographs placed in an album.

Lulu walked into The Barn and stood a moment to admire the special fall and Thanksgiving offerings for sale. They would remain in place through Thanksgiving. The following day, the entire staff would cooperate to convert the décor of the interior to a winter wonderland of offerings. Lettie had always insisted the seasonal transition be handled this way, and Cami was keeping to that schedule. The Christmas catalog, however, was available at the store months ahead of time, building pre-orders.

Gwen Chapman, the manager, came over to her. "We received those photo albums you ordered. I'm hoping you'll get permission from a bridal couple to use their photos in one of them for display."

"Nice idea, but I don't think this is the right couple. Neither set of parents is happy about the wedding, which is why the wedding party consists of only the bridal couple, a matron of honor, a best man, and two others. But you should see Chandler Hall. Cynthia has done a great job of dressing up a small section of the room for this occasion."

"I understand that even though only six people will be in attendance, everything is going to be first class, including the meal Chef Darren is making for them," said Gwen. "It's too bad their families can't agree to put issues aside and allow the couple a special time. I've heard through the grapevine they are adorable together."

Lulu couldn't help the chuckle that escaped her. She'd learned early on there were no secrets in the hospitality business, that news among staff spread faster than wildfire. "They seem very much in love."

Assured everything was available for her first official presentation of a wedding album of photographs, Lulu went back to her office to check on things there before going home.

An email message had come in from the printer regarding a delay in adding the new offerings to the Christmas catalog. Someone had left a sticky note beside her computer telling of a telephone call from someone named Ross Coughlin. Lulu frowned at the name and then remembered he was Becca's teacher friend who was in charge of the after-school programs for the local elementary schools. He was someone she definitely wanted to meet.

She picked up her desk phone and punched in the number. A deep voice said, "Hello?"

Lulu, who was used to talking to strangers regarding her father's campaign, suddenly felt hesitant. "Hi, this is Lulu Kingsley returning your call. I'm a friend of Becca's, the substitute teacher ..." her voice trailed off.

"Oh, yeah, that's why I called. I thought maybe we could meet up sometime, maybe catch a quick cup of coffee together sometime. I want to ask you about some of the incentives the L.A. schools were using for their after-school programs. I need to come up with more ideas if I'm to keep the kids interested."

"I'm happy to share any information I have. Though I'm busy at the Chandler Hill Inn, I promise to make time for you."

"Great. How about coffee next week? I have some time then."

"I can manage that," said Lulu, wondering at the way her pulse was sprinting. It was just a voice. A very sexy voice.

"Okay, there's a great coffee shop downtown on the main street. I'll meet you there at two o'clock on Monday. Is that doable for you?"

"Yes, that's fine. Most of our weekend guests will be checked out by then."

After saying goodbye, Lulu hung up the phone, intrigued about the man behind the voice. She checked her watch and let out a gasp. She had to get moving in order to get the photos she wanted of the wedding party. The four of them were scheduled to arrive at four o'clock.

She hurried out of the inn to her car. Above her, the sky was clinging to the last strands of pink that threaded through the clouds, promising a good day tomorrow.

As she drove up the driveway to Cami's house, her heart

lifted. The house couldn't compare in size to the one in California she'd always called home, but it was the warmest, most welcoming place in which she'd ever lived.

She got out of the car and hurried inside, stopping to pet Sophie on the head. There was no question about who ruled the house. Like any dachshund Lulu had ever met, Sophie was in charge.

The guest wing, away from the main part of the house, was quiet. She stripped out of her work clothes, raced into the bathroom to freshen up, and emerged with a clean face, fresh makeup and the flowery scent of an expensive perfume she loved.

She was standing in the middle of the closet trying to select the perfect dress for the wedding when Cami knocked and stuck her head inside.

"Getting ready to go back to the hotel?"

"Yes. It's going to be a small ceremony as you know, but everything is being done with no expense spared. The flowers alone must have cost a fortune. I heard they hired a trio to play romantic music. Do you know who they are?"

Cami's smile was sly. "Yes, I do. That's all I'm going to say. I think you're in for a little surprise."

CHAPTER THREE

Lulu hurried into the lobby of the inn in time to see two couples heading for the registration desk. One of the women was a petite, beautiful Asian dressed in dark slacks and a furry white jacket. The other woman and her two athletic companions looked like an ad for a sports magazine with their hiking boots, jeans, and lightweight parkas.

Before Lulu could reach them, Sarah bounded into the lobby, followed by Lee. "At last! You're here," she cried. As Sarah hugged each woman, Lee shook hands with the men and thanked the women for coming.

Laurel came up behind Lulu and watched the group from the sidelines with her.

Sarah noticed them and waved them forward. "I'd like you to meet my best friends." She glanced at Lee. "*Our* best friends. And everyone, this is Laurel Nelson, the wedding coordinator. And our special photographer, Louise Kingsley."

A look of recognition crossed the taller woman's face. She studied Lulu with interest, but to Lulu's relief, she didn't say anything.

Sarah put her arm around the Asian woman. "This is Amy Chou. She was my roomie in my freshman year at Boise State and is still one of my besties, even in grad school." She indicated the other woman. "And this is Mindy Peters, our mutual close friend." She turned to the men and indicated the shorter of the two. "Sam Dwyer is Lee's lab partner and buddy, and Elliot Brinkman is their TA."

"We're working together on a genetic research project at

the university," said Lee. "We've been good friends for a few years now."

Taking pictures, Lulu liked the ease between the men. They might dress in a casual outdoorsy style, but she bet these men were brilliant at their work. Their eyes shone with intelligence. She focused on the women, taking plenty of photos. The excited buzz of their conversation was nice to hear, and she loved the happy expressions on their faces.

The sound of a phone ringing stopped their talk. Sarah lifted one from her pocket, looked at it, and frowned.

"Is it your mother?" asked Amy, giving her a worried look.

Tears filled Sarah's eyes. "She's furious that I've gone ahead with these plans, but that woman doesn't have a kind bone in her body. No wonder my father left her years ago."

After taking a couple of shots, Lulu stopped aiming her camera at them.

Mindy turned to Lulu and explained, "Her mother is prejudiced and has warned Sarah that if she goes ahead and marries Lee, she'll never speak to her again."

Even though Lulu told herself to stay quiet, she thought, *Easy choice. Marry Lee.* She'd seen enough bigotry and hate to last a lifetime.

Amy's gaze rested on her. "Sad, isn't it? Worse yet, Lee's family has already selected someone else to be his bride. Me." She glanced at Lee. "We would be a poor match. We're not interested in each other." She turned and smiled shyly at Sam.

"Right," said Lee. "All the old-fashioned ideas have to go away."

"Besides, Amy and Sam are great together," Sara said. "Like Lee and me."

Lulu snapped a picture as Amy and Sam smiled at one another.

"Now that everyone is here, let's have some fun," said

Sarah. "Lee has arranged a little pre-ceremony party."

"That sounds good. Remember, if you need anything, please let me know. We want this wedding to be perfect for you," said Laurel, who'd been standing by.

After they'd left the area, Laurel turned to Lulu. "It's sad to have such unhappy overtones to the occasion. But Lee has done every imaginable thing to make it memorable for everyone. Wait until you see the jade jewelry he bought all three women! And the men are receiving gift cards of some kind."

"Too bad Sarah's mother is being so awful about the wedding. I wonder what Lee's family will say to his marrying her."

"As far as we're concerned, it's none of our business," said Laurel. "There's a note at the registration desk that no calls are to be sent through to their room for either Sarah or Lee."

"Just a few more hours and they'll be safely married."

"Yes, and I'll be able to breathe a little easier." Laurel let out a sigh. "I don't like secret weddings."

Lulu was in the kitchen talking to Darren about the special meal he'd prepared for the wedding party, when Cami walked into the room.

"We need to move up dinner. Lee's father is on his way to the inn. He sent Lee a text saying he expects to get here within two hours."

"Where are Sarah and Lee now?" Lulu asked. "I was supposed to get pictures of Sarah as she dressed."

"They're in Chandler Hall going ahead with the wedding ceremony. Take as many photos as you can because we cannot reach the videographer Lee hired to tell him of the change in plans."

Lulu ran to her office, grabbed her cameras, and hurried to Chandler Hall.

She opened the door quietly and stepped inside. Reverend James Bliss, who'd performed many weddings at the inn was speaking. "I now pronounce you man and wife."

Lulu checked her watch. It'd had only been an hour and a half since she'd seen the group in the lobby. She hurried over to the scene of the wedding and began snapping pictures of the happy couple, the setting, and the bridal party.

"Sarah, your dress is gorgeous," said Lulu. "Stand still and I'll get a few photos of you in it." She gave Sarah a quick hug and stepped back to get a good look at her.

Though not beautiful, Sarah had a wholesomeness about her that was very attractive—a ready smile, shining blue eyes, and hair the color of pale wheat. Her dress was a sheath in a white, satiny fabric with capped sleeves. A beaded border of flowers edged the hemline which reached just below her knees. Simple but elegant, the dress was a perfect choice for this small ceremony. A jade and gold bracelet surrounded Sarah's right wrist, and jade earrings shone on her earlobes, no doubt gifts from Lee. The other two women, she noted, wore jade earrings too.

When she'd taken enough shots of Sarah, Lulu called to Lee. "Come stand beside her. Then let's get a picture of all of you together." The girls wore simple A-line dresses in gold. The men wore gold ties with their navy blazers and gray pants.

After she'd captured several photos, Lulu approached Sarah. "Why didn't you call me? I would've taken photos of you getting dressed with the girls helping you."

Sarah fanned her face, trying to hold back tears. "I'm sorry, but I didn't want anyone to get the wrong impression of my crying as I got dressed. This is such a happy time for me. Or, it should be. Neither family is making it easy."

Lee approached them. "We're going ahead with the dinner right now. Darren has assured me everything is as close to what I wanted as he could make it." He put an arm around Sarah's shoulder and hugged her to him. "I hope you'll be happy with it."

She smiled up at him. "I know I will be. It's our wedding dinner."

Lulu observed the flurry of activity as kitchen staff and servers worked together to arrange food on a large, round Lazy Susan set up in the middle of the table.

Lee turned to her. "Please get a photo of each item as I'm explaining it. I want my parents to know I followed some of the traditions."

"I can't wait to learn about them," said Lulu. "It's interesting to discover different cultural traditions. We might even incorporate some of them into our wedding program here."

"I'll try to explain them carefully." Lee held a chair for Sarah and then sat as the others lowered themselves into chairs at the table.

"Instead of serving one course after another like you might do at a large wedding, I've asked Darren to serve the dishes together so we can taste what we like. But I'll explain what each dish means." He pointed to a plate of crispy-skinned pieces of pork. "The pork represents the purity of the bride, especially the crispness of the skin."

As everyone helped themselves to a taste of it, Lee continued.

"The crab claws represent the groom's side, the Dragon. The scallops with asparagus are for lots of children because the word for scallops in Chinese sounds a lot like the word for children. The lobster is stir fried with ginger and onions and topped with coriander. But it's the lobster's red color that's important. The color red is for good luck, which is why we have so much red at this table and for the wedding flowers. We couldn't get pigeons, but the chicken we're serving symbolizes peace."

"We'd all better eat a lot of chicken," quipped Sam.

Laughter rang around the table, and the tension that had hovered above it disappeared. After wine and beer were poured, everyone settled down to taste the interesting collection of food that symbolized so much for the bride and groom.

Lulu took photos of the food and the group celebrating at the table and then said to Lee. "Enjoy your meal. I'll be available whenever you need me. Just buzz me on my cell."

Lulu was grabbing a bite to eat in the kitchen when the staff member handling the registration desk came hurrying into the room. "Lulu, come quickly! Cami needs your help."

She dropped the sandwich she'd been about to taste onto her plate and raced out of the kitchen.

In the lobby, Cami was standing face to face with an angry man. She gave Lulu a look of desperation.

"Mr. Wing would like to speak to us about his son's wedding. I've tried to explain that Lee and Sarah are guests, and we don't want them disturbed. I've told him he's certainly welcome to call his son on his cell and wait for him here, but we can't allow him to interrupt them without their permission. We have a requirement to protect the privacy of our guests."

"I see," said Lulu, giving herself a moment to come up with a plan. She held out her hand. "Mr. Wing, I'm Louise Kingsley, the photographer your son and daughter-in-law have hired. May we offer you some refreshments?"

"Why don't I have a tray of appetizers brought out?" said Cami, giving her a grateful smile. "And, Mr. Wing, what could we offer to you to drink? Tea? Coffee? Wine?"

He let out a long breath of frustration and then quietly said, "A glass of wine might be nice. I've rushed to get here. Now that I know it's too late, I need time to think things through."

Lulu led Mr. Wing to a couch in the living room. "We can sit here. And, if you're interested, I can show you some of the photos I captured."

He sat down on the couch and held his head in his hands. When he looked up at her, his eyes reflected sadness. "Tradition isn't always easy to follow, I understand that. But the young people today don't have any idea how free they are compared to those of my generation."

Lulu studied him. He was a well-dressed, handsome man with gray hair at his temples. As stern-looking as he'd first appeared, she noticed laugh lines around his eyes, and relaxed.

Cami returned to them carrying Lulu's cameras. "I thought you might need these." She turned as a waitress approached carrying a tray holding a selection of appetizers, two glasses, and an opened bottle of wine.

Lulu moved the coffee table closer to the couch and helped place the tray on top of it.

Cami poured the wine into the two glasses and, after exchanging reassuring glances with her, left.

Lulu raised her glass. "Here's to your health and happiness, Mr. Wing."

He bobbed his head. "And to yours."

As the wine slid down her throat, Lulu kept an eye on him. Observing the tightness in his face relax the tiniest bit, she thought Cami was right to offer this gesture of hospitality as a counter to her refusing to permit him to interrupt Lee and

Sarah's wedding. Normally, she would not be drinking wine with a guest, but she knew it might seem rude for Mr. Wing to drink alone.

They sipped the wine and tasted the appetizers in silence and then Mr. Wing spoke. "I understand what it is to challenge tradition. People in my generation have been told by our elders how irreverent we are, and yet my children test me even further."

"Let me show you a few of the photographs. I think you might find an answer to your dilemma there." She lifted her digital camera and began going through the photographs with him. As modest as she was, Lulu could see she'd captured how alive, how happy, how spontaneous Lee and Sarah were together.

Mr. Wing remained silent until she came to the pictures of the food and then, his eyes moist, he uttered, "My son has not forgotten everything. I see the red colors, the food choices ..."

"And their love?" Lulu couldn't help saying.

"I see that too." He got to his feet and walked over to one of the front windows and gazed out.

She sat quietly as Mr. Wing continued to stare out at the darkness.

"Father?"

At the sound of his son's voice, Mr. Wing whirled around. "Son?"

Holding hands with Sarah, Lee walked toward him. Facing his father, he said in a shaky voice, "Sarah and I are married now. We hope to have your blessing."

Lee's father stared at him and then ever so slightly bobbed his head. "I will not stand in your way, but you will do me the courtesy of writing to Mr. Chou to tell him of your choice. Understand?"

"Yes, but there's no need. Amy is here with us. She's part of our wedding and with her boyfriend. This is what we both wanted."

Mr. Wing's eyes widened and quickly returned to normal. "We'll talk later. Now, I ask Sarah to forgive my rudeness. My wife and I will welcome you into our home as Lee's wife." His smile was brief. "I'm sure Mei will want to celebrate in style when you can come to San Francisco."

"Thank you," Sarah said. "I am honored."

"Thank you, Father," added Lee.

Though the exchanges were all formal, Lulu understood what giant steps had been taken to move forward.

"Won't you join us? We're having cake and enjoying some nice music," Sarah said to Lee's father. She turned to Lulu. "Will you come too?"

Lulu grabbed her cameras, and with Mr. Wing, she followed Lee and Sarah to Chandler Hall. She was curious about the band Cami had talked about. It had been an evening of surprises and yet, according to her sister, another one awaited her.

The strands of soft music wafted out of the building to greet her as Lulu approached Chandler Hall.

Even though only a portion of the building had been set aside for the wedding and celebration, the entire exterior of the building was lit with twinkling lights. Inside, she found the same attention had been given as a welcome to the guests.

Sarah and Lee led them to the enclosed section by the fireplace.

Lulu froze. A keyboard player, a drummer, and a guitar player were working together to produce a nice, mellow jazz sound. The man playing guitar caught her eye and winked.

Her breath escaped in a soft gasp. Even though he wasn't playing the right music, Miguel Lopez looked like the hottest rock star ever.

"Cami said you'd be surprised to see Miguel," Laurel said coming to her side. "Though he denies it, he's actually very good. He certainly looks the part."

"Yes," Lulu replied automatically. Her mind was still spinning at the sight of him in dark, tight jeans and a white, long-sleeved shirt that showed every bulging muscle from his work in the vineyards.

"Surprised?" Cami's smile was like that of an imp as she approached. "Better get lots of pictures. I had a hard time convincing Miguel to substitute for the guy who usually plays with this group.

"A good choice," said Laurel. "Mindy looks ready to swoon."

The three of them laughed. Weddings could be very interesting.

CHAPTER FOUR

The soft, romantic sound of the music stirred Lulu. She hoped one day to find the man of her dreams and enjoy a quiet celebration like this. Something small, intimate.

She looked up to find Miguel's eyes on her and felt heat creep up her face. It wasn't only his appearance that was so attractive to her. He'd protected her from the angry man at the restaurant. And that meant a lot to her.

Mr. Wing rose from his chair at the table and asked Sarah to dance with him. The look of surprise on her face was telling, as was the grateful expression Lee wore. Standing quietly on the sidelines snapping photos as Lee's father danced with Sarah, Lulu noticed the tears in both sets of eyes. For different reasons, she supposed, but a few tender moments she hoped to capture.

Studying the people who surrounded her father like moths drawn to a light, Lulu had been trained to see what others might miss. That's what made her photography of people so compelling. Tonight she was grateful for it.

After the music stopped, Mr. Wing approached Amy. Lulu overheard him say, "I'll speak to your father tomorrow."

Amy clasped her hands in front of her chest in a prayerful pose. "I called him myself after the ceremony, but it would be helpful if you two talked. I'm sorry if I offended you or your family. I would never wish to dishonor you or them."

He gave Amy a steady look. "Honor among families is very important. I will speak to your father about what I've seen and heard. I wish you the happiness my son has found." He turned to watch Lee and Sarah dance. "Ah, to be so young, so brave, so bold."

As he spoke, Lulu captured the way regret had entered his eyes and knew a sad story lingered there.

"I must leave," he announced, walking up to Lee.

Laurel hurried over to him. "Won't you stay the night? We have a room ready for you."

Mr. Wing shook his head. "I must get back to Portland. I have an early morning flight home tomorrow. There are things to be done."

"I understand. Is there anything we can do to make the drive to Portland more enjoyable? Perhaps bottled water and a snack?"

He shook his head. "Thank you, but my driver has all that."

Laurel shot him a look of concern. "A driver? Oh my! Has he been waiting all this time?"

"Yes, but he's fine. I told him it might take a while."

Hearing this, Lulu realized that the evening which had turned out as well as it had could have been a huge disaster. Lee's father was used to having things go exactly as he directed. She knew then how much he loved his son.

Lee and Sarah left the room with his father.

"Wow! I'm glad that's over," said Amy sinking into a chair at the table. "I've never been so nervous in my life. Mr. Wing might've been my father-in-law."

"He seems like a nice man," Laurel said.

"He is, but he's even more old-fashioned than my father. And, besides, I love Sam. My parents already know I wouldn't marry Lee, but I couldn't tell Mr. Wing that."

A while later, Lee returned to the group. "Sarah and I are going to call it a night, but you're welcome to stay and dance and enjoy yourselves."

"Amy and I are tired from the trip. We're going to our

room." The look Sam gave Amy indicated they weren't so tired they couldn't have a little fun.

Mindy turned to Elliott. "How about you?"

Elliott put his arm around her. "I'm ready to retire too."

Laurel called in the waitstaff to clean up. Lulu snapped a few photos of the cake that remained and shots of the band putting away their instruments. The Pendleton/Wing wedding was over. She'd take a few shots of the group in the morning, and then her work would be done.

Lulu swung the two cameras over her shoulder and prepared to leave.

"Hey! Where are you going?" said Miguel, walking over to her.

"I thought I'd go home. My work is over for the night."

He lifted her chin and gave her a crooked grin. "That last song? I was playing it for you. Don't end the evening now. Let's go down to the Green Grape. I want to get to know you a lot better."

Every instinct told her to say no. His hand on her chin had sent disturbing heat waves through her.

"Come on. Please. You haven't let me apologize to you for the last time we were there. Give me a chance to make it up to you now."

Lulu sighed. "Okay. I need to drop the cameras off in my office and then I'll meet you out front."

He beamed at her. "That's a deal. I'll have the truck warmed up for you." His expression told her that's not all he wanted to warm up.

It being a Saturday night, the Green Grape was jammed. Miguel took hold of her hand and tugged her through the crowd.

"Where are we going?" Lulu asked, weaving with him through the dancers.

"I called and reserved a table," he said. "I know one of the girls at the bar."

"Of course, you do," she said wryly, suddenly wondering why she'd allowed herself to be talked into a date with him. As he cleared the way for her, Miguel reminded her of some of the security people who worked for her father. Lulu was pleased to see that the table that had been reserved for them was a small one in an out-of-the way corner.

"What can I get you? Wine? Beer?"

"Beer sounds good. Whatever you choose is fine." Everyone once in a while she liked a beer, and with all the micro-breweries in the northwest, she'd learned that some beer drinkers were as fussy with their beer as she was with her wine.

"I'll be right back," Miguel said, making his way to the bar.

Lulu was deep in thought about Lee and his father when she sensed someone approaching. She turned. A young woman with long, dark hair slid into the empty chair at the table.

"I'm sorry, this table is taken," said Lulu.

"I'm well aware of that," the woman said smoothly. "I just wanted to get a good look at you and warn you that Miguel and I have an understanding. After he gets all this foolishness out of his system, he and I are going to be married."

"Who are you?" Lulu asked wondering why no one had warned her about Miguel's engagement.

Glancing into the crowd around them, the woman rose. "I'm Maria Ramos. Don't you forget it."

As she hurried away, Miguel appeared with their drinks. "Who was that?"

"Didn't you recognize your fiancée?

He set down the drinks with more force than necessary and faced the crowd. After a moment he turned back to her and sat down. "If you're talking about Maria, she's not my fiancée!" Miguel dragged a hand through his glossy black hair. "It was a mistake. The whole thing."

"You don't need to explain your love life to me," said Lulu, shaken by the encounter.

Miguel's dark-brown eyes studied her with an expression of disbelief. "You're going to accuse me of something without knowing all the facts? You, of all people?"

Lulu's cheeks burned. She was acting as terrible as the reporters and other members of the news media who decided something was the truth whether they'd investigated or not. She reached over and touched his hand. "I'm sorry. Please go ahead."

"Maria and I were together in high school. A cheerleader/football player kind of thing. At the end of our senior year before we went away to college, she wanted to get married. I told her no, that I had a lot of growing up to do."

"She thinks you're just sowing wild oats, so to speak, before settling down with her."

Miguel's sigh spoke volumes. "I've tried to explain that's not going to happen, but she won't listen. I have no intention of marrying anyone until I'm sure I'm ready. I do my best to ignore her, though sometimes I feel as if she's stalking me."

Listening to him, Lulu filled with sympathy. Because she'd seen this kind of thing with her father, she understood how he felt. "Let's simply enjoy ourselves. It's been a busy, emotional day for me with the wedding, and I need to relax."

As they sipped their beers, they began to talk about the vineyards and how the three of them—Chandler Hill, Taunton Estates, and Lone Creek could do exciting things together. One beer led to two and then three.

Lulu enjoyed the buzz and the chance to get a guy's perspective on life in the valley. She recognized how knowledgeable Miguel was about grape growing. And he had a way of listening to her questions that made her feel as if she was the only person in the world.

His gaze settled on her. "Now, you know a little about me and my work. What should I know about you besides your being your father's daughter, Cami's half-sister and working at Chandler Hill? What are your hobbies? What are some of your favorite things?"

Flattered, she said, "Well, I love photography and catching people on camera at unexpected times. Cami asked me to help with the wedding party tonight and I liked doing it. I'm hoping to do more. Favorite things? I love Belgian chocolate and, like Cami, I love pink roses the best. There, is that enough?" She'd learned in politics not to give away too much information about herself.

Laughing, he shook his head. "It's a beginning. That's all. I want to learn a whole lot more about you. Do you have brothers and sisters?"

He listened quietly, his expression growing sad, as she told him about Teddy.

"Sorry. I can't imagine losing a sibling. That's tough."

"What about you? Do you have any brothers and sisters?"

Me? I have three older sisters." He chuckled. "You can imagine my life growing up with those three trying to boss me around."

She laughed with him. No doubt they'd coddled him. He must have been an adorable little boy. He certainly was a handsome man.

He leaned forward. "Say, I want your opinion on an idea I have about fixing up the farmhouse at Taunton Estates. Are you willing to help me?"

"Sure. Anytime." She was much more comfortable with him and was curious to see what he had in mind.

"How about right now?" Miguel said, grinning at her.

She gave him a quizzical look. "Are you kidding? It's dark out."

"I know. That's why I want to show you something now. It's an idea of mine that might seem far out, but after talking to you, I'm willing to take a chance that you won't laugh at me."

"Okay," said Lulu, more relaxed, more open to fun than she'd been in many months.

After paying their bill and leaving the bar, Miguel helped Lulu into his truck. As he climbed into the driver's seat, he turned to her. "Are you okay with this? I can show you another time. We've both had a lot of beer."

"Are you insulting me?" Lulu said. "I can hold my drinks very well, thank you."

He laughed. "I didn't mean to insinuate you were drunk. I just meant ... oh, never mind. You're fine. I'm fine. Everything's great."

As they drove to Taunton Estates, Lulu laid her head back against the headrest and sighed with contentment. She felt so relaxed. Though she hadn't done much serious dating, she couldn't remember the last time she'd been so intrigued by a man. She'd had a fling with Kirk Ketcham, a college student working on her father's campaign, and she knew Wilson Chambers was definitely interested in her. But she attributed his attention to his fascination with the political connections he might gain from being with her. He was already talking about running for local office.

"We're here," said Miguel jarring her out of her thoughts.

The air was crisp as she stepped out of the truck. She looked up at the dark, September sky. The full moon glowed as it floated above them like a light welcoming them home.

Stars twinkled in the sky giving her silent winks.

"Come inside," said Miguel. "Then you'll be able to see what I'm talking about." He held out his hand, and she accepted it. "We four owners of Lone Creek Winery are going to fix this house up as a place for me to live and for occasional use for social events. So, while it might be bigger than I'd normally choose, I want to make it uniquely mine."

"I understand they've committed to working on the house. Drew is excited about it." Of all the three houses at the different vineyards, including Cami's, this was Lulu's favorite. A white stucco finish and a mansard roof made it look European in flavor.

"All the technicalities of ownership will be worked out with lawyers, but it will be mine to live in for as long as I choose, in the same way the house at Lone Creek is available to Dan and Becca."

"Sounds like it's been well thought out."

He led her up the front porch steps, flicked on exterior and interior lights, and welcomed her inside.

She blinked in the brightness of the lights and glanced around. At the moment, it was a guy's kind of place. Nothing fancy, just the basic furnishings, off-white walls and nondescript carpeting.

"Looking at it with you now, I see how much work will need to go into the place to make it as nice as the houses at the other vineyards," said Miguel. "But, as I told the other guys, the bones of this house are good. Right now, it has four bedrooms and two and a half baths. We're going to change that, add another bathroom or two. Dan is very good at figuring that stuff out."

"I'm curious. What did you want to show me?" She could already envision some interior decorating changes she'd make.

"Upstairs. Follow me."

Lulu gave him a quizzical look and trailed him up the stairway. When she realized she was focusing on his butt, she told herself to stop fantasizing. This was a man who wasn't serious about anyone and wanted to remain that way for the time being.

At the doorway to a large bedroom, she paused behind him, her heart sinking. "Is this it? Your way to get someone up here?"

"What? No! This is where I want to make the biggest change. Come here."

He walked her to a sliding-glass door and led her out onto a deck. Standing beside him, she gazed with appreciation at her surroundings. The moonlight coated the hills and vines below with a silvery glow that was breathtaking.

"I saw this idea on television, and I want to do it here. Tell me what you think. First, we'd expand the deck, and instead of leaving it open, I want to build a roof with a skylight over it and enclose the whole thing with large, sliding-glass windows that would make up most of the walls surrounding the deck. The master bedroom would go here. The space inside the house could be used as a private dressing room, more closets, an expansion of the bathroom, whatever."

"It would be like camping out under the stars," Lulu said softly, looking up at the sky, imagining what it might feel like to sleep here surrounded by the night, the moon, and the stars. Arms out, she twirled around as if to embrace it all.

"I knew you'd like it!" Miguel beamed at her. "The other guys are trying to talk me out of doing this. They're worried about heating the area in the winter and keeping it cool in the summer. But I believe that problem can be solved with solar panels, baseboard heating, and adequate air conditioning."

Staring up at the stars, Lulu said, "If not, make this an old-fashioned sleeping porch that can be used most of the year without those problems. It's too good an idea to give up."

Miguel's face lit, washed with the light of the moon. "I'm so glad you understand what I'm trying to do here." He drew her into his arms and lowered his lips to hers.

At his touch, a powerful tug of longing traveled through Lulu's body and settled at her core. She reached up and wrapped her arms around his neck, wanting to hold onto the delicious feeling new to her.

His lips met hers gently then became more demanding.

When they finally broke apart, Lulu struggled to catch her breath, but her heart was pounding so hard, she could only try.

"Wow!" said Miguel softly. "Come here."

Lulu didn't hesitate to move into his arms. She'd never felt this way and wanted more. Much more.

CHAPTER FIVE

Later, marveling at what had just happened between them, Lulu lay on the bedroom carpet just inside the sliding door leading to the deck. She'd had only one other man make love to her, but this was a very different experience. On his back beside her, Miguel wore an expression of satisfaction on his face, which was highlighted by the moon's gauzy glow glistening on their bare bodies.

Miguel rolled over and drew her against him. "You're so beautiful," he murmured, "and not at all what I expected."

"Oh? What was that?" She wasn't experienced and worried she hadn't been a good lover.

He clasped his hands around her face and gazed at her with a tender expression. "You're one hell of a woman, Weezie Lopez!"

Lulu chuckled. "I can't imagine how Cami came up with that name so quickly, but it's a good cover for me."

"I like it." A smile curved his lips as he looked down at her. "But I also like Lulu Kingsley, the woman by my side. You're very special."

This time, his lovemaking was slow and easy, building into another explosion of sensations.

Lulu awoke sometime later and, realizing the hour, forced herself to move away from Miguel's warm body and head into the bathroom. She freshened and quickly dressed.

As she was running her fingers through her hair, Miguel padded into the bathroom. "What's up?"

"I'm sorry. I can't spend the night here. I don't want any

gossip spreading about us. I've had enough of that kind of thing. Please, will you take me home?"

"Really?" His voice held hurt, but she chose to stand by her wish. She wasn't ready for a relationship until she picked up the pieces of her life and put them back together. Especially a relationship ruled by sensations and not common sense. The depth of her feelings, her need for him frightened her.

The next morning, when Lulu walked into the kitchen, Cami looked up at her with a smile. "A late night, I heard. Becca said you and Miguel left the Green Grape together."

Lulu propped her hands on her hips. "Does everyone in this town know what everyone else is doing?"

"Pretty much," Cami said giving her a teasing smile.

"Well, all talk can stop about Miguel and me. Neither one of us is ready to do any serious dating. Besides, I'm still trying to resolve things following my father's death. Personal issues I have to address."

The smile left Cami's face. "I'm sorry for teasing you. I was simply happy to know you were going out with someone."

"It's okay." Lulu sighed and stared out the window. "There are so many things still to take care of. Mostly my mother." She turned back to Cami. "I can't tell you how grateful I am to be here."

The shrill ring of the phone ended their talk. Cami rose to answer it.

Lulu poured herself a cup of coffee and headed out to the deck. Even though the air was cool, she was comfortable in the pink, furry robe she'd recently bought. She'd just settled in one of the rocking chairs, when Cami hurried over to her carrying the phone.

"This call is for you. You need to take it now." She handed

her the phone and rather than leave, Cami sat in a chair next to hers, gripping her hands and giving her a worried look.

"Hello? Miss Kingsley? This is Dr. Cleveland from the Steelman Rehabilitation Clinic. Your mother was admitted this morning after attempting to take her life with prescription medication. Fortunately, her housekeeper found her in time and was able to get medical help right away. As you've been given power of attorney, you'll need to sign some papers. It also would be a good idea for us to sit down together to talk about the case."

Lulu felt as if someone had just kicked her in the gut. "Of course, I'll come right away. I was just taking a break ..."

"No need to explain," Dr. Cleveland said kindly. "When you get into town, give my office a call, and we'll set up a time to meet. Your housekeeper has my phone number and the number of the clinic. I suggest you don't try to talk to your mother until you and I have discussed the matter."

Lulu bobbed her head as if he could see her, ended the call, and sat there in stunned silence.

Cami immediately put her arms around her. "What is it?"

"It's my mother. She tried to kill herself again. I should've been there for her. I have to go home now."

"Oh, no! I'm sorry, hon," Cami said. "What can I do to help you?"

"Can you check flights out of Portland?" Her voice quivered. "I need the earliest flight you can get." She felt so conflicted. She knew she had a responsibility to her mother, but she'd hoped to build a strong relationship with her sister. Tears blurred her vision. "I'm sorry I won't be around to help when the holidays are this close."

"Don't worry about that now. Take care of your mother, and we'll see you as soon as you can arrange it. We'll keep your room ready for you."

"May I leave my car here? That way, I know I'll be back."

"It'll be here waiting for you. We all will."

"Some girls dream of fairy godmothers. I always dreamed of having a sister. I'm so glad I found you," Lulu said, giving Cami a hug before hurrying to her room to get ready for her trip home.

She was in the midst of packing when Cami knocked on her door and entered. "A flight leaves Portland at eleven o'clock. You have time for breakfast and a shower. Then I'll take you to the airport."

"Thanks. I'm not hungry. I'll try to eat something later."

She undressed, stepped into the bathroom, and headed into the walk-in shower.

Feeling the warm water sluice over her skin, Lulu imagined the water as her tears. She lifted her face to the stream of water. She knew depression was a horrible thing for anyone to bear, yet her mother didn't seem to want to help herself. All she wanted to do was to be with her dead son—another indication that her mother was so wrapped in her own sorrow she hadn't cared enough about living to be there for Lulu.

She finished washing and dried herself off. *Time to get off the pity pot*, she reminded herself. She had to take care of what was left of the Kingsley family.

the plane, Lulu thought of her date with Miguel. Self-doubt ate at her. It was a fantasy to think anything could or should come from it. Considering who she was and her responsibilities to her mother in California, it would remain a happy memory of an evening when she'd let her worries go and enjoyed being with a man whose gentleness was a bit of a surprise to her.

After the plane landed, she saw that Miguel had tried to call her twice and had left a short text message saying simply "Please call me. I miss you already."

Lulu read and reread his message, then reminded herself that thoughts of Miguel Lopez and Chandler Hill needed to be pushed aside until her mother was squared away. Besides, she worried that this was Miguel's usual next-morning message to the women he'd been with the night before.

As she waited for her luggage at the airport, she sent him a message telling him she'd been called suddenly to California to care for her mother and that she'd be in touch when she got back to Oregon. She hoped to have him out of her system by the time she returned. The last thing she needed was another charismatic man like her father in her life. Women were constantly throwing themselves at Miguel. Someone else was bound to come along. What she felt for him was too quick, too much, a disaster waiting to happen.

Later, she met with Dr. Cleveland, a kind, older gentleman who greeted her with sympathy.

"Let's sit and talk. I'm well aware of the difficulties you face now and have faced in the past. I'd like to set up a new protocol to balance your mother's medications. It's all about the meds," he said. "We'll have to work together to make sure they're doing what they need to do for her. I suggest we discuss a plan with your mother, the housekeeper, whom she trusts, and you."

"What if we fail?" Lulu said, blinking away the tears that threatened.

Dr. Cleveland's blue gaze rested on her. "You're not responsible for keeping her alive, Louise. You can help, but in the end, if things go bad, you're not to blame."

"But my father always told me to keep an eye on her. I've

tried, and then when I went to visit my sister, this happened."

"It's unfortunate you were handed such a burden," he said. "I'm relieving you of that right now. We'll cooperate to keep her as healthy as possible, but that's all we can do. The choices she makes are hers alone."

"But won't I have to be there for her? Stay at home for a while?"

"It would be helpful," Dr. Cleveland admitted.

"All right, that's what I'll do," Lulu said, wishing she could grow magical wings and fly away, back to Oregon.

Melba Milner, the housekeeper the family had employed for many years, was a stunning woman of mixed heritage—both African American and Native American. Aside from being one of the most giving people Lulu knew, Melba was a bright, happily married woman with two successfully raised sons—one was a doctor, the other, a lawyer. Lulu had always thought her father might have been a little in love with Melba, though Melba would never do anything to harm her mother. Melba adored Rosalie Stockton Kingsley. In the good times, they were as close as sisters, and when the bad times came, Melba was the one Rosalie wanted near her.

Lulu sat with Melba in the living room of the palatial home in Brentwood she'd always known. After being at Chandler Hill for a couple of months, this house seemed overdone with its fussy furniture and heavily-framed artwork.

"Don't worry," Melba now said. "We'll work together to help your mother, as Dr. Cleveland asked."

"I honestly believe she's always wished *I'd* drowned, not Teddy," said Lulu, unable to hide her sorrow.

Melba reached across the space between them on the couch and clasped her hand. "No, Lulu, I don't want you ever to think that. You surely know that from the good times you were able to share with her."

"I guess," she said. "God! I sound like a crybaby."

Melba's lips spread into a loving smile. "No, sweetie. You sound like a young woman who wishes she'd had more time with her mother."

Lulu's eyes filled. "Do you know how often I wished *you* were my mother?"

"Come here," Melba said, drawing Lulu into a warm embrace. "You are the daughter of my heart."

Lulu leaned into Melba's body and sighed, grateful to the woman who'd more or less kept the family together. "I love you, Melba," she said, meaning it with her whole being.

"Love you too, baby girl," Melba said. "I always have. Now, let's talk about the plan Dr. Cleveland wants us to work on."

Lulu straightened and drew a deep breath. "We're going to need to keep a record of her medications, what she eats and when, and what, if any, mood swings she demonstrates."

"And then what?"

"Once a pattern is established, we can hopefully anticipate when her meds need to be upped for that period of time. We should eventually be able to tell when the next swing is going to happen and catch it early. That's our hope, anyway. My mother has always been able to talk to you honestly, which Dr. Cleveland feels will be very helpful in our oversight of her meds and mood swings."

"I can take care of the hours during the day," said Melba. "But you'll have to speak to the night nurse you're hiring. It should be a matter of routine for her to note those things and to maintain control over the medications. You'll be there to help us when we need you to do that. Right?"

"Yes, I'll stay here through Thanksgiving for certain," said Lulu, wishing things were different. "But if everyone, including my mother, Dr. Cleveland, and you, are okay with it, I'd like to go back to Chandler Hill at the beginning of the new year or before."

Melba eyes lit with excitement. "It's going well between you and your newly found sister? She's such a pretty little thing."

"Cami is a wonderful person. And so is her grandfather, Rafe Lopez. I've never felt more welcomed, more accepted for who I am. I can't let that relationship dissolve."

"Of course not," said Melba. "We'll get through the next several weeks, and then we'll get you back there. In the meantime, what are you going to do while you're here?"

"I'm going to see if I can work with a professional photographer or at least take some online courses. There's so much more I want to learn. I started taking candid shots for wedding parties at the inn, and I've discovered I have a good eye for it."

"I imagine you are expert at reading others," Melba said. "You've been involved with your father's activities and all kinds of people since you were little."

"It's helped me discover the special little differences in them." Lulu smiled. "Everyone at Chandler Hill is excited about what I'm doing with the camera and the marketing program. I am too."

"It's good for you to keep busy while you're here. And a certain gentleman will be happy you're home."

Lulu cocked an eyebrow at Melba. "Are you talking about Wilson Chambers?" Melba had always liked him.

Melba's smile reached her eyes. "Yes. I promised to let him know when you were coming back to L.A. I haven't called him yet. I figured you'd want to do that yourself. You know, your father always thought he was the perfect match for you."

"I'm not ready to settle down with anyone," Lulu said, uncertain how she felt about Wilson. Will, as he preferred to be called, was a good-looking, smart man with a lot of ambition. Life with him would be a whirlwind adventure, just like her life with her father had been.

"You're still very young, but it wouldn't hurt for you to go out with him, have the chance to get to know him better," said Melba. "My point is for you to go on living and not be tied down by your mother's illness."

"Maybe you're right." Her thoughts turned to Miguel. She had received another, polite text from him saying he was sorry about her mother and telling her he was there if she needed him. And since then, no word from him at all.

A couple of days later, Lulu sat with Dr. Cleveland in her mother's private room at the rehabilitation clinic. A nurse had helped Rosalie get dressed to come home. Even with her body too thin and her expression guarded, Lulu's mother was a beautiful, but frail-looking woman. It was her eyes, Lulu decided, that seemed the most damaged of all. They were as lifeless, as empty as the woman who sat in the chair clutching a sheaf of papers as if they could tell her how to go on living.

"The key to setting up the schedule will be honesty and trust," said Dr. Cleveland. "We need Lulu and Melba to make note of everything, and we need you, Rosalie, to be totally honest about how you're feeling. You'll soon find it's easier to be open about your emotions than hiding and trying to fight your demons alone."

"I want you to feel better, Mom. For my sake, too. We've missed out on so many things."

Rosalie sighed. "I've failed you, Lulu."

"No," Lulu said, taking her mother's thin hand in her own. "Let's not think that way. Let's decide it's a new beginning, for the two of us."

Dr. Cleveland gave Lulu a smile. "Good idea. What do you say, Rosalie? Are you willing to give it a try?"

Rosalie glanced at him and Lulu. "Melba will be there with me too. Right?"

Disappointment stabbed Lulu. Once more she felt she wasn't enough for her mother. She forced the hurt from her voice. "Yes, Melba will be there for both of us."

"Good," said Rosalie. "She knows what I like to eat."

"Eating will be good for you," said Dr. Cleveland. "But no medicine other than what I've prescribed and no alcohol. Understand?"

Rosalie's shoulders drooped with defeat. "Yes," she answered quietly.

Rosalie seemed more comfortable at home. She sat in the kitchen with Lulu and watched as Melba stirred the homemade chicken soup Rosalie loved.

"We'll start slowly with easily digested foods," Melba said. "Once we get your strength back we'll go on to other things. I know you like your sweets, Rosalie, and I've got a new recipe for a chocolate cake I'm sure you're going to like."

"You always know best, Melba."

Lulu listened to their conversation and understood how much these two must have gone through together. She remembered the nights Melba slept over following the death of her brother, comforting her mother. Lulu got up out of her chair, went to Melba, and gave her a hug. As she turned away, Lulu noticed the look of surprise on her mother's face and realized why. She and her mother almost never hugged.

CHAPTER SIX

Sometime later in her stay, while her mother was napping, Lulu, bored and restless, decided she needed a distraction. She scrolled through her contacts and called Will.

The sound of Will's deep "hello" seemed so familiar and comforting. He was a nice guy who'd been devoted to her father. From a wealthy family, he'd always had his eye on a political office. "Will, this is Lulu. I'm back in town for a while. Melba suggested I call you; she had promised to let you know when I was here."

He chuckled. "I had to be sure I wouldn't miss you. You took off under everyone's radar. How is your sister and life at Chandler Hill?"

"Cami is wonderful. I'm very lucky. She and her grandfather, Rafe Lopez, have treated me as part of their family. I feel more at home there than I do here. How are you? Still working for the county prosecutor?"

"Yes, but I'm ready to move on. I've arranged to work with underprivileged clients at my father's law office. It's discouraging to see how many people aren't able to get good and fair representation on either side—defense or prosecution. I'm taking on clients who need a better chance for fairness."

"I've always admired your outlook, just as my father did."

Will's sigh was full of regret. "If only we'd known his heart was in such bad shape. I'm sure he and I could have done a lot of good things for the country. That's why I've vowed to carry on his message."

"Not all of it, I hope," Lulu said with a bitterness she sometimes felt.

"No, no. None of that."

In the silence that followed, Lulu said, "It's been nice talking to you. I hear Melba calling me. I'd better go."

"Wait! May I call you?"

"Sure. It seems as if I'm going to be here for a while."

"Your mother?"

"Yes. She needs me." Lulu didn't say more, didn't need to.

"I'll call you soon. Good to know you're back."

Lulu hung up, pleased she'd made the connection. Will knew more about her family than most and still accepted her. After being ripped apart in the press, that meant a lot to her.

She set her phone down and hurried into the living room to find Melba.

"What is it?" Lulu asked.

"Your mother is hungry for ice cream. Will you go to the store for her? She wants coffee ice cream and chocolate ice cream bars." Melba winked at her. "I thought you might enjoy getting out of the house."

"Thanks. I'll use Mom's car."

Lulu grabbed the car keys and went to the garage where her mother's silver Mercedes convertible sat. She climbed into it, wondering how often her mother used this vehicle. She'd become such a recluse after the first of the bad news about her father broke. Lulu paired her phone to the car's bluetooth system. If she was going to be here for some time, she might as well make things easy for herself. She felt so isolated here.

As she headed for the Whole Foods Market on San Vicente Boulevard, Lulu passed by many beautiful homes. She'd always loved living in this neighborhood, but after staying with Cami, a much simpler lifestyle appealed to her. She couldn't wait to get back to it.

Her cell rang and the name of the caller appeared on the screen on the dashboard. She pushed the button to accept the call and said, "Hi, Cami! How are you?"

"Concerned about you. How are things going in L.A.?"

"As well as can be expected. I'm in my mom's car on my way to pick up some ice cream for her. Melba is doing her best to make sure my mother is eating. The new medicines seem to be working, but I've been there with her before and can't be sure how long it will last."

"It was Melba who found her, right?"

"Yes, after all my mother and our family have gone through for the past twenty years or so, she and my mother are extremely close. In many ways, Melba is the person who's kept our family together."

"She sounds lovely. When do you think you'll be able to return to Chandler Hill?"

"Probably not until after the holidays. Then, if she's doing well, I'd like to return and stay with you until I figure things out for myself. I want so much to be a part of the Chandler Hill Inn and Winery."

"You can be, Lulu. If not now, later. I'll always have a place for you here."

Tears blurred Lulu's vision. She blinked to keep them at bay. "Thanks. I'm glad to hear that. No matter what happens to my mother, I have no reason to want to stay in L.A."

"What about Will, that guy you once told me about?"

"Oh, that's different. I talked to him, and we're going to get together sometime."

"Hmmm," said Cami, and Lulu could envision her raised eyebrows and sassy smile.

Lulu laughed. "We'll see what happens."

"Good talking to you," said Cami. "I've got to run, but you know you can call and ask for help anytime."

"Thanks. I'll pick up my car after the holidays. Okay, if I keep it there?"

"Absolutely. Can't wait to see you again! I've missed you!"

After Cami ended the call, Lulu sat in the car feeling so alone she wanted to cry.

A few nights later, Lulu stood in front of the mirror studying the simple, long-sleeved black dress she wore. If offset her dark hair and dark eyes nicely. She wore her hair long and straight, and though she wore diamond earrings, she didn't want attention brought to them because she, like Cami, had misshapen ear lobes. It was one of the characteristics that tied them together through their father.

She wrapped a green-silk scarf around her neck, slipped silver bangles onto her wrist, and decided the black, ankle-high boots worn with black tights were a nice addition. She enjoyed getting dressed for the evening, something she hadn't done much of recently.

At the sound of the doorbell, she hurried to answer it. Melba had gone for the day. Her mother was resting in her bedroom, and the night nurse was with her.

She opened the door and felt a smile cross her face. Wilson "Will" Chambers was a decidedly handsome man. Tall and well-built, he had sun-streaked brown hair he'd brushed away from facial features that contained a Roman nose, a strong chin, and an intriguing, wide smile that showed straight, white teeth. Sparkling green eyes shone through horn-rimmed glasses. At thirty-two, and with his well-to-do background and ambition for the future, he was considered a very eligible bachelor.

"Lulu, so good to see you," he said, and swept her up into his arms.

Laughing with sheer pleasure, she hugged him back.

He set her down before him. "You look terrific. I can't wait to show you off."

"We're just having dinner, right?"

"As a fresh beginning. Though I've respected your wish to have some time on your own, I've missed you." He cupped her face in his hands. "You resemble your father."

"Cami does as well, if you ever meet her," said Lulu. "Aside from our coloring, we do look a lot alike."

"I hope to meet her someday." He drew her close for a warm kiss and then said, "Are you ready to go?"

"I will be in a moment. I have to let my mother and her nurse know I'm leaving."

The expression on Will's face became somber. "How's she doing?"

Lulu shrugged. "She seems much better, a lot happier. But I'm afraid to get my hopes up."

"Maybe this time will work," Will commented. "I'll wait for you here."

"Thanks." Lulu hurried up to her mother's bedroom. She knocked on the door and opened it. Her mother was lying on top of a chaise lounge upholstered in an off-white fabric.

"Yes? What is it?" Her mother's voice held a hint of irritation that Lulu ignored. Some of the medications could sometimes make her difficult.

"I'm leaving to go out for the evening. See you tomorrow. Have a pleasant night."

"Such as it is," her mother sighed. "But thank you. Have fun."

Lulu quietly shut the door and hurried down the stairs. She couldn't wait to get out of the house.

"All set?" Will asked.

She let out a long breath. "Yes. I'm ready for a little fun."

Will led her to his black BMW and helped her into the passenger seat. Lulu rested against the leather seat and emitted a sigh of pleasure. She needed this evening to relax.

As they drove toward Rodeo Drive, anticipation filled her. She was with a man she admired, and Cosima was one of her favorite restaurants. Their food was fantastic.

"You look beautiful, Lulu. All that fresh air in Oregon must have been wonderful."

"Thanks. I've grown to love Chandler Hill and the entire Willamette Valley."

He squeezed her hand. "I hope you're happy to be back. We have so much work to do together. Remember how we talked about that with your father?"

She frowned. "I didn't realize you were serious. I thought that idea was just talk over dinner one night."

Will pulled over to the curb so fast, she had to grab hold of the armrest beside her.

His look was almost stern. "Lulu, I was serious about you, our plans, everything. Now, more than ever. While we were going through all the fallout from your father's accusers and then his death, I knew you were too upset to deal with a relationship between us, but I need you to understand how sincere I was and still am about all of it."

Caught off guard, she said, "But you and I ... we never really dated."

He shook his head. "Only because I never had the chance. By the time I decided I wanted to make a serious play for you, everything fell apart. I'm not going to let other things stop me now. I want you for my partner now and in the future."

Lulu's pulse sprinted. "Whoa! Are you asking me to marry you?"

"Not yet. Oh, hell, I might as well tell you here rather than over dinner. I'm going to run for Congress next year, and I want you to work with me on my campaign. More than that, I want to see if we can build a future together. We've been friends, and we've dated casually. But I want more than that." His green-eyed gaze settled on her. "Will you at least give it, give us a try?"

A flush of adrenalin flooded her body. She'd always liked Will, had once even fantasized about having a closer relationship with him. But this was different. This was between just the two of them without her father beside them encouraging such an idea. "I need time to think about it," she answered honestly.

"Fair enough," said Will. "And even if a deeper relationship between the two of us doesn't work out, maybe you'd consider taking on the job of my campaign manager."

"You've got to be kidding! What do I know about it?"

Will's lopsided grin turned into soft laughter. "You're one of the savviest politicians I know. And with all the experience with your father's work, you're a perfect one to do it."

Lulu's senses came alive. She suddenly remembered what it was like to see a crowd of people react to one of her father's ideas. He may have sometimes behaved in a foolhardy manner, but he had creative ideas on how to help others in a meaningful way.

Sensing her feelings, Will shot her a satisfied smile, checked for traffic, and pulled away from the curb. "I really blew how I wanted this evening to be, but I hope you'll relax and enjoy it. Like I said, I want to see where our relationship can go. We've already started as friends ..." His voice trailed off.

She studied him, seeing him in a different light. There was so much to admire. The idea of his genuine interest in a future with her made her feel good. She was well aware of how women used to flock around him at various political gatherings. He, like her father, had a certain charisma about him. She'd always considered him as her father's employee, but she was intrigued by the idea that he'd been truly interested in her all along.

Will led her inside the restaurant. Following the maître d' to a coveted corner table, Lulu heard hushed murmurs and observed the attention that was being given to them. Her stomach twisted. In recent months, she'd become uncomfortable at being noticed. Tonight, was no different.

She forced a calm she didn't feel as she was seated opposite Will. Some of those very same people who were now nodding and smiling at them were people who'd turned against her, judging her for the things her father had done.

"Guess it's official," said Will, smiling and reaching for her hand. "We're dating."

The waiter arrived, gave them menus, asked for water orders, and told Will the wine steward would be over to help him select the wine for the evening.

Lulu studied the people in the room, feeling as if she was in a play she'd rehearsed for a long time. The aromas wafting through the air were tantalizing. But she already knew what she would order as her entrée.

"If I remember correctly, you're going to go with a veal dish. Right?" Will said.

She blinked, surprised he'd remember such a thing. "Probably the veal piccata." The veal dishes at Cosima were legendary.

He turned to greet the sommelier who'd arrived with a leather-bound wine list.

"May I help you, sir?" the man said.

Will lifted the menu. "My date is thinking of the veal

piccata, and I'm thinking I'll go with the veal saltimbocca."

As the two men perused the wine list, Lulu studied her surroundings. Dark-paneled walls met a thick, ruby-red carpet. Crisp, pink linen covered the tabletops and hosted cut-crystal candle holders and a single red rose in a crystal glass. She recognized one or two movie stars but looked away. She had no interest in making visual contact with anyone else. She needed this evening to be about Will and her.

"We're thinking of a nice Barolo for the wine. It should pair well with the veal. Is that okay with you?" Will asked, turning her attention to him.

"It sounds lovely," she replied, pleased he'd included her in the decision. He'd always been generous that way.

After the sommelier left, Will said, "Thank you for agreeing to see me tonight and on such short notice."

"I'm glad to be out of the house and pleased to be here."

He chuckled. "You've always been very honest. I appreciate that." A sadness washed his face. "I've felt so adrift with your father gone. Then I remembered all that he'd taught me and decided to go forward with his ideas."

"It's a way to honor him, I suppose, when no one else is willing to take on his role," Lulu said, realizing the struggle he might have in running for office.

He gave her a steady look. "How are you doing with everything?"

She let out a long sigh. "I've gone through so many emotions—anger, hurt, regret, and partial acceptance. I'm still working on that. Right now, I'm trying to deal with my mother and her illness. In a way, I lost her a long time ago."

"You haven't had an easy time of it, for sure," he said.

"Yes," she replied, grateful he didn't say more.

Their wine arrived. After it was sampled and approved, the wine steward poured some into Lulu's glass and then Will's before quietly leaving.

Will raised his glass. "Here's to us!"

She took a sip of the wine, uncertain about her feelings.

"What do you think of the wine?" Will asked. "Now that you've lived in wine country, has it changed your opinion of many of them?"

"This is a nice wine. I like it, but I've grown fond of pinot noir, and Chandler Hill wines are particularly good. The process of growing grapes and making wine is fascinating. You'll have to visit someday."

As they made their way through the menu, Lulu relaxed. Conversation with Will was lively. He was well educated and interested in many things. He also, she discovered, had a wicked sense of humor.

She'd just finished her veal piccata when her cell rang. She checked caller ID. *Her home number.* She clicked on the call. "Hello?"

"Louise?" an unfamiliar voice asked.

"Yes. Who's calling, and why?"

"This is Mrs. Sampson. Your mother has become ill with flu-like symptoms and is asking for you. I think you'd better come home. She's quite agitated."

"Oh, I'm sorry. I understand. I'll be there as soon as possible." Lulu clicked off the call with mixed emotions. She was both frustrated and pleased by the fact that her mother was choosing to reach out to her even though all she wanted was one evening out, away from the house.

"What is it?" Will asked giving her a look of concern.

"That was the night nurse. My mother is ill and is calling for me."

"I'm sorry." Will gave her hand a squeeze. "It must be so hard for you."

Hearing the empathy in his voice, Lulu dabbed at

unexpected tears. "I have to get home. I hope you understand."

Though he didn't look happy, he nodded. "We can leave if you need to."

"Yes, I think it's best. I don't want to make a scene here, and I certainly don't want anyone to think you've made me cry."

His eyes widened. "No! We don't want that to happen." He signaled the waiter, explained that Lulu wasn't feeling well, and paid the bill.

The waiter held her chair as she got to her feet.

They quickly exited the restaurant and waited for the valet to bring Will's BMW to the front entrance.

In the car on the way home, silence reigned. Lulu was glad Will didn't try to fill the quiet with a lot of chatter.

He pulled up to the front of her house and turned off the car's engine. "I'll walk you to the door."

Lulu waited for him to come around the back of the car to open the door for her.

She stepped out of the car and into his arms. Resting her head against his strong chest she sighed. "I'm sorry to end the evening this way."

"Me, too," he said, "but we'll have other times." He lifted her chin and gazed into her eyes. His lips came down on hers, sending a number of delicious sensations through her.

She wrapped her arms around his neck, giving in to the pleasure of having strong arms surround her while his lips sent a message of their own. She knew how much she needed this kind of support and kissed him back.

When they stepped apart, Will's smile lit his face. "I've wanted to do this so many times. Now, we can. And I know your father would be pleased."

Lulu couldn't hold back the sudden discomfort she felt.

"This isn't about my father."

"No, no. I didn't mean to make it seem that way. Somehow, though, I like thinking he'd be excited by our dating and the plans I have for us."

As their lips met again, she relaxed into the kiss. There was something very nice between them. When they broke apart, Will said, "I guess I'd better leave. Maybe next time we can try my condo for privacy."

"We'll see how things go." She wasn't going to rush into anything. He was assuming she was ready to move to the next level, and she wasn't.

He laughed. "Spoken like a true politician."

He led her up the front steps of the house and waited as she opened the door and then turned to him. "Good night. Thank you for a nice evening."

After closing the door, Lulu leaned against its solid surface, wondering what had just happened. Will was being totally honest with her about his vision for the future, but she wasn't sure it was what she wanted. That would have to wait. At the moment she needed to see to her mother. Even with the night nurse there, she wanted Melba or Lulu around.

CHAPTER SEVEN

As Thanksgiving approached, Lulu concentrated on spending time with her mother. One afternoon, with encouragement from Lulu, her mother agreed to help her bake a pumpkin pie in anticipation of the holiday. They'd already decided to stay in and order dinner from one of the best restaurants around.

Melba stayed with them as they worked with the pie crust they'd made from scratch.

"Remember to handle your dough carefully," Melba warned them. "And when you're rolling it out, stop the minute the dough sticks to the surface and doesn't move with you. Then, sprinkle a light dusting of flour beneath the dough and begin rolling again."

"I used to love making pies," her mother said. "But it's been years since I've done it."

Lulu smiled her encouragement. "This is a good time to begin."

"Yes," added Melba. "A time to start doing many things." She stood back and studied them. "It's nice to see you two like this. I remember how you used to love to do things together."

"Really? I don't remember many moments like that," said Lulu.

"You don't?" Her mother's surprise startled Lulu.

"I guess I was too little. Once Teddy was born, we didn't do much together at all." Lulu's matter-of-fact statement caused her mother to cover her face.

"It's okay, Mom. I understand," said Lulu, hoping she

hadn't started a downward spiral of emotion in her mother.

When her mother lifted her face, silvery trails of tears glistened on her cheeks. "Losing Teddy almost killed me. After his death, I had nothing left to offer you or your father. Nothing. Absolutely nothing."

Lulu exchanged worried glances with Melba.

"Now, Rosalie, you know that's not true," Melba said firmly. "Think of all the volunteer work you did and the foundation you set up in Teddy's name."

"Yeah, Mom. You've given a lot to the community through the years."

Rosalie's laugh was bitter. "Only on those days when I managed to get out of bed. It sounds so easy to someone who doesn't know how darkness can drag you down." She reached over and caressed Lulu's cheek. "I wish I'd been a better mother to you."

Lulu knew it would be dishonest to protest. Instead, she said, "I love you, Mom."

Her mother wrapped her arms around Lulu. "You are the best thing I've ever done. Now, I'm going to go upstairs and lie down."

Touched by the conversation and the hug, Lulu said, "I'll walk you up."

Her mother's smile was sad. "Thanks, but I know my way. All too well."

After her mother left the kitchen, Melba said, "She's always loved you. She just didn't know how she could compete against the darkness that hid inside her."

Lulu plopped down into a kitchen chair feeling as if she didn't know who she or her parents were. Everything she thought she knew about them now seemed out of kilter.

Melba put a hand on Lulu's shoulder. It felt right. Melba had been the one person she could trust to be there for her.

She looked up at her now.

"I'm so confused. It's all so complicated."

"Yes, life itself is complicated. It helps to remember the good times, the nice things that happened. Your mother told me earlier that you had a date with Will. How did that go?"

Lulu exhaled a long sigh. "That's another thing I'm confused about. After the Thanksgiving celebration here, I'm going back to Chandler Hill to get my car and take time to think things over. You'll be here with my mother. Right?"

"Like always," Melba said. "I told both your parents I'd always be there for them and you."

"Thanks," Lulu whispered, wondering how one family could be so full of hurt.

Thanksgiving was bright and sunny—a day Lulu would always remember because her mother was experiencing one of her "up" days. With Melba off for the holiday, Lulu and her mother shared breakfast in the kitchen and then spent the afternoon outside in the garden resting and reading.

In this island of calmness, Lulu told her mother about Will's wanting to build a relationship with her.

"Ah, Will. Your father's favorite planet circling his sun." Her mother's lips curved. "Will was always kind to me, which I appreciated. He has a lot to offer you, but politics is a nasty business. Is that what you want? Whether you merely work on his campaign or end up marrying him, it will be difficult."

"But think of the good work we can do, Mom. Dad may have hurt us both, but he did a lot of good for others. And now I have the chance to help Will do good things for the country."

Her mother studied her. "You'll know if it's the right choice. Whatever that decision, be sure it's good for you, not for him."

Emboldened by their conversation, Lulu said, "I hope I haven't hurt you by becoming friends with Cami Chandler."

Her mother's laugh was soft, sad. "I've known about her for a long time. Not too long after we were married, I found a letter written by her mother in your father's desk. I put it back without discussing it with him. By then, I was pregnant with you, and he was running for office. As painful as it might have once been for me, I'm glad you're getting to know her. It's the closure of one circle of life."

Stunned by the news, Lulu gaped at her mother. "You knew about the letter way back then and about Cami and her mother? After Dad died, I found it too but kept it hidden from you so you wouldn't be hurt."

"Yes. I never thought you and she would find one another and saw no need for you to meet. Not really. But life can sometimes unfold in ways you never dreamed."

Lulu reached for her mother's hand and leaned over to kiss her cheek. "Mom, I'm just beginning to truly know you. I'm very glad we've had this chance to talk. It means the world to me."

"And to me," her mother said, smiling shyly at her. "Let's go see about getting that dinner. For once, I'm hungry."

Feeling as if she was in a dream of normalcy, Lulu went inside to check on their food order.

After they'd eaten dinner, stored the leftovers in the refrigerator, and served coffee, Lulu decided to ask her mother if it was okay for her to make the trip back to Chandler Hill.

"I thought I'd leave sometime this weekend for Chandler Hill to pick up my car. Is that all right with you?"

"You're a grown woman, Lulu. You can make those plans

on your own."

"Yes, but, Mom, I need to know you'll be all right. I promised ..."

Her mother's eyes widened. She cut Lulu off. "Oh my God! You promised your father you'd take care of me? Is that it?"

Lulu hesitated, uncertain how to answer.

"Never mind. I know it's true." Her mother shook her head sadly. "My sweet child, what a burden you've been given. Yes! By all means go! Take time to think things through. Melba is here with me, along with that godforsaken night nurse you both insisted on hiring even though I told you I'm feeling better than I have in years and years." Her mother rose from her chair at the dining room table and paced the room. "I hate being like this. I really do."

Lulu pushed to her feet and took hold her mother's arm. "It's been a wonderful day. Come sit with me in the den. We'll find a television program or a movie."

Her mother's shoulders drooped. "Sorry. Yes, it's been a lovely day. Now, let's watch a movie."

They sank onto the couch in the den together. Relieved the tense moment had passed, Lulu searched for a lighthearted movie. Soon they were engrossed in a tale about two friends visiting Italy together and finding love.

The next morning, Lulu rose and stretched with renewed optimism. If everything was still okay, she hoped to catch a flight to Portland. It was such a busy weekend at the inn, she intended to take a limo from there and surprise everyone at Chandler Hill.

After Melba arrived, Lulu told her about the day she and her mother had shared and then said, "Do you think I can leave today for Oregon? Things seem so good, and Mom told me to go ahead and go. Did you know she knew about Cami all along?"

Melba studied her. "Yes, I've known about her too. Your father loved her mother so much."

"Is there anything else I need to know?" Lulu said with dismay. Everyone else seemed to know much more about her parents than she did.

"No, sweetheart. I think all the secrets have been exposed. Now it's time for you to leave them behind and make your own journey through life."

"That's one reason I need to go back to Chandler Hill."

Melba laughed. "Well, then, I think you'd better go ahead and make the call. We'll be fine here."

With a great deal of effort, Lulu finally secured a reservation, packed, said her goodbyes, and caught a cab to the airport.

Waiting for her flight, she called Will. "Happy Thanksgiving again!" They'd talked yesterday, but only briefly, and she'd sent him a quick text this morning.

He laughed. "I missed you at my family's dinner. Maybe next year. How did the afternoon and evening go with your mother?"

"It was amazing. She and I talked about a lot of things. She's so much wiser than I knew," Lulu continued to babble. "Of course, I know this mood swing might not last, but it's pretty wonderful."

"I'm glad you had this time together. Rosalie's a lovely woman."

Lulu chuckled happily. "She called you a planet around my father's sun."

"Very apt comparison," he said good-naturedly. "I'm honored to be part of the Kingsley solar system. Seriously, I've realized I've cared for you for a long time."

"I had the biggest crush on you when I was little," said Lulu, "but I never dreamed you'd feel this way about me. This time away will allow me to do some serious thinking."

"Have a safe trip. Can't wait to see you again."

"Me, either. Talk to you later." Lulu clicked off the call with a sense of satisfaction. A bright future beckoned to her.

CHAPTER EIGHT

Walking through the terminal at the Portland International Airport, Lulu felt her spirits lift. Soon she'd be back at Chandler Hill with her newly discovered half-sister and the group of family and friends who already meant so much to her. She loved her mother, but being with her sometimes felt as if she were in a play without a script.

The gray, rainy weather outside the terminal did nothing to dampen her enthusiasm. The cool, moist air smelling so fresh compared to home felt good against her skin. Best of all, she felt free of the burden of her life in California.

Thankfully, the driver she hired was quiet as they made the trip to McMinnville and to Chandler Hill. As he pulled the car up to the front of the inn, he said, "I've heard about this place. It looks nice."

"Oh, it is," Lulu assured him, feeling a sense of pride that she was part of the fascinating family that had changed it from a small, country bed-and-breakfast to the luxurious property it was today.

She paid the driver and got out of the car, standing a moment to take in the pleasure of being here again.

Lulu had no sooner entered the inn when she heard her name being called. She turned to see Cami running toward her. "Lulu! So glad you're back!" Cami cried, giving her a hug. "How's everything at home? Come, let's go into my office. We can catch up with one another there."

Arm in arm they headed into Cami's office, which had been recently renovated. The soft-green and hibiscus-green color scheme was pleasing to the eye.

"I love this office," said Lulu. "It always makes me think of spring."

"Me too. It's why I chose it. Gray, rainy days can be depressing." Cami stopped talking and turned to her. "How's your mother? Did you have a good time away? We haven't talked much on the phone, but I wanted to give you some time to see things settled."

"I understand. That's why I'm here—for time to think a few things over. There's a man I want you to meet. He worked for my father's campaign, and he and I ... well, he and I want to see where we can take our relationship."

"Is this Wilson Chambers by any chance?" Cami asked, giving her a sly smile.

"Yes. How did you know?"

"There was a blurb on last night's west coast news. You were seen with him last week, and speculation is that there is an Edward Kingsley follower trying to carry on with his message."

Lulu's jaw dropped. She stood a moment, not knowing what to say.

Cami wrapped her in a hug. "He's a hottie, and if this is what you want, I say go for it."

"But that's the thing," she protested. "I don't know if it's what I want. That's why I'm here."

Cami gazed into her eyes. "Okay. I'll give you all the space you need. But in the meantime, can I put you to work?"

"I thought you'd never ask," Lulu said, pleased to be part of this family operation again.

Hearing a knock at the door, they turned.

Becca opened the door, let out a little squeal, and hurried to Lulu to give her a warm hug. "I heard you were back. How are you, Weezie Lopez?"

Lulu laughed. No one at Chandler Hill was going to let her forget their name for her. "I'm fine. I'm here for a little while. My mother seems to be doing better, and I need time to think things over."

"Time to decide if that handsome guy on television, the one her name has been associated with, is what she wants," Cami said, giving her a playful nudge.

Becca fanned her face. "He looked hot to me. What's the problem?"

Lulu sighed and gave them a steady look. "Will wants me to run his campaign to carry on some of my father's ideas and wants to see if our relationship can grow. We've worked together in the past, had a few dates, and he knows we'd make a good team."

"Is it true, then, that you're going to help him?" Cami asked.

"I don't know. I'm not sure if I want a political life again." The thought of it spun in her head, circling with irritating uncertainty.

Becca and Cami exchanged worried looks.

"Marriage isn't a business relationship," said Cami. "How does he make you feel?"

Lulu's lips spread into a smile. "Nice. Very nice. He and I are naturally comfortable with one another."

Becca and Cami exchanged more worried looks.

"What? Go ahead and say it," Lulu said, unnerved by their reaction.

"The spark between the two of you better be real if it's going to last." Becca gave Lulu an impish grin. "Why don't you invite him here sometime? Cami and I will make sure he's the right one for you."

"No way," said Lulu, laughing along with them.

"How about working in The Barn?" Cami said to her.

"You're excellent at selling, and we've got a lot of merchandise to move for the holidays."

"My pleasure to help you out," said Lulu. "First, let me get my things settled at the house, and then I'll check in with Gwen."

"I'm so happy to have you back, sis," Cami said, giving her another hug.

Lulu left the office humming softly under her breath and headed to Cami's house to change her clothes and get settled.

She was about to head to The Barn when Rafe appeared at the house.

"Hi, I saw your car and thought I'd stop by to say hello." He embraced her. "It's very nice to have you here with Cami. My two favorites."

"And you're my favorite, darling old man," she joked.

Chuckling softly, he stepped back and gave her a penetrating look. "How're things at home with your mother?"

"Better than I thought they'd be. We're working on getting her medications regulated. I see a big change already."

"Ah, that's good to hear. How long are you staying this time?"

"I'm not sure," she told him honestly. "Hopefully through the holidays, and then I'll see. I've been invited to work on my father's protégé's campaign."

"An interesting challenge," he said.

"What do you think about it?" Lulu asked, knowing he would be straightforward with her.

"If it's done for the right reason it could be very healing for you. But it's a life decision you can make for only yourself, not for others."

She gave him a quick hug. "I love having you for my grandfather."

His eyes were moist as he smiled at her. "And I, you,

Cariño. You are my other gift from heaven."

They walked out of the house together.

For the next few days, Lulu enjoyed working with customers at The Barn. She loved seeing the things she'd suggested to them leave the store.

One afternoon, Gwen came over to her. "You're a natural salesperson. I'm glad you're here to help through the holidays. And I know how happy Cami is to have you back. For sisters who haven't known of each other for years, you are very caring to one another, which is touching to see."

"Both of us always wanted a sister," Lulu said, giving her manager a smile. "Who knew we had one all along? Life sure is crazy sometimes."

"Indeed. For everyone," said Gwen. "Let's go over some inventory figures, and then you can help me decide on reorders."

Soon, Lulu was immersed in numbers and facts.

Later, as she prepared to head to Cami's for dinner and a lazy evening of watching television, Cami buzzed her on her cell. "A group of us are going to order pizza and meet at my house. What kind do you want? And, yes, we're ordering salad too."

"Oriental chicken pizza," Lulu said without hesitation. She missed some of the restaurants in L.A., and having a taste of Asian flavoring was a treat.

"Great, I'll place the orders. Drew said he'd pick them up on his way home."

As Lulu clicked off the call, she was forced to recognize that she had few close friends left in L.A.—friends who would do something as simple as an impromptu pizza party. Some of her so-called friends had ditched her during her father's troubles; others no longer lived in L.A. after their marriages.

She set aside her thoughts and hurried to Cami's to help her get ready.

Standing in the kitchen with Sophie underfoot, Lulu got plates out of the cupboard. "How many?" she asked Cami.

"Let's see, Drew and me, Becca and Dan, Miguel and a woman named Caro. She's someone new."

A stab of disappointment made Lulu gasp. She hadn't realized how much she'd hoped to see Miguel again. It had been only a few days since her return and she'd yet to call him, but now that she knew he already was interested in someone else, it hurt. This scenario was exactly as she'd feared. She told herself to stop thinking of him, that the single evening with him would remain just that—a sexual fling.

"Oh, I almost forgot. I've invited Ross Coughlin," said Cami. "During school breaks and on weekends, he works for Drew."

"Nice. I had to cancel coffee with him. I promised I'd tell him about some of the innovative after-school programs I've worked on in L.A."

"Great," Cami said as Becca, Dan, and Drew entered the house.

Sophie barked and raced to greet them.

A few minutes later, Miguel arrived with a tall, willowy blonde who stood beside him with a wide smile. Introduced as Caro Schinder, she seemed both nice and smart as she exchanged greetings and comments with everyone. Lulu learned she was a new teacher in town, taking over for another on maternity leave.

Ross arrived, and after greeting everyone, turned to her. "So glad to finally meet you, Lulu. Maybe we can do coffee this week. Sorry you had to cancel the other one. How's your mother?"

Lulu's smile was heartfelt. "She's doing much better, thank you. Depression is a tough thing to deal with."

"I guess it's all about the meds," Ross said. "One of my students is dealing with the same issue with his mother, and he told me that."

"Yes, that's it. The meds," Lulu said, happy she could be open with someone who knew about the difficulty with it.

The group grew noisy as beer was given out with the pizza. The party spread from the kitchen into the living room, where people took seats wherever they could find them. Extra chairs were brought in, and soon the noise died down as people dug into the food.

From her seat across the room, Lulu noticed Miguel's gaze on her from time to time, but did her best to ignore it. She was the kind of person who needed a steady, trustworthy man, someone devoted to her and her alone. Miguel Lopez did not appear to be ready to settle down. As soon as she finished her pizza, she moved into the kitchen to get away from him.

She was standing at the sink stacking her plate inside when she felt a movement behind her.

"How are you?" Miguel asked quietly. "I didn't know you were back in town. You said you'd call me."

Heat raced through her until she reminded herself that he was already dating someone else. She stiffened and slowly turned around, forcing a smile. "I'm fine, thank you. And you? Have you been able to start construction on your house?" She knew she sounded cold and awkward, but she needed to play it safe with him. She'd thought they might have something special, but he'd already moved along.

He shrugged. "Some inside construction stuff is being worked on. We're waiting for warmer, drier weather before adding the addition I showed you." His eyes softened. "I thought we could get together again, but I didn't know you and Ross were seeing one another."

"We're not. Not really. But you're with Caro."

"We just started dating. I'm helping her get to know the area."

Lulu didn't know how to respond. The silence between them pounded in her ear, and then she said, "Guess I'd better help Cami." She turned to go.

He held her back. "Why didn't you call me like you said you would?" His gaze stayed on her, making her wish things were simpler between them.

"I'm sorry, I was going to, but I thought if you wanted to talk to me, you'd have been in touch."

"But I left a message saying to call me if you needed me," he said, sounding disappointed. "And then, when you said you'd call me, I took you at your word." He turned and walked away, leaving her to wonder why she suddenly wanted to cry.

Later, after most of the food had been eaten, they all sat around drinking beer and talking.

Beside her, Ross asked about the work she'd done in L.A. She told him about the need for after-school programs there and how they used them to make sure the kids had enough food to eat at home.

"Some restaurants in the area provide us with snacks, and those not eaten at school are sent home with the kids. It's all tactfully done. Of course, it's handled without being part of a school program per se. By keeping it independent but on school grounds we have more flexibility."

"Yes, I can see the need to do something like that here."

"I worked at one of the programs a few years ago. It's very

important. In fact, a man I know who is running for Congress has some ideas about expanding services like that not only for children, but their entire families. He's asked me to help him."

"Yes, he wants her to marry him and run his campaign," blurted Becca.

Lulu felt her cheeks grow as hot as burning coals as everyone stared at her. "Hold on! I don't know if I'm going to do that. I just want programs like these to succeed."

"We need to give her time to think things through," Cami reminded Becca, frowning at her.

"So, you're probably not staying here? Weezie Lopez was a short-term joke?" Miguel said with enough sharpness in his voice to make everyone turn and stare at him.

"Don't be so quick to judge," Cami said. "My sister has a lot to handle, more than you'd guess. I'm hoping she decides to stay right here because I love her, but that is her choice to make and hers alone."

"Thanks, Cami." Lulu was touched by Cami's quick defense.

The silence that followed was broken by Dan's announcing that he had to get up early and better go home to bed. He wiggled his eyebrows at Becca, and Lulu, like the others, grinned at them. Their wedding was tentatively planned for February.

With their departure, Ross announced it was time for him to go too. He turned to Caro. "I'll see you tomorrow at school. Remember, if you need anything, I'm available."

"Thanks," Caro said to him. "I'm still finding my way around the school and might need your help."

"I'm showing her around the town and making sure she's comfortable here," Miguel said. He glanced at Lulu. "One of my nephews is in her class."

After everyone had left, Lulu quickly said goodnight and

went to her room. She may have tried to ignore Miguel's glances, but she wasn't fooled by the way her body had reacted to him in the kitchen. She'd come to Chandler Hill to gain clarity on her future only to find it more complicated than ever.

She changed into her pajamas and climbed into bed wondering what she was going to do about her feelings for Miguel.

A knock on the door brought her out of her thoughts.

Cami cracked the door open. "Okay, if I come in?"

"Sure, I'm just lying here as confused as ever."

Cami walked into the room, and when Lulu indicated a place for her on the bed, Cami sat down beside her.

"I'm sorry Becca brought up the business about Will and your decision. I noticed how embarrassed you were."

"Yeah, I'm not ready to talk about it yet."

"And what was the thing about Miguel being so judgmental? You just went out on one date with him, right?"

"That's it." No way was she going to admit to Cami that it was the most wonderful night of her life. "You're not upset with me for thinking of going back to L.A., are you?"

"No," said Cami. "Honestly, I wish you'd stay here permanently, but I know how you feel about doing some good things for families. That's important."

"Will is going to try to do that no matter what decision I make, but I can be a big help to him. Like I said, we've worked together before. He's got the same way with people as my father. He could be very successful in a political career."

"You were all set to help your father's presidential campaign. Do you feel the same way about Will running for office, maybe even running for president someday?"

Lulu made a face. "I'm not sure. My mother reminded me that a political life is a difficult one. Look what it did to her!"

"That, and her depression," Cami said softly.

"Right," Lulu admitted. "But hiding behind facades is exhausting and disheartening. I know it all too well."

Cami got to her feet and studied her. "I don't envy you the decisions you're facing. I hope I get to meet Will. Have you invited him to come visit?"

Lulu shook her head. "Not yet. I need more time before I do. Maybe after the holidays. He's got a busy schedule right now doing year-end legal work, and I think it's better if I wait."

Cami leaned over and kissed her cheek. "Good night, Lulu. Glad you're here."

"Good night," Lulu said softly.

After Cami left the room, Lulu lay in bed staring up at the ceiling thinking about why she'd been so quick to tell Cami she needed more time before inviting Will to Chandler Hill. Though she was conflicted about the idea, she was pretty sure it had something to do with Miguel. That man brought out feelings in her that scared her to death, especially when she knew she wasn't the only one he made feel that way.

CHAPTER NINE

Lulu found herself drawn into the Christmas spirit in a new way at the inn. All the glitz of L.A. seemed overdone compared to the simpler, more-alive decorations that were displayed all around her. Following her family tradition, Cami used live evergreens for Christmas trees and sold wreaths made of fresh, woven boughs of pine. Homemade, decorated candles in a variety of scents became best sellers at The Barn. Though they were former employees who had moved away, Abby and Lisa still made them for the store. And Lulu's favorite chocolates imported from Belgium were another traditional hit.

During this busy time, Lulu still checked in every couple of days with Melba and her mother. With an adjustment of her medication, her mother pulled through a down period, and for the first time in a long while, Rosalie was looking forward to Christmas.

When Lulu heard this, she went to Cami. "Is it okay with you if I reserve a room for my mother at the inn?"

"No, it isn't," Cami replied, giving her a mock frown. "I'd like to offer her the second guest room at my house where she might be more comfortable and have more privacy."

Lulu gave Cami a quick hug. "Thank you! That would be perfect. I can keep an eye on her and be there for her if any problems arise."

Cami sent her a worried look. "You sure she won't be uncomfortable with me, considering the family history?"

"I am. Apparently, my mother found out about you and

your mother at one point pretty early in her marriage, but did and said nothing about it. Pretty surprising, but then my parents' marriage wasn't like most others. It was a political alliance."

"I'll go out of my way to make certain she's comfortable," said Cami. "I know what a big step it is for her to make the trip and how much it means to you."

Lulu's heart burst with love for her. "You're the best sister ever."

They gave one another quick hugs.

Later, when Melba and her mother heard the offer, they were both delighted. Lulu was especially happy to know that Melba would have some quality time over Christmas with her family without worrying about her commitment to be available to help Rosalie.

As the days went by, Lulu grew anxious. Her mother was continuing to have good days. Lulu worried it might mean by the time her mother came to Chandler Hill, she'd be in a downswing of emotions.

When Christmas Eve arrived, Lulu called Melba. "How is she?" Her mother was due to fly to Portland that afternoon.

"Your mother is doing fine. The new medications she's on seem to be working, and I think her being away from here will be a tremendous boost. I haven't seen her this excited for a long, long time."

"I don't want her too excited," said Lulu, remembering how quickly one of her mother's highs could change to a low.

"This time it's different, sweetie," Melba said. "But if you see any changes, you know what you need to do."

"Yes." Lulu and Melba had arranged to keep in touch with Rosalie's doctor during her time away. He was pleased to know that she was going to be with Lulu for the holidays.

Late that afternoon, Lulu paced back and forth inside the terminal at the Portland International Airport. She'd agreed to meet her mother in the baggage claim area. When she finally saw her mother among the group of disembarked passengers heading her way, she breathed a sigh of relief.

Her mother was dressed conservatively in gray slacks and a soft-blue sweater coat. Large sunglasses covered her eyes and helped to keep people from recognizing her.

Lulu rushed forward and wrapped her arms around her mother. During this visit, Lulu hoped to bridge the gap that still existed between them, especially after learning how much her mother had suffered being married to a man who didn't love her.

Her mother returned her hug and stepped back to look at her. "My! What a nice greeting! And you look so healthy and so happy. Being away from L.A. has been good for you."

"I love it here, Mom, and I'm hoping you will too. Wait until you meet Cami. She's wonderful."

A momentary stillness on her mother's features alerted Lulu that it would take a great deal of diplomacy on everyone's part to get over the initial awkwardness of meeting her husband's love child.

"How many bags did you bring?" Lulu asked, taking a small carry-on from her mother's hands.

"I brought just one suitcase, but it's rather big and heavy," her mother confessed, giving her a sheepish look.

"No problem," Lulu answered cheerfully. At the moment she felt as if she could move mountains.

###

The drive to the inn was filled with small talk. Lulu explained what little she'd learned about grape growing and how she was fascinated she was by it all.

"All that hard work for a glass of wine," her mother commented, giving her a smile.

"Wait until you see the inn. It's beautiful and another instance of a lot of hard work. I don't know how Cami does it, but she's very organized and good at keeping everything going."

Her mother remained quiet.

They started up the long driveway to the inn. As they reached the top of the hill and her mother saw the inn, she let out a gasp of delight. "It's beautiful!"

Lulu and her mother exchanged smiles. "I'm so glad you agreed to spend Christmas here. I think it will be good for all of us. Cami is worried you might resent her, but I assured her that wouldn't happen. Right, Mom?"

Rosalie sighed. "It wasn't her fault my husband fell in love with her mother."

"What happened, Mom? Why did you marry Dad?"

Her mother pointed to the inn just ahead. "We're here, sweetie."

"Okay, maybe another time. I'm trying to understand because I don't want to make the same mistake."

Her mother studied her. "I'll find a time to answer your questions. I promise."

Lulu drove past the inn to Cami's house and parked in the driveway. "Here's where you'll be staying. It's nice and peaceful. If you want more activity, it's close by."

"Perfect," said her mother. "I think I'm going to love it."

Lulu paused a moment to study the house. A huge wreath hung on the dark-red door. Mini-lights twinkled from the shrubbery that softened the base of the house whose gray-painted clapboards blended in with its surroundings, making it appear to be a natural part of the scene. Battery-lit candles flickered in the windows, offering a warm welcome.

"What a lovely home," said Lulu's mother, surprising her.

Compared to their house in California, this one seemed simple, small. Lulu had loved it the first time she saw it. But she'd always thought the house in L.A. was something her mother had chosen.

Her mother noticed her look of confusion. "Another story for later."

"Okay." Lulu shook her head. Apparently, this was another instance that proved she didn't know her mother at all.

Cami opened the front door.

Sophie ran toward the car at full speed, her short, crooked legs moving as fast as they could.

"Here's Sophie. And there's Cami," Lulu announced.

Her mother sat in the passenger seat staring at Cami. "My God," she whispered. "It's remarkable how much the two of you look alike."

"Come on. Let's go meet her."

Lulu unbuckled her seatbelt and climbed out of the car. Hurrying to her side, she held onto her mother's arm. Together they walked toward Cami waiting for them on the front porch. At Lulu's wave, Cami approached them.

"Hello, Mrs. Kingsley, I'm so happy you could make the trip to Chandler Hill. I hope you'll be comfortable here."

"Thank you. And please, call me Rosalie."

Lulu beamed at them as they shook hands.

Sophie barked and looked up at Rosalie with dark eyes, wagging her tail so hard her backend moved back and forth.

"Ah, Sophie is it? Hello." Rosalie bent over and patted the dachshund's head and gently rubbed her ears.

Lulu smiled at them. "I think you've made a friend, Mom."

Rosalie turned to Lulu. "A good beginning, don't you think?"

The tension that had pinched her neck eased a bit. Lulu shot Cami a hopeful look. "It's going to be a good visit. I can tell."

"Rafe, Drew, and I have been looking forward to it," Cami said, smiling at Rosalie.

"Rafe is Cami's grandfather and Drew, her fiancé," prompted Lulu.

"Oh, yes," said Rosalie. "I remember hearing you say that."

"Here comes Rafe now," Cami said, and they all turned to watch him make his way toward them.

Observing the smile on his handsome face and feeling a surge of love for him, Lulu ran to greet him. They hugged, and then Lulu led him by the hand to her mother.

"This is Rafe," Lulu said proudly. "He's been wonderful to me."

Rafe gave Rosalie a little bow. "I'm pleased to meet you. I hope during your stay here, I'll have the opportunity to show you around."

"Thank you. I'd like that," Rosalie responded in a cheery voice that pleased Lulu.

She and Cami exchanged silent looks. *Maybe*, thought Lulu, *this visit will be even better than I'd hoped.*

When they went inside, Sophie stayed right at Rosalie's heels.

Sitting at the dining room table, Lulu filled with a whole new appreciation for her sister and Cami's grandfather. Each made sure Rosalie was part of the conversation. Drew, sweet guy that he was, tried too.

Rafe talked about his family, how they'd lived in the valley for generations, and how he'd always wanted to have his own land to grow grapes.

"He's been very successful at it," said Lulu. "Cami too."

"I couldn't go wrong," said Cami. "As Nonnee used to say, I'm a Chandler and a Lopez."

"I see," said Rosalie. "After hearing about your grandmother and meeting Rafe, I'm certain it's a wonderful combination." She smiled at Rafe.

"What a surprise she was to me. You can't imagine my joy." Rafe's cheeks flushed with emotion. "Guess this old man is getting sentimental in his golden years."

"I think it's sweet," said Rosalie.

Conversation turned to the weather. A warm front was hitting the area.

"Perhaps you'd like a tour of the vineyards," Rafe said to Rosalie. "After our usual Christmas breakfast, you might need a good walk."

"Cami makes a mean hollandaise sauce for the eggs benedict," said Drew. He grinned at Cami. "She's a great cook."

"I think that's the reason he's marrying me," she teased.

"You know better," said Drew giving her a grin that could only be called sexy.

Lulu chuckled with the others at their antics. She wanted a man to look at her the way Drew was doing now with Cami. Her thoughts flew to Miguel and away. It was obvious he had no serious interest in her.

"Did you hear about Miguel?" Drew asked Rafe. "He's going to Chile for three months or more. Being the only single guy of the four of us at Lone Creek Winery, he's agreed to travel there to work with a wine grower we know to see if there's a way to come up with a new, distinctive wine for Lone Creek that would set us apart from everyone here."

Rafe's eyebrows rose. "I didn't know about it, but it would,

I think, be an interesting trip. He'll be able to see parts of the process first hand."

"You might even want to visit him there," said Drew. "Now, that you've started to travel."

"My grandmother had a fear of flying which is why Rafe's first trip to Europe was last summer," Cami explained.

"Oh, I see," said Rosalie. "I used to do a lot of traveling in my younger years, but grew to detest being part of an entourage."

"Understandable," commented Rafe.

While they chatted, Lulu's thoughts returned to Miguel. Three months was a long time to be away, proving to herself that he didn't care enough to try to spend more time with her.

CHAPTER TEN

Christmas Day was as the weatherman had predicted—unseasonably warm with a bright sunny sky. A gift, he'd called it, and Lulu agreed.

She got up and hurried into the shower, anxious to see what the day held. She'd carefully selected Christmas gifts for the family and couldn't wait to hand them out.

Dressed and ready to go, she walked into the kitchen to find Cami in her pajamas setting the table for breakfast. Cami turned to Lulu with a smile. "Hope you don't mind, but I've invited Becca and Dan and Miguel for breakfast. Nonnee always liked having a crowd, and I do too."

"It sounds wonderful. Too many of my past Christmases have been pretty lonely. Can I help with anything?"

"No, thanks, unless you want to fix a cup of tea or coffee for your mother and take it into her."

"I'll be happy to do that," said Lulu, glad for something to do. This would also give her an opportunity to gauge how her mother was faring.

She fixed a small tray with a cup of hot tea and a plate with a couple of pieces of toast and knocked on her mother's door. When she heard no answer, she pushed the door open and gaped at the dark, cold room and the empty bed.

Her heart bumping in her chest, she set the tray down on a bureau and went to find her mother. As she hurried toward the bathroom, she noticed a movement outside and observed her mother sitting on the deck outside her room. Lulu stepped outdoors. "Good morning, Mom. How are you?"

Her mother looked up at her with curved lips. "I'm fine. I'm enjoying the quiet, peaceful scene. It's so lovely."

Lulu sat down beside her mother and studied her. "Are you feeling all right?"

Smiling, her mother nodded. "I'll let you know if I start to go in either direction. I promised you and Melba that I would do that. But, thanks."

"I brought you some tea and toast. Let me get some for myself and I'll join you."

Her mother's eyes lit with pleasure. "That would be nice, sweetheart."

Pleased, Lulu hurried into the kitchen.

"Is your mother okay?" Cami asked, noticing her fixing the tea.

"She's wonderful. Grab a cup of coffee and come say hello to her."

Cami followed Lulu out to the deck and pulled up a third chair. "Good morning, Rosalie. Isn't it a beautiful morning?"

"Perfect," Rosalie said. "I feel like I'm in a place far, far away from my usual surroundings." She smiled at Cami. "I have you to thank for that."

"I'm so glad you could come and stay here." Cami spoke in a wobbly voice. "I was worried you'd blame me for something my mother did."

"Oh, my dear, that's not your fault. But like I've told Lulu, I've known for years all about Edward and the woman he loved. Ours was an arranged marriage of sorts. Unlike your grandfather, Rafe, Lulu's grandfather was an opinionated, dominant man who was ambitious for his son. My father and he were business partners and didn't always see eye to eye. But when my engagement was unexpectedly broken by my fiancé, the father I adored convinced me that I could do great things for the world with Edward by helping him reach his goals. But, truth be told, neither of us was ever more than a little in love. "

"Why didn't you leave him, Mom?" Lulu held back tears.

Her mother's eyes widened. "How could I? I had you and then Teddy. And after Teddy died, I was too broken ..." she stopped talking, and in the silence that followed, unspoken words fluttered between them like butterflies searching for a place to land.

"Another time, if you're willing, I'd like to know more about my father," said Cami softly, breaking into the quiet between them. "Right now, I don't know what to think about him."

"Another time," Rosalie agreed. She stood and drew in a deep breath. "I think I'll go and prepare for the day. If I'm to go walking with Rafe later, I guess I'd better wear comfortable clothes."

"Yes," said Lulu. "I can't wait for you to get to know him better."

Cami picked up Rosalie's dishes from the table and headed indoors with her, leaving Lulu with her thoughts.

Hearing her mother's story, Lulu was determined to hold off on any plans with Will. If in a few months she was still interested, she'd begin work on his campaign.

The others were due to arrive at eleven. Lulu carried her gifts into the living room and set them down by the live tree in the corner of the room. Cami, Drew, and she had decorated the tree with family ornaments. Nonnee's Santa Claus collection lined the mantlepiece, and candles and other decorations were carefully placed around the room. Lulu admired the simplicity.

Observing her mother reading on the couch, Lulu picked out one of the gifts and carried it over to her. "Before the others come, I'd like you to open this."

Her mother's eyes widened. "For me?"

"Yes. I hope you like it." Lulu's stomach churned at the thought of her mother's rejection.

Cami walked into the living room with Drew. "Opening presents?"

"This is a special one I wanted my mother to have before our guests arrive," said Lulu.

The three of them watched as Rosalie carefully unwrapped the gift. Staring at the label on the box, she lifted her face to Lulu. "Me? Really?"

Unsure whether her mother liked it, Lulu blurted out. "I remember you used to take photographs of Teddy and me. I thought you'd like to photograph the scenery around here and get interested in photography again. It's a very simple digital camera to use."

"Why, Lulu, I didn't think you'd remember that. How thoughtful. This is the perfect place for me to begin again." She hugged her. "You might have to show me a few things about it. But, I'd like to try. Somewhere at home, I have boxes of photos of some of the people your father and I met."

Lulu felt as if a huge weight had been lifted from her shoulders. If she could get her mother interested in things outside the home, she might feel better, be more positive about life. She turned to Cami.

"Can I give you your present now? I can't wait."

Cami grinned. "Sure. I love surprises."

Lulu handed Cami the package and squirmed as Cami ripped the paper off. When Cami opened the box and saw the silver and gold pendant on a silver chain, she turned to Lulu and grinned.

"You have the other half?"

Lulu pulled the half-heart pendant out from under her

sweater. "They match perfectly."

Cami's eyes filled. "What a thoughtful gift. Thank you so much!" She hooked the chain around her neck and hugged Lulu. "Sisters forever."

"Sisters forever," responded Lulu, still finding it hard to believe that her wish of long ago was finally true.

Rafe arrived, and more gifts were exchanged.

When Rafe saw the gift Cami and Drew gave him, he laughed out loud. "You want to get rid of me again?"

"We know how much you liked the river cruise last summer. We thought you'd like another one," said Cami.

"I would," Rafe said, easily. "Yes, indeed." He turned to Rosalie. "Ever been on a river cruise?"

She shook her head.

"Maybe we can plan one together as friends traveling separately. Singles are welcome, of course, but having a friend along would be even better."

The surprised look on Rosalie's face turned to pleasure. "I'd like to think about it, but a river cruise sounds nice. We can talk about it. Some of my friends have gone and loved it."

"It sounds nice, Mom." Observing the pleased look Rosalie exchanged with Rafe, Lulu felt her heart fill. She knew Rafe well enough to know he was not making a play for her mother, but was just trying to help get her back into a normal life away from the struggles that had shaped her. Everyone who knew Rafe knew he'd given his heart to Lettie forever.

Lulu was surprised when Rafe handed her a package. "For me?"

His expression was full of excitement. "From Nonnee and me."

Before she even opened the package, tears filled Lulu's eyes. She blindly opened the small box and stared at the tasteful, solitaire diamond earrings.

Rafe's smile was touching. "I discovered these in one of my drawers and thought they were the perfect gift for you. Cami and I both agreed that Nonnee would be pleased to see you have them."

"Thank you," murmured Lulu, trying not to cry. She'd had bigger, more expensive gifts in her life, but none so meaningful.

"How lovely," her mother said softly, giving Lulu a tender smile. She turned to Cami and then looked at Rafe. "You've made my daughter feel welcome and such a big part of your family. I can't thank you enough."

"I've got a present for you, Rosalie," said Cami, handing her a gaily wrapped package with shiny stars.

Rosalie opened the box and lifted out a gray fleece jacket with the Chandler Hill Inn logo and grinned. "I'll put it right on. Thank you." She unzipped the jacket and slid her arms into it.

"It fits you perfectly," said Lulu, noticing how touched her mother was.

Amid laughter and warm sentiments, Lulu thought it was the best Christmas ever. And when she saw Cami become weepy over the picture frame filled with a photograph Lulu had taken of Cami and Drew together, she knew she'd made some wise choices.

They'd just cleaned up the mess when Becca, Dan, and Miguel arrived.

"Merry Christmas!" Becca cried, entering the house. Dan walked beside her carrying a huge palm tree.

"We thought you could use this, Cami. You mentioned you needed a plant to fill the space by the sliding door on the south side of the house," said Becca, directing Dan to set it down at the far end of the living room.

Miguel followed, carrying a small, brightly-wrapped box

and a red stocking full of dog treats. "And we didn't forget Sophie. Here, Soph!"

The dog trotted right over to him, grabbed the end of the stocking, and ran to the far corner with it.

Miguel laughed. "Guess I got that right." He handed the box to Cami. "I heard some people especially like Belgian chocolate."

Lulu hid her surprise. She knew he was referring to her and was touched by his thoughtfulness. She glanced at him but he'd already turned to Drew.

Cami and Lulu introduced Rosalie to everyone, and then the house filled with chatter as Cami and Rafe handed a fruit punch to Rosalie and mimosas to everyone else.

Lulu sat in a chair opposite her mother, who was resting on the couch next to Rafe. From her viewpoint, she saw her mother as the attractive woman she was. The air, change of place, and new medications were working their magic. And to be fair, maybe the freedom from worry over what her husband might or might not be doing with another woman was another factor.

Becca was full of stories about the puppy she'd given Dan for Christmas. A black lab, Daisy was already a big girl weighing eighteen pounds at ten weeks.

"She's going to be a great dog on the farm," said Dan. "Old Mike, the golden retriever we inherited from Rod Mitchell, the original owner of Lone Creek Winery, is starting to show his age."

Cami lifted Sophie into her lap. "She might not be as big as your dogs, but she's a great little hunter. Right, Sophie?"

The dog wagged her tail and barked on cue, bringing laughter to the room.

"She's great with the guests at the inn," said Becca, laughing. "I almost gave my mother a heart attack when I told her that Dan and I had a secret baby. But she calmed down when she realized I was talking about a puppy I'd bought for him."

"Once we complete work on the house at Taunton Estates, I'll get a puppy," said Miguel. "Not until then."

"How is the house coming along?" asked Rafe.

"We've done as much interior work as we can. Come spring, we'll do the addition." He turned to Lulu with a grin. "You're the one who made me decide to go ahead with it."

As all eyes turned to her, Lulu felt heat rise to her cheeks. "He showed me what it would be like," she said awkwardly.

"I agree it's a very romantic idea," said Becca, sitting next to Miguel. She nudged his arm. "But then he's such a romantic guy."

"All the girls in the valley think so," Cami said, continuing to tease him. "How many hearts are you going to break when you leave next week?"

Miguel held up his hands. "Stop!" The smile that had been on his face was gone. "You know I don't play around when it comes to the serious stuff. Sure, I date a lot and have fun, but that's because I haven't met the right girl yet. I'll let you know when I do."

Lulu's body tensed at his hurtful words. She worked hard to maintain a neutral expression while her body felt as if it had been pierced with an arrow.

Cami stood. "Who's ready for another mimosa?"

Lulu raised her hand. "I am," she said, ignoring the frown on her mother's face.

After a delicious brunch, Lulu helped Cami with the dishes and then announced she was going to lie down. Maybe it was all the emotions of the day, but she was exhausted. Rafe and her mother had already left for their walk through the vineyards.

As she lay atop the bed, Lulu decided as soon as the holidays were over, she'd invite Will to visit Chandler Hill so they could have a chance to talk seriously about the future. Then maybe she would have a better idea of what it might be like to share a life with him. It was obvious that a relationship between Miguel and her was not going to happen. He'd stated very clearly that he hadn't met the right girl yet. Pain squeezed her heart.

CHAPTER ELEVEN

Over coffee the next morning, Rosalie asked Cami for permission to stay until January 2nd instead of returning to L.A. on the twenty-seventh of December as planned.

"Rafe suggested I spend New Year's Eve and day here at Chandler Hill. He knows how hard the holidays can be," Rosalie explained to Cami and Lulu together. "He's such a sweet man and still so in love with his Lettie."

"Of course, you may stay! I'm very happy you want to." Cami's eyes filled. "The relationship between Rafe and my grandmother is the kind I want with Drew. Loving and lasting."

"A good man is hard to find," said Rosalie. "But your Drew seems very nice. And the two of you look happy together."

"I'm thinking of inviting Will here after the holidays," said Lulu. "I'm still not sure whether I want to help him with his campaign or not."

In the silence that followed, Rosalie said to Cami, "Rafe also spoke to me about you and your need to know information about your father. He told me you've wondered about him for a long time and began searching for information right after you met Lulu."

"I feel like I didn't know the real man very much myself," Lulu said. "Is it going to hurt you to talk about him, Mom? If not, I'd like to hear too."

"It's a good idea for both of you to know more about him. Human beings are complex. He wasn't all bad like the press would make you believe. You, Lulu, know more than most that he truly wanted to do good things for our country, the world."

"Yes," Lulu agreed. She turned to Cami. "Is this a good time to sit and talk? I know you usually head to the inn at this time."

Cami checked the clock on the microwave. "Let me call Becca to tell her I'll be late and we can do it now. Are you ready, Rosalie?"

Lulu's mother let out a long sigh. "I suppose now is as good a time as any, and I do believe Rafe is right. Both of you should have a chance to know about your father from someone other than political junkies or the press."

"I'll fix more coffee," said Lulu.

"And I'll refresh the plate of biscuits," added Cami. "Even though my stomach is whirling with excitement, I think we should all be as comfortable as possible. Why don't we go into the living room? I'll get a fire going, making the room nice and cozy."

As Lulu prepared the coffee, her stomach was as unsettled as it had been for weeks. She realized how nervous she was about her mother remaining well and glanced over at her. Except for the way her mother's eyebrows were drawn into a frown, she seemed at ease about the upcoming conversation.

Lulu settled on the couch next to her mother; Cami curled up on a wide chair angled at the end of the couch toward them.

"Rosalie, I'm so grateful for your agreeing to do this," said Cami. "You have no idea how often I've wondered who my father was, what he looked like, why my mother refused to talk about him, and all the questions I had about him since I was a child. Nonnee and Rafe agreed to abide by my mother's wishes not to press for information, but I've always had a need to know about him."

"I can imagine your curiosity, your desire to find out more. We all want to know about family." Rosalie was quiet and then spoke softly. "As I've mentioned, I grew up an only child with parents who adored me. My father and I were always close and grew even closer after my mother died of cancer when I was twelve. Without my mother around, as I became older I grew into the role of hostess for my father. He was a successful businessman and was a part of society."

Lulu looked to Cami and made a face. "My mother made sure I did all those social things. Cotillion and all that."

"Yes, well I thought it best. At any rate, my father and Edward's father decided Edward and I would make the perfect pair. William Kingsley had great political ambition for his only son and needed a wife for him who had the right connections and could oversee the social requirements necessary to help him succeed in politics. I'd just broken up with a man I truly loved when Bill Kingsley and my father approached me. Devastated at losing who I'd thought was my one true love, I agreed to meet Edward."

Rosalie took a sip of coffee and sat back against the couch lost in memory. "Edward was always an impressive man—good looking, bright, full of energy, and with the ability to appear to listen to others. I was intrigued from the beginning." She let out a little laugh. "Who wasn't?"

"Did you know about his trip to Africa?" Cami asked, leaning forward.

"That trip to Africa and Asia was all he could talk about for months, and then just after we were married, he grew quiet about it. We had Lulu right away and tried for more children immediately after that. But Teddy didn't appear for some time."

The look her mother gave her was full of such sadness, Lulu held her breath.

"We both loved that boy. And, Lulu, we loved you too. You were our first child. Teddy came at a time when we were trying to hold things together. We had a few good years and then ..."

her voice trailed off.

"Then he died," Lulu said bluntly.

Rosalie fought tears. "That was the end," she said simply. "I knew Edward was having affairs. Believe it or not, that was something I could accept. But I couldn't deal with the fact that I knew he'd always loved another woman more than me. That letter I once found from her was something he read over and over." She turned to Cami. "Though he tried, he was never able to hide that."

"I'm sorry," Cami said softly.

"Oh, sweetheart, there's nothing for you to be sorry about. I knew from the beginning that we'd both made a mistake by marrying. And after all we'd been through together, I grew tired of trying to be the picture of a perfect wife. I wanted a man who loved me just for being me. But, of course, divorce wasn't an option. In politics, you hang onto a bad marriage to reach long-range goals. But one thing I want the two of you to know is that you were both loved. Your father was bright and dedicated, a lot like the two of you."

"Did he ever talk about me or my mother?" Cami asked, and then was appalled by her question. "I'm sorry, that may be insensitive of me to ask—"

Rosalie cut her off. "We talked about her once, right after he came back from Africa, before we were married. Then we vowed never to speak of her again. And we didn't. I had no idea about a child until I found the letter from Autumn. One reason I wanted to come to Chandler Hill now was to be able to reach out to you." Tears trailed down Rosalie's cheeks. "If your mother was anything like you, Cami, I can understand why Edward loved her."

Cami let out a soft cry and covered her face with her hands.

Lulu went to her and sat on the edge of the seat of the chair. Hugging her, Lulu whispered, "I think our father would be pleased we are together." She straightened. "And, Mom, Dad would be proud of the way you've handled this. You're a true class act."

"Thank you, darling. I've always wanted more children. Maybe in time, Cami will accept me as part of the family."

Cami lifted her tear-streaked face. "I already do."

The three of them were still dabbing at their eyes with tissues when Rafe knocked on the door and entered the house. He gaped at them and blanched. "What's wrong?"

Cami ran over to her grandfather. "We've increased our family by two. Is that okay with you?"

He glanced over to Rosalie and Lulu and nodded. "Lettie would love it."

"How about some coffee?" Cami asked.

He shook his head. "I'm here to see if Rosalie wants to go see Taunton Estates. Thought we'd better get out this morning. Cold and rain are due here this afternoon."

Rosalie stood. "Give me some time to get ready, and I'd love to see your winery."

"Better take Cami up on her offer for coffee," said Lulu with a teasing smile. "It might take a while for Mom to get ready."

"Okay, I'll do that," Rafe said agreeably, following Cami into the kitchen.

Lulu left them and hurried to her mother's room. Her mother was standing at the sliding-glass door leading to the deck outside her room.

"Are you all right?" Lulu asked, coming up behind her.

Her mother turned to her. "Just a little sad about all that's happened. But I'll get over it. Rafe understands what a difficult situation we've been through. While we weren't a love match, I loved your father as a person—a flawed, controlling man I spent over half of my life married to. I still am struggling with his death. Rafe understands that too. He's not over Lettie's death. Truthfully, he probably never will be."

"Is there anything I can do for you?" Lulu said. "Have you taken your meds?"

"Yes, Lulu, I have," her mother said with an unmistakable edge to her voice.

She hid her annoyance and forced a smile. "Just checking."

Her mother cupped Lulu's cheek. "Thanks."

As Lulu walked her mother out of the room to meet Rafe, she felt more like the mother than the child. Then, seeing the smile that crossed her mother's face, she pushed away her anxiety. Chandler Hill was such a magical place.

Lulu saw little of her mother for the remaining days of her visit,. The inn was busy with guests arriving for the New Year's Eve celebration that had become the "in" place to be on that evening. The Barn was busy with after-holiday sales, freshening the store with new merchandise, and blending catalog items in with the regular inventory.

By the time New Year's Eve came, Lulu decided she was too tired to go to the inn. She'd been having headaches on and off, along with a nervous stomach, and she longed to spend the evening in her PJs reading a book or crying over a movie. Will had called and suggested coming to see her in Oregon for the holiday, but Lulu had nicely but firmly told him not to come until after her mother had gone, and she could concentrate on him.

"Are you sure you want to stay home? After the party here, staff and friends get together to celebrate on our own," said Cami. She was dressed in a long-sleeved, forest-green, silky sheath that complemented her strawberry-blond hair and trim body beautifully.

"I'm sure," Lulu said, stifling a yawn. "The thought of

alcohol and rich food is nauseating. My mother and I are going to share a simple supper here. Besides, I have to work the morning shift at The Barn and want to be rested to do that. I have the next day off to take my mother to the airport. Rafe offered, but I told him it was important to me to do this for her."

"It's been nice that they've become friends," Cami said. "I think they've really enjoyed one another."

"Yes," replied Lulu cautiously. Her mother had been doing so well, she was worried about her.

At the airport before the flight home, Lulu's mother began to fret. "I don't want to go back to my old life. But I can't leave California. Not now. I have Melba to take care of."

"Mom, Melba is the one who takes care of you. Not the other way around."

Her mother waved Lulu's comments away. "Oh, I know that. But I keep an eye on her too. She's like the sister I've always wanted. And what would I do if I left L.A.? All my friends are there."

"The one or two who have stuck with you through all the mess with Dad?" said Lulu, unable to hide her disgust. Her stomach roiled. "After you get home and get settled, you and I can talk about things. Hopefully by then, I'll have come to some decision about Will and his campaign."

Her mother sighed. "All right. That sounds sensible."

When at last it was time for her mother to enter the security line, Lulu gave her mother another hug and kiss and said, "I love you. Safe trip."

Her mother's eyes grew moist. "I love you too."

Before the scene could become maudlin, Lulu turned and walked away.

CHAPTER TWELVE

When Lulu returned to Chandler Hill, she went right to the inn. Most of the guests had left, leaving staff behind busily cleaning the rooms.

Lulu knocked on the door to Cami's office and, when invited to "Come on in," opened the door.

Cami beamed at her. "Hi! Becca and I are talking about her wedding. She's always been thinking of a winter wedding, but now she's considering putting it off until nicer weather."

Lulu glanced at Becca. "That makes sense. It's a pretty miserable day today—cold and cloudy. Guess I got spoiled by all the mild weather, but I gather from the news this weather is more typical for this time of year."

"It's hard to wait to get married, but Dan and I are living together anyway. I just don't want to get pregnant before my wedding."

The headache that had hovered earlier broke loose in Lulu's head with a burst of bright stars. She grabbed onto the edge of the chair and closed her eyes.

"Are you all right?" asked Cami. Her voice sounded as if it was coming through a hollow pipe.

Lulu started to answer and felt herself falling.

When Lulu opened her eyes, a stranger in a blue sweater and dark pants was staring down at her with concern. Kneeling beside her, he was holding onto her wrist with one hand and feeling her forehead with the other.

"Hello, I'm Dr. Miller, a guest at the hotel. How are you doing? Can you tell me what happened?"

She turned her head. She was still in Cami's office. Cami and Becca were staring down at her wide-eyed. "Dr. Miller was passing by when I went to get help," explained Cami.

"I'm okay. Guess I got a little dizzy, probably from the headaches I've been having. That, or maybe I'm catching the flu. I haven't been feeling well."

Dr. Miller stood and helped her sit up. "Doing okay now?"

She nodded. "I just feel a little foolish. That's all."

"Your temperature and heart rate are fine. You might be a little dehydrated. It happens at this time of year with all the celebrations, rich food, and alcohol."

"That must be it," Lulu said, knowing that wasn't the case at all. She hadn't been drinking alcohol or eating rich foods lately. No, it was probably much worse than anything he'd described. The only thing she wanted to do was to leave Cami's office and go home to bed.

After helping her to her feet and leading her to a chair, Dr. Miller turned to Cami. "I think your sister will be fine. She just needs to take it easy for the rest of the day."

"Okay. Thanks for coming to our aid." Cami shook his hand. "I appreciate it."

As he turned to leave, Lulu tugged on Cami's arm. "How long was I out?"

"Just a few seconds. He was right outside the office when I called for help."

"It's nothing." Lulu's wobbly voice turned into a wail before she burst into tears.

Cami wrapped her arms around Lulu. "My God! What's going on?"

Lulu slowly drew several deep breaths in and out, trying to

calm herself. Feeling sicker than she had for the past few weeks, she managed to say, "I think I'm pregnant." She pushed past Cami and Becca, raced into the office's private bathroom, and threw up.

"Oh, sweetie," said Cami, coming up behind her and handing her a cold cloth. "I'm so sorry."

"I'll have to tell Will," Lulu said, aware she couldn't be part of his campaign now. The rumors would kill his chances of winning, especially when the talk concerned the daughter of a man disgraced by his actions.

Lulu grabbed Cami's extended hand and got to her feet. Facing Cami and Becca, she felt a new strength come to her.

"Please don't mention this to anyone. I haven't figured out what I'm going to do. Right now, I feel as if my world has just collapsed."

"Okay," said Cami. "We're here for you."

"Absolutely," Becca said, giving her a little hug.

"You both promise me you won't even mention it to your guys?"

Cami and Becca held up their right hands.

"Okay, thanks. Now, I'd like to go home and get some rest," Lulu said with as much dignity as she could muster. She felt like curling up into a fetal position and staying there until she faded away into a memory.

"I'll drive you," said Cami with a firmness Lulu wasn't even going to try to challenge.

They walked out of the inn together.

Cami gave her a look of such concern, it brought tears to her eyes. "Are you going to be all right?"

Lulu shrugged. "Is it okay if I stay with you until I make a decision?"

"Oh, hon, of course. The way the house is designed you can come and go as you wish without disturbing Drew and me, and maintain the privacy you've always wanted."

"Thanks," Lulu replied, fighting fresh tears. After the news about the possibility of her working with Will had come out, she'd have to think of a way to gracefully back out of that job. She clutched her hands, feeling sick all over again. She was in such a mess.

Cami pulled into her driveway. "Remember, I'm only minutes away if you need me."

Lulu nodded and managed a smile. "Thanks, sis."

Walking into the empty house, Lulu felt more alone than she ever had. She didn't need to take a pregnancy test. Now that she thought about it, all the symptoms were there. The underlying nausea she'd felt for weeks, her tiredness, even the change in her breasts, which she'd attributed it to the weight she'd gained from all the good food. And there was only one man responsible. But how? He'd made sure of protection. Had a condom broke?

She turned around and headed down the hill to the special grove of trees reserved for family. The peaceful atmosphere there was something everyone in the family sought when they were troubled, and she was more than troubled. She'd made the worst mistake of her life.

There, among the pines whose scented boughs whispered in the breeze and the hardwood trees whose sterile branches seemed as empty as her future, Lulu paced back and forth.

When she heard the sound of footsteps behind her, she knew who it was. She turned and fought back tears.

"What is it, *Cariño?*" asked Rafe.

The tender expression on his face broke the dam of her resolve. Crying, she ran into his outstretched arms.

"Oh, Rafe, I've made such a mess of my life. I don't know what I'm going to do," she sobbed.

Rafe patted her back. "Let's start by finding out what the

problem is. Come, sit with me."

She found a place beside him on the bench and stared at him through blurred vision. "I'm pretty sure I'm pregnant. All the signs are there. I've ruined my life."

"Well, now, I've always thought a baby added to life," he said calmly. "If you're pregnant, it doesn't have to be a catastrophe."

"Oh, but I'll have to tell Will I can't help him with his campaign, and I certainly can't marry him."

"It's not his baby?"

Lulu shook her head. "No. And I don't want the father to know. I'll raise the baby alone."

"Whoever the father is, he has a right to know," said Rafe. The edge to his voice reminded Lulu of his own circumstances with his daughter, Autumn.

She gasped. "Oh, Rafe, I'm sorry I forgot ..."

"Any man has the right to know about such things and then take responsibility for his actions." His steady gaze made her shift uncomfortably.

"Who is it?" Rafe asked quietly. "Someone we know?"

She emitted a long, painful sigh. "It's Miguel. We went out one evening. We got carried away standing in the moonlight talking about the plans he has for his house. And then, later, he was so ... tender ... and..."

"He's an honorable man. He'll want to do the right thing by you," said Rafe, squeezing her arm with encouragement.

Miserable, Lulu sniffed. "At Christmas, you heard him say he hasn't met the right person yet. I don't want any man to feel obligated to marry me. If you insist, I'll tell him about the baby, but that won't change my thinking."

"One step at a time, dear one," said Rafe.

She caught a sob in her throat. "Cami's lucky to have you for a grandfather."

His smile was sweet. "You've forgotten. Cami and I have already included you and your mother in the family."

Lulu hesitated and then asked, "Are you and my mother ..."

"Just friends. She's the same age as Autumn would be if she'd lived. I like to think that Rosalie is allowing me to get to know what it might have felt like to have my daughter here. She can talk to me about most anything because she knows it won't go any further. And I can offer her some of the wisdom I've picked up along the way. She still misses her father, you know."

"I barely remember him. He died before Teddy was born."

"Death is part of living," said Rafe. "That's why it's important to embrace new life."

Lulu's blood rushed from her head. "You wouldn't think ... Oh, Rafe! I would never end this one."

"All right," said Rafe calmly. "You've taken care of step one. Now you can move on to other decisions. Decisions you have to make alone." He rose. "How about a cup of hot tea? My bones are getting chilled."

"Do you have any decaf? I'm going to have to be careful."

Rafe patted her on the back. "Good girl."

After spending more time with Rafe and being reassured he'd tell no one, Lulu felt much better, stronger. She drove into town to the drug store and picked up the test that she felt would be positive. Still, she wanted to be absolutely certain.

Back at home, Lulu sat on the edge of the tub in the bathroom and stared at the test with a calmness that came from knowing the results all along. She figured she was seven weeks or so along. That would mean her baby would be born in August.

Lulu discarded the test and the material that came with it

and went to get her computer. She wasn't made of campaign manager material for nothing.

Sitting at the kitchen table, she made a list of all the things she'd need to do. The call to Will would wait until she was certain everything else was in order.

She made an appointment with an OB/GYN doctor, left a message for a realtor, and made a note to ask Drew about his rental. He had left some of his things there and might be willing to sublease it to her.

With each notation she became more confident of the future. She'd either rent or buy an apartment or condo, work at Chandler Hill Inn, and raise this child alone. Yes, she would tell Miguel about the baby, but not until after he came back from Chile. By then, she'd be settled.

"Keep things simple," she reminded herself aloud. In another week, things should be in order. In the meantime, she'd once again swear Cami and Becca to secrecy. She didn't want anyone else to know about her predicament. In time, it would become all too obvious.

CHAPTER THIRTEEN

When Lulu talked to Drew about the house he was renting, he explained he was leasing it from Abby and Lisa. He gave her their phone number in Arizona and offered to help in any way.

"Thanks," she said, giving him a quick hug. "I've decided to stay in the area and am considering renting or buying a place convenient to the vineyards. I appreciate your help. Cami sure knows how to pick a great guy."

"No problem. Come on by this afternoon, and I'll give you a tour of the place. It's kind of messy, but you'll get the idea. It's a very nice house. I'd buy it myself, but I'm overextended as it is with Lone Creek Winery."

"I understand." Her thoughts flew to Miguel. Thank God she'd elicited promises from Cami and Becca to keep quiet about her predicament. None of them would suspect Miguel was the baby's father, and that's how she wanted to keep it for as long as possible.

That afternoon, she toured the house Drew was renting with growing enthusiasm. Conveniently located between the wineries and town, it was a perfect place for her. The two-story house had three bedrooms, one of which was a master suite on the first floor, a small office, a nice kitchen, and an open living-dining area with a fireplace. A front porch caught the morning sun, and the back deck was the perfect place to view a sunset.

After she toured the house, she gave Abby a call, explaining who she was. "Drew has moved into Cami's house, so I was wondering if you'd be willing to rent it to me. And if you ever decide to sell it, I'd definitely be interested."

They chatted some more about the family and her work at The Barn. "Cami has told us so much about you that we'd be delighted to rent the house to you," said Abby. "As for selling it, I don't think we're ready to do that just yet."

"Thanks so much," Lulu gushed, filled with gratitude. Her circumstance might not be what she wanted, but the vibes of the valley were working in her favor.

"We'll email the paperwork to you. Once a deposit has been made and the paperwork signed, you'll be all set," Abby said.

Lulu ended the call and sat on her bed, weak with relief. Now all that was left was a call to Will and later, after things were settled with him, she'd call her mother.

One week later, Lulu waited at the airport for Will to arrive. When she had told him they needed to talk, he insisted on coming to Chandler Hill against her wishes. Standing among others waiting for disembarked passengers, Lulu's body hummed with nervous energy. She knew very well she and Will would make a great political team, but after spending time at Chandler Hill with Rafe, Cami, and the others, she realized that was not a good reason to decide to marry. And as for the campaign, she'd stay away from it. Will already had enough of a struggle to win a political race because of his connection to her father.

As the minutes for his arrival dragged on, she gazed into space and told herself everything would be all right. Even if their discussion went badly, she was happy with her future life in the valley.

She looked over to find Will striding toward her with a wide smile. Her heartbeat bumped to a stop and sprang ahead to cover the missed tempo. He moved with confidence and looked every bit the handsome, successful man he was striving to be. People automatically turned to him in the crowd, no doubt wondering who he was.

She stepped to one side and greeted him with a quick hug, praying he would understand what she had to tell him.

"Hey, beautiful," he said, snuggling her against his tall, solid body. As he bent down to kiss her, she quickly moved her head to offer her cheek.

He stepped back and studied her. "Should I be worried?"

Reluctantly, she nodded. "Let's get to Chandler Hill, and we'll talk then. I've reserved a room for you. We'll have more privacy."

They were quiet as they headed to Lulu's car. And even after they were settled inside, the silence between them pulsed with unspoken questions and answers. Lulu attempted to fill the time with talk about winemaking, growing grapes, and her job marketing for the wineries.

"Wait until you see what Cami's grandmother and she have created. The Chandler Hill Inn is beautiful, and you'll get a nice taste of Chandler Hill wines."

"I looked it up on the internet, of course. It's a gorgeous piece of property. I can understand why you told me you want to live there, but you're right. We definitely need to talk. I can't let you make a mistake like this."

Lulu bristled at the authoritative tone he'd begun to use, but remained silent. She did not want to have this conversation in a car midway between the airport and the place where she felt safest.

When they finally began to drive up the hill leading to the inn, Will's attention was caught by the scenery. She pulled her car to a stop in front of the inn's entrance.

Will let out a soft, "Wow! Even better than the photographs."

"You're going to feel very pampered here," Lulu said. "Let's go in. I'm sure Cami and Becca have put you in one of my favorite rooms in the original building."

Will got out, grabbed his carry-on bag from the backseat, and followed Lulu to the front entrance. As she did each time she stepped inside, Lulu felt a sense of pride at being related to Cami Chandler. Hers was a proud, successful family who deserved a lot of respect and praise for all their hard work. The end result was stunning.

As soon as they stepped up to the front desk, Lulu heard her name being called and turned to find Cami walking toward them, Becca at her heels.

"You're back," said Cami giving her a hug for a few extra seconds. She glanced at Will, who was staring at her with unconcealed astonishment.

"My God! The two of you could be twins!" He offered Cami his hand. "I'm Wilson Chambers."

"So glad to meet you. And this is Becca Withers, my assistant. Please let us know if we can do anything for you during your stay." Cami grinned at him. "You're with family, and that means a lot."

"I'm here to help you, too," said Becca, smiling and shaking hands with him. She turned as new arrivals headed their way.

Lulu handled the arrangement at the reception desk and then led Will up to one of the upstairs rooms she'd requested. This one had a small balcony off the back of the house and a fireplace in the room. Lulu liked the fact that they'd be able to warm the chill of their conversation with a glowing fire.

She'd tried to analyze her position from all angles, but no matter the direction she followed, it didn't work. She liked

Will a lot, but she didn't love him. Respect wasn't enough of a reason to dedicate her life to him and his work. Because of the affection she did have for him, she didn't want to be in his way, with both her family history and her latest development.

She stepped onto the balcony and wrapped her arms around herself. The sun would soon be going down, but in the growing dusk, the rows and rows of grapevines were impressive.

Will came up behind her. "It's beautiful, isn't it? Full of promise."

Lulu's eyes stung with tears. It was that kind of thinking that touched her.

"Come on inside," he said gently. "We'll both feel better when we know what we're dealing with."

She drew a deep breath. She knew he'd be disappointed in her for so many reasons.

"Let's have a glass of wine," he suggested. He went over to the bottle of wine and basket of treats sitting on a table next to the loveseat in front of the fire.

"You go ahead," Lulu said. "I'll just have water."

Nervous, she waited while he opened the bottle of wine. He hadn't commented on her request for water which meant he was going to be totally unaware of what she had to tell him.

He poured wine into one of the wine glasses and lifted it up. "Beautiful color."

"Oh, yes," said Lulu. "And a beautiful bouquet and smooth finish. It's one of my favorites—light and fruity."

He turned to her with a surprised look. "Wow! You're learning a lot. I'm impressed."

She waited until he'd taken a couple of tastes and then poured more into his glass before patting the place on the couch next to her.

"This would be so much easier if I could say this on the

phone, but I'm glad now that you insisted that we talk here at the Chandler Hill Inn."

"What is it? All I know is that you want to live in Oregon. I've come up with a way for you to do both—live in California and stay at the winery part-time."

She sighed. "I never had the chance to finish our conversation. There are several reasons why I can't contemplate thinking about growing our relationship or working with you on your campaign. I'll just say it. I'm pregnant."

"What? How? I mean ... who?"

"That is going to remain private information because I intend to raise this baby alone."

Will jumped to his feet and began pacing the room. "This is crazy. I didn't know you were dating anyone. And any baby needs a father. If you're intending to raise the baby by yourself, why don't you let me help you?"

"But the campaign ..."

"The public will love it—me helping you with your mystery baby." His eyes widened. "Oh, Lulu, I didn't mean that the way it sounded."

Her eyes misted. "Of course, you did. You have your mind on the campaign. Though it's painful, I understand. Besides, I think the issue would bring up all sorts of bad things about my father. Can you imagine? Like father, like daughter." Her laugh was bitter. "I'm not going through anything like that again."

Will knelt down in front of her. "You need me. What are you going to do here in the middle of nowhere? You need to be by my side."

"No, I need to stand on my own two feet, take care of the situation myself, and build a life I truly want." Lulu surprised herself with her calm, firm words.

He rose and stared down at her. "Yeah? How?"

She got to her feet and faced him. "I'm helping Cami and the others by taking charge of marketing for all three wineries. It's a big job, a challenging one I intend to do well. I've already rented a house and will be settling in soon. I appreciate your offer, Will, but I'm sorry. I can't do what you want."

He sank into the couch and covered his face with his hands. When he looked up, the sadness on his face was gut-wrenching for her to see. "I've loved you for a long time, Lulu. I should've told you before now, but with everything going on with your father, I knew I couldn't. Now, it's too late."

Lulu sat down beside him and put her arm around him. "I'm so sorry, Will. But I can't be less than honest with you. It wouldn't work between us for many reasons."

"You've never loved me?" His handsome features contorted with misery.

Lulu swallowed hard at the pain in his voice. "You've been a loyal friend to my family and for that, I'll always love you, but not in the way you want."

His sigh said it all. "I should probably get going. No use in my staying." He rose to his feet.

Lulu followed. "Don't go. I want us always to be friends, and I need you to understand what Chandler Hill and my new family mean to me."

He paused.

In an attempt at humor, she added, "Besides, if you're going to run for president one day, you need to know as many people as possible."

With obvious effort, he tried to smile. "Do they know about the baby and us?"

"I'm keeping quiet about the pregnancy, so please don't mention it. They know how much I admire you, and even though they know I've chosen to stay in the valley, they're anxious to get to spend some time with you. It's a wonderful group of people."

He sighed. "As long as I'm here, I might as well take a couple of days off from work and try to enjoy myself."

She lifted on her toes and kissed his cheek. "I do care about you, you know."

"Maybe I hesitated because I was concerned all along that it wouldn't work," he said, tilting his head in confusion. "Some guy is going to be very lucky to have you for his partner one day. I'm sorry it isn't me."

She hugged him and lay her head against his chest for a moment, well aware she was letting go of a man with whom she could've built a good life.

CHAPTER FOURTEEN

Like any true politician, Will seemed to let go of his dashed hopes easily and enter into the spirit of the weekend. Only Lulu, who knew him well, was aware of his deep disappointment in her. She tried to make it up to him by introducing him to the family, the inn, and the area, hoping he'd understand some of her decision.

On Sunday morning, Lulu sat with Cami in her office.

"I think it would be nice to gather family and friends together to meet Will on his last night with us," said Cami.

"Very nice. I'm sure he'd like that."

"I want to hold the party at the inn so I can spend quality time with Will. Because he knew our father so well, I'm hoping to get some information about him from Will."

"Of course," said Lulu. "I'll feel better knowing you're not stuck in the kitchen at home while everyone else is relaxing. Can I do anything to help set this up?"

Cami shook her head. "No, thanks. I'm going to have Darren and his wife, Liz,work their magic in the kitchen and come up with anything they want. It's a slow time of year, and they're anxious to keep busy."

Lulu squeezed her affectionately. "Thanks for being so understanding. I think Will is beginning to see how lucky I am to have found you."

Cami hesitated, then said, "Are you sure you're doing the right thing?"

"Yes, I've thought it through, and this is the best resolution for me. If your Nonnee could raise a child alone, I can too."

Cami studied her. "Will seems nice. I'm a little surprised he's let you go so easily."

Lulu arched her brows. "Doesn't that tell you something? He wanted me for a partner. I suspect for his campaign more than anything else. And he never actually got down on one knee to ask me to marry him. When the time comes for something like that, I want it to be perfect."

"When he proposed, Drew caught me off guard and then was so sweet about it. I understand you'd want the same thing." Cami smiled at the memory.

Lulu remained quiet. Only Rafe knew who the father of her baby was, and that was how she intended to keep it.

That night, Lulu dressed in black slacks and a long-sleeved silk blouse in a rich, deep shade of green that went well with the emerald and diamond earrings her mother had given her for Christmas. The simplicity of the outfit showed the tiniest expansion in her abdomen. Frowning at her outline in the full-length mirror, Lulu realized she'd have to purchase some new clothes—ones that would better hide her condition.

Cami knocked on her door and stuck her head inside. "Ready?"

"Coming," Lulu replied, pleased by her sister's excitement. Hospitality came so easily to Cami.

At the inn, a few guests lingered in the library enjoying drinks and conversation. Lulu and Cami stopped to say hello and then proceeded to the small dining room. As promised, Lulu texted Will they'd arrived.

Moments later, Will walked into the dining room looking as polished as ever. The clean, country air had added color to his cheeks, and the sadness that had coated his features had disappeared. Though Lulu was pleased to see it, she wondered how deep his proclaimed love had really been.

"You ladies look lovely. Where are the others?"

"I wanted to come early to greet some of the inn's guests and to make sure things were set for this evening. I've given Darren and Liz *carte blanche* to create whatever they wanted for the meal."

A movement at the door caught their attention. Imani, Cami's assistant, walked into the room with Gwen and Laurel, followed by Rafe, Drew, Becca, and Dan.

"Ah, the party has arrived, I see," said Will. He went over to greet everyone. Lulu watched the way flushes of pink colored the women's cheeks as he spoke to them and understood that's the way it would always be with him. Like her father, he had the ability to charm anyone.

"What are you thinking?" Cami asked softly. "I noticed you staring at him. Are you sorry about the choice you made?"

Lulu shook her head. "Not at all. I'm actually relieved."

"I'm sure things will work out." Cami turned as Drew walked over to her and gave her a kiss on the cheek.

"How's my favorite girl," he said, drawing her into her arms.

Cami laughed and hugged him before stepping away to answer Darren's beckoning wave.

Drew turned to her. "You're looking nice, Lulu. Cami tells me you're going through a rough time. Anything we can do to help?"

Lulu shook her head. "Thanks, but I'll get through it. By the way, I've signed the lease for the house so I can move in anytime."

"I'll get the rest of my things out of there," Drew said. "Like I said before, it's a great house. I think you'll be happy there."

"Me, too," Lulu said with determination.

Cami announced it was time to find seats at the table. Name cards had been placed by each table setting. Lulu was pleased to see she was seated between Rafe and Becca.

Liz oversaw the waitstaff as bowls of soup were carried in and placed before them.

"We're starting with Butternut Squash Apple Soup with Sage Parmesan Croutons," Liz announced. "I think you'll find it a nice beginning to your meal on this chilly, rainy day."

She left the room, and it was quiet as everyone tasted the soup. Satisfied murmuring followed.

"How's that puppy of yours doing?" Rafe asked Becca.

She laughed and shook her head. "He's into everything. But, like Dan says, he's going to be a very nice dog."

Conversation remained light among the group. Seated opposite Will, Lulu saw how much fun he and Imani seemed to be having as they talked to one another. On his other side, Gwen was looking as if she wasn't feeling well.

When she got up, Lulu followed her to the ladies' room. "Are you all right?" she asked Gwen, alarmed by how pale she'd become.

"It must be the flu," Gwen said. "I haven't been able to shake it."

"Let me know if there's anything I can do," Lulu said. "Do you need to go home now?"

Gwen shook her head. "I'll just put cold water on my face and then I'm sure I'll feel better."

Lulu returned to the dining room just as Liz was announcing that their main course was Cornish Hen with Garlic and Rosemary, accompanied by a mélange of winter vegetables and rice.

Cami shot her a look of concern as Lulu took her seat. "Is Gwen okay?"

"I think so," said Lulu, even as a niggling worry buried inside her.

Gwen returned. After she was settled, Rafe lifted his wine glass. "Here's to us! We've come together for different reasons, but we share an affection for one another that is and always will be there."

"Yes!" said Cami, raising her glass. "We've only just begun to know you, Will, but I'm sure we'll see more of you in the future."

Lulu shot Cami a look of horror at what Cami might be implying. She hadn't told Cami the father of her baby wasn't Will.

Cami noticed and quickly added. "I meant with the political race on which you're about to embark."

As they raised their glasses and enjoyed sips of the wine, no one else at the table seemed to notice her discomfort, or the fact she'd held her glass but hadn't take a sip.

Rafe placed his hand on hers and she drew a deep breath. It was silly, she knew, to try to hide the fact of what had happened, but in this group of wine lovers, sooner or later they'd notice.

This special evening was a lovely gesture, Lulu thought as she sipped her tea after dinner. Not only for Will, but for Imani, Gwen, Becca, and Laurel. Cami had put together a capable, loyal team. She glanced at Gwen and was relieved to see she was acting more like herself.

"Thank you, everyone, for coming," Cami said, getting to her feet as people began to prepare to leave. "Hopefully, Will, this has given you a nice send-off with all our thoughts on what we'd like to see happening in government."

He glanced at her with a warm smile. "I now have a very good idea of what it's like to live here. I understand completely why Lulu has chosen to stay."

Lulu listened to his easy banter, thinking how much he acted like her father and if her father were alive, how proud he'd be of his student.

Will came over to her. "I've arranged for a driver to pick me up early tomorrow morning. Want to join me for a few private minutes to say goodbye?"

"Sure. I'd like that." Will was a friend and, she hoped, he always would be.

They walked up to his room, and, as before, sat in front of the fireplace facing one another.

"I'm glad my family liked you, Will." Lulu said. "And I'm even happier that you liked them."

"They're great! But, Lulu, you could be doing something so much more meaningful with your life. It's nice to be what Rafe laughingly calls a "grape farmer," but together we could be doing things that would really matter to everyone."

"At what cost to family?" said Lulu. "You love the spotlight. I don't. And what so many politicians forget is that this nation was built on core values of virtue, hard work, and a belief in doing for others in what little ways one can. My new family epitomizes that."

Will sighed and shook his head. "I can see that I'm not going to be able to change your mind. I think your father would be disappointed."

A torrent of feelings rushed through Lulu and spilled out of her. "My father was a lying, cheating bastard who all but destroyed my mother and me! Don't you get it? I try to be fair about the good things he did, but bottom line, he's someone who can't even begin to compare to a man like Rafe."

"Whoa! Where did that come from?" Will said, holding his hands in front of him to ward off her anger.

"It came from my heart," Lulu said softly and blinked back tears. She stood. "I'm sorry, but I have to go. I wish you well with everything. I know you'll give it your best."

He stood, leaned down and kissed her cheek. "Good luck with the baby. I wish it were mine."

Unable to find words, she gave him a little hug, and left the room.

CHAPTER FIFTEEN

The following morning, Lulu awoke with a new sense of purpose. In the coming days, she was moving out of Cami's home and into the rental down the road. She hadn't wanted to do it while Will was around because, to her, it symbolized a new beginning.

With it being a slow time of year, she had the day off to begin cleaning the house. Far from the portrait the press had painted of her, she knew very well how to clean a house. Melba had made sure of that.

Thinking of Melba, she punched in her cell number.

Melba's cheery "Hello" brought a smile to Lulu.

"How are you?" Lulu asked her. "And how is my mother?"

"I'm fine, thank you, and so is your mother. After all these years of trying to come up with the right combination of medicines, we've finally found one that is keeping her steady."

"She was wonderful here at Christmas. I kept waiting for things to change, but they didn't," admitted Lulu.

"What's going on with you?" Melba asked.

Lulu wished she could be honest, but she wasn't ready to tell Melba or her mother about the baby. "I'm moving into a rental house. In fact, I was going to ask you about that cleaning solution you use for the bathroom."

"You're cleaning the house yourself?"

"As much as possible," Lulu said. "It's part of my plan for making a fresh start."

"Good girl," said Melba. "I'll email you a list of my favorite products. Here's your mother. She wants to say hello."

"Lulu, I'm so glad you called. I've been thinking of you and everyone there. I want to make another visit as soon as possible. I felt so well, so happy there."

"I've rented a three-bedroom house. When you come, you can stay with me."

"How lovely. I take it everything is settled between you and Will. He told me he was going to convince you to join him, but it sounds as if that isn't happening."

"No," said Lulu. "I don't want the kind of life you had with Dad."

"I'm so glad," Rosalie said. "I wanted you to make your own choice, but I was worried about it."

A new tenderness filled Lulu. She and her mother were building a stronger relationship. As her stomach rumbled, she wondered if news of the baby would destroy it.

"Well, my darling. Have a good day. Talk to you later."

Lulu clicked off the call and padded into the kitchen. Drew had already left for work but Cami was sitting at the kitchen table sipping a cup of coffee. She looked up at Lulu and smiled.

"You're cleaning the house today?"

"Yes," said Lulu. "If it gets overwhelming, I'll do as you suggested and hire some of the inn staff to help, but I'm thinking of this process as a cleansing of sorts."

"I like that," said Cami. "I have to admit, though, I'm going to miss you around here. Especially in the morning when we sit like this and talk."

"Yeah, I will too. But it's only fair that you and Drew have the place to yourself."

They talked about the weather and the plans to do an inventory for The Barn.

"I'm worried about Gwen," Lulu said. "Last night she looked terrible."

"Yes, I've noticed," said Cami. "I'm going to suggest she see a doctor. You might have to take over for her. You and one of the other women."

"Gwen and I have already processed orders for new items, so that's been taken care of. I can help you decide about themes and changes in the layout of the store to enhance the new merchandise."

"That would be great." Cami rose. "I'd better get ready for work. Good luck today."

Lulu fixed herself a cup of decaf coffee, mixed some raspberries and granola with yogurt, and sat at the breakfast table to plot out a plan. The house was mostly furnished, but Lulu wanted to add some new furniture pieces to the space. And she needed to buy sheets, towels, and other small things. Drew hadn't fussed much with the house and had eaten out or at Cami's most of the time he'd rented the house.

After breakfast, Lulu put on jeans and a sweatshirt and tied her hair in a long ponytail. After checking Melba's email for cleaning suggestions, her first stop would be one of the local stores for supplies. She'd pick up bottled water and a few light, healthy snacks.

Later, as she pulled up to the house, Lulu turned off the ignition and studied the house that was to be her home for the next year.

The tan-painted clapboards of the sprawling two-story house reminded Lulu of the color of her mother's house in California. But all similarities ended there. Towering red alder and bigleaf maple trees, evergreen bushes, and flowering plants surrounded the house nestled between two rolling hills. The two tall, arched windows facing her resembled inquisitive eyes studying its new occupant. A wide front door whose red-wine hue was the perfect bright touch was welcoming. Though the design of the exterior was simple, Lulu knew from her previous visit how lovely it was inside. Sliding-glass doors led from the large living area to a patio over which a vine-covered pergola gave some protection from rain and sun. The view from inside looked out over a large yard that contained a vegetable and herb garden, perennial flowers, and an apple tree. Lisa, who loved gardening, had created something very special. Lulu couldn't wait to see it abloom.

As Lulu unloaded her bags of groceries and cleaning supplies in the kitchen, she admired what Abby had done with the interior decorating. Throughout the living area, walls painted a pale, pale gold served as a background for the few paintings Abby and Lisa had left behind.

The large, river-rock fireplace had a wide hearth for sitting and was flanked by bookshelves that still displayed a number of books along with several metal and wood art pieces. Lulu supposed when it came time to rent or sell the house to someone outside of the Chandler Hill family, everything of Abby's and Lisa's would be removed. In the meantime, she was grateful for the few homey touches left behind.

Lulu cheerfully started with the kitchen, excited about the prospect of having her own private space. Drew hadn't cooked much, but he'd still left a mess behind.

After she got the kitchen pretty much the way she wanted it, Lulu started another list, this time adding groceries and kitchen items. Following research online, she decided to skip cleaning the rest of the house and drive to Keiser where Bed Bath and Beyond and Target stores were located. Besides, after spending the morning cleaning the kitchen, she was ready for a break.

Hours later, Lulu drove up the driveway to her house exhausted. One purchase had led to another. Her car was loaded with all kinds of things required for her new living arrangement. Thankfully, her savings account covered most of the cost. But she was glad for the job she had at Chandler Hill.

As she headed to the front door, she noticed movement in the house and stopped. Not sure whether it was safe or not, she pulled out her phone in case she needed to call 911.

The front door opened and her mother, Melba, and Cami emerged wearing wide smiles.

"Surprise!" Cami cried.

Lulu dropped the packages she'd been holding and ran toward them. "Mom! Melba! What are you doing here?" She exchanged hugs with them and turned to Cami. "Did you set this up? I see now that you pulled your car out back."

"No, Cami didn't do this," Melba said. "After your mother and I talked to you on the phone this morning, we both agreed you were holding something back. Rosalie and I decided to hop onto a plane and come see what is going on with you."

Her mother wrapped an arm around Lulu's shoulder. "Are you all right?"

Lulu nodded, but couldn't stop the tears streaming from her eyes.

Cami said quietly. "It's all going to be all right, but I'm glad the two of you are here."

"Yes, oh yes," said Lulu, sniffing and wiping her eyes.

"I've already got them settled at my house," Cami explained to her. "And tonight, you can either go to the inn or order dinner in."

"Cami, dear, that's so nice of you," Rosalie commented.

"Yes, indeed," said Melba, giving Cami a grateful smile.

Melba was a striking woman. Mahogany skin, smooth as silk, covered a tall, trim body and fine facial features. Lulu knew from the past that Melba had been offered a role in a movie, which she didn't hesitate to turn down. She was a woman who didn't like subterfuge and yet had lived through it with her dearest friend. Lulu filled with a sense of gratitude and love for her.

"What did Jerome say about your taking off like this, Melba?" Lulu asked her.

Melba laughed. "I think he was as relieved as I to have some time apart. Since he retired a few months ago, we both want more space. Love that man, but 24/7 is a few hours too many."

Lulu chuckled. Their devotion to one another was well known.

"Mom, while you're here I'm hoping you'll help me fix up the house."

Rosalie's eyes shone and then became moist. "Oh, I'd love to do that. And I want Melba to meet Rafe. He was so helpful to me over Christmas. Such a dear friend."

Lulu and Melba exchanged glances. Her mother was continuing to make progress.

"Okay, I've got to go back to the inn. I'll see the three of you this evening." Cami gave them a little wave and left.

Melba took Lulu's hand. "Let's sit for a while and talk. Like I said, both your mother and I know something's wrong. What is it?"

The soft, reassuring tone of Melba's voice undid Lulu. She began sobbing.

Her mother guided her to the couch, and the three of them sat together, with Lulu in the middle. Her mother held one hand, Melba the other.

Lulu inhaled several deep, shuddering breaths and then blurted out, "I'm pregnant!"

"What? With Will?" said her mother.

"Oh, honey. It's not that bad. He's a good man," said Melba.

Lulu sniffed, pulled out a tissue from her pocket and dabbed at her eyes. "It's not Will."

"Then who is it?" asked her mother.

"It doesn't matter. I'm going to raise this baby alone," said Lulu doing her best to hide her misery.

"When is the baby due?" Melba's dark eyes were full of concern.

"August."

"Then it happened here," said Melba.

"Yes." Lulu blinked rapidly. "It was just one night. The whole evening with him was special."

"Does the father know?" asked her mother, her brow creased with concern.

"No, he's away in Chile."

Her mother's eyes widened. "Oh, my! Are you talking about Rafe's nephew, the one who owns the Lone Creek Winery with Drew? He was charming."

Surprise stopped Lulu from speaking. She'd forgotten her mother had met Miguel at Christmastime. "Yes. When he's in a room, he commands attention. Women are drawn to him. Sort of like ..."

"... your father," her mother finished for her.

"Oh, Mom, I'm sorry. I didn't mean ..."

"It's all right, darling. We both know what it was like. Best that you not get involved with a man like that."

"No, he isn't like Dad," Lulu protested, rising to his defense. "Not really." She remembered how Miguel had texted her, how he'd brought Belgian chocolates to Christmas dinner at Cami's, how he'd waited for her call.

"What is he like, Lulu?" asked Melba softly.

Lulu sighed. "For one thing, he's kind. At a restaurant, he protected me from a man angry about Dad, and even though one woman thinks he's going to marry her, he's tried to explain that's never going to happen. He offered to take me home because I had a couple of beers and wasn't as steady as usual. He works hard. Cami and Becca tease him about dating so many women, but like he said at Christmas, he hasn't met the right one yet." Lulu's eyes welled with tears at the stab of pain she still experienced when she thought of it.

Melba grasped her hand. "Oh, my! You care for him."

Lulu gasped and jumped to her feet. "Why would you say that?"

Melba and her mother exchanged glances, and then her mother said, "Sweetie, you should see your face when you speak about him."

Lulu collapsed in a nearby chair. She hadn't meant to be so obvious. She wanted everyone to think there was nothing between Miguel and her. She had to think and act that way if she was going to raise his child alone.

"Even if he asks, I won't marry him. I don't want anyone marrying me out of any sense of obligation. Rafe said he'd do the right thing, but that's not what I want."

"Rafe knows?" her mother asked.

"Yes, he is the only other person who knows the father is Miguel. Cami, Becca and the others think it's Will's baby. That's how I have to keep it until I have a chance to talk to Miguel. I promised Rafe I'd tell him, but the two of you can't say a word about it to anyone else. Understand?"

"Hmmm, Rosalie, no wonder you want me to meet Rafe," said Melba. "He's got to be something special if Lulu trusts him like this."

"He is," said Rosalie. "Rafe reminds me so much of my own father. He's a very good man who still mourns the death of his beloved Lettie—Cami's grandmother and the woman behind the Chandler Hill Inn and Winery."

"That must be the reason Cami is the way she is—kind and hardworking." Melba smiled at them both. "You have a lovely new family. What a nice departure from all the grief and disappointment of the past."

"Yes, I suppose that's so." Lulu's mother glanced at Lulu. "Let's go back to Cami's house. Tomorrow, I intend to help you get settled here. You say the owners don't want to sell even though they're now living in Arizona?"

"That's what they said."

"Ready?" Her mother stood.

Melba and Lulu exchanged surprised glances. Lulu's mother was acting as if she were in charge. Maybe, thought Lulu, this is what her mother used to be like without being constantly embarrassed and hurt by both her husband and the media.

CHAPTER SIXTEEN

Lulu couldn't hide a smile as she watched Melba teasing Rafe about something he said. As she'd suspected, the two of them liked one another from the beginning. Both were sensitive about including her mother in their light-hearted conversation about Rafe's life at a vineyard.

As her mother grew tired, she became quieter. Sensing that, Lulu rose from her seat in the living room and said, "I'm going to turn in for the night. How about you, Mom?"

Her mother's smile held relief. "That sounds good, if you don't mind, Cami?"

Cami got to her feet. "Actually, I'm going to call it a night too. It's an early morning at the inn. A local group is holding a breakfast meeting." She turned and held out a hand to Drew. "Coming?"

"You bet!" Amid the gentle laughter that followed, he jumped to his feet.

"I'm on my way," Rafe said. "Good night to one and all." Lulu stood with her mother and Melba as they made plans with Rafe for a walk among the vineyards and an early supper the following day.

"I'm still a pretty good cook," Rafe said.

"Yes, you are," Lulu's mother said, bringing a smile to his face.

After seeing him out of the house, Lulu walked her mother and Melba to their rooms. She gave each of the women a hug and a kiss. "Thanks for being here. I didn't realize how much your support would mean to me."

"We women have to stick together," said Melba, her expression soft with tenderness. "Hardly seems possible you're going to have a baby. I was holding you in my arms not that long ago."

"What would we ever have done without you?" said Lulu's mother to Melba. "Even now I count on you for support. It doesn't seem fair."

"Life isn't fair. If I hadn't been given a very good job in your home, I might never have had the kind of life I have now. I was a mixed-up young kid when, over the objections of everyone else, you gave me a chance, Rosalie."

The two of them smiled sweetly at one another.

Soul sisters. That's what they were, Lulu thought.

The next day, Lulu watched with amazement as her mother, dressed in jeans and a nice sweater, ran the vacuum over the rugs in the house. She'd never seen her mother work like this. Seeing Melba now, scrubbing out a tub, tears misted Lulu's vision. Melba ran the house in California but didn't do any deep cleaning. That was left up to a company that came in once a week.

Standing on a ladder, dusting the light fixtures and the tops of cabinets in the kitchen, Lulu thought back to the night with Miguel. She hadn't dared to admit to her mother and Melba how fuzzy parts of it seemed. And yet there was nothing sordid about it. Theirs had been a sweet lovemaking unlike anything she'd known. Miguel, she remembered very well, was a generous lover who'd made sure she was completely satisfied. At the memory, her cheeks felt fiery.

Her mother walked into the kitchen and shot her a look of concern. "What are you doing up on a ladder? And look at your cheeks; they're flushed."

Lulu gave a last swipe of her duster and climbed down. "Mom, I'm not suddenly made of glass. I'm just having a baby."

"Oh, yes. Right. Well, you have to be careful now."

Carrying a bucket filled with cleaning supplies, Melba joined them. "The bathrooms are beautiful, if I say so myself."

"The vacuuming is done. I've rearranged a few things, but I think you'll like it," said Lulu's mother. She smiled brightly. "I've made a mental list of what I'd like to purchase for you for this house. Can we talk about it?"

Lulu studied the excitement on her mother's face and paused. She glanced at Melba.

"Let's take a break, Rosalie," said Melba. "We've been working hard."

Rosalie groaned. "Okay. I know where this is going. How about a cup of hot tea and a cookie? That always makes me feel calm."

The three of them sat at the kitchen table chatting comfortably. After a while, Lulu brought out a pad of paper and a pen. "Okay, Mom. What are some of your ideas?"

Rosalie eagerly told them about her suggestions.

"Wow! You're very good at this," Lulu told her mother, realizing she had an uncanny ability to see what was missing in each room and how to make it better designed and coordinated.

Rosalie laughed. "I've looked at each room in our house and wished I could change it many times."

Lulu choked on her tea. "What? I always thought the house was exactly the way you wanted it."

"No, it was exactly how your father insisted he wanted it. It was much too fussy for me, but a lot of those expensive pieces came from his family home, and he wanted to work everything around them."

Lulu shook her head in amazement. "I grew up with a stranger. I like the new you much better."

"It's taken me a while to be comfortable with myself, after living with your father," her mother said.

"You never had the chance to be yourself," Melba quickly corrected. "I tried to encourage you, but as long as Edward controlled things, I could only try to make it easier for you."

"My God! What a monster he turned out to be," said Lulu with dismay.

Her mother placed a hand on Lulu's arm. "Don't be too judgmental. I was to blame, too, soaking myself in drugs and depression, allowing him to take complete control over my life. I'm on the right road now. I may stumble and fall, but I have you, Melba, and my support groups to rely on. The new combination of medications is working well."

"Wow! You sound like superwoman!" said Lulu, genuinely impressed with all her mother was doing to change her life.

Her mother's response was a sad look. "We both know I'll have my 'down days' too. But they're farther and farther apart."

"Coming to Oregon has been good for you," said Melba. "You should visit as often as possible.

A smile crossed her mother's face. "Good idea. And then I'll be around to help with my grandchild."

They turned to Lulu with expectant expressions.

Lulu hesitated. She was so accustomed to feeling responsible for her mother. Having her here wouldn't change that, but it might make it easier for them both. "That might work very well."

"One step at a time," her mother said. "I want to sell the house in California first. I've seen a condo I like."

"Sell the house?" It felt somehow like robbing Lulu of her childhood. Most of her early memories had happened there.

"It's time, Lulu. I don't want to live there anymore. That home never felt like mine." Her mother's voice was gentle. "One of my friends suggested a condo in Hollywood, and I like it. That area is enjoying a revival, and I'm ready for a change."

"Of course. I'm being silly. It will be good for you, Mom," Lulu said contritely.

"Tomorrow, let's go shopping!" Melba said. "I can't wait to see what Rosalie comes up with next."

"Right, tomorrow." A flush of pleasure coated the cheeks of Lulu's mother. "In a while, we have to meet up with Rafe for that walk through the vineyards and dinner."

The next morning, the three of them decided to head toward Eugene, where several shopping areas were located. They agreed to buy practical but fun things that could be moved into another environment. Lulu had a one-year lease and didn't know for certain if she could continue to rent Abby and Lisa's home at the end of that time.

As she drove, Lulu listened with interest to the conversation between Melba and her mother.

"Rafe thinks it's a good idea for you to buy a house here, Rosalie. I believe you should look into it. As he says, you have Chandler Hill family now."

"I'm thinking about it. I just want Lulu to be happy." Her mother called to her from the back seat. "Lulu, will you be okay with my buying a house here? Honestly?"

Lulu didn't hesitate. "Yes, Mom. It's fine with me. I probably can use your help with the baby. I'll have to work and don't intend to stay at home."

"See, Rosalie? It's something to consider," said Melba. "And then I can come visit you. I love the countryside here."

Lulu knew Cami would love to hear those words. She and

her grandmother had shared a love of the land.

After shopping with her mother and Melba, Lulu's idea of her mother being fragile ended. Her mother was a bundle of energy as she quickly surveyed her surroundings in a store and either left it or homed in on a few things of interest. Their visit to the furniture store in Albany was the most successful. Everything from bar stools for the kitchen to end tables in the living room to lamps and a chaise lounge for the bedroom were purchased without any fuss.

Lulu was both mentally and physically exhausted by the time they headed home. The furniture was scheduled to be delivered in the next few days, but everything else was packed into the back of her car. Melba and her mother stared out the car windows in a daze.

"I'm going to bed early," said Melba.

"Me, too," Lulu's mother agreed. "I can't remember when I've felt so tired from all the physical activity."

"I'll drop you off at Cami's," Lulu offered. "No need to stop at my house."

As Lulu drove up to the driveway to Cami's house, she noticed Drew's truck, Becca's SUV, and a couple of other trucks parked outside.

"What's the occasion?" said Melba.

Lulu shrugged. "I don't know. Let's go see."

She led her mother and Melba up the front stairs and opened the front door. "Hello?"

A group had gathered in the kitchen. When Cami noticed them, she hurried over. "Hi! We're celebrating. Miguel is back for a short visit, and he's brought someone from the vineyards where he's staying. Come say hello."

Lulu's heart began to beat erratically. She caught the

worried looks her mother and Melba shot her and wondered how she could gracefully leave the house.

Unaware of the panic Lulu felt, Cami took her hand. "I want you to meet her." She signaled Lulu's mother and Melba to come with them.

Walking into the kitchen Lulu felt her stomach whirl in sickening circles. She hadn't fought morning sickness like so many others, but, at the moment, she could hardly stand.

"Are you all right?" Cami asked.

Lulu swallowed hard. She couldn't let anyone else know how upset she was.

She looked up to find Miguel's eyes on her. He nudged the beautiful Latino woman next to him in a gesture Lulu thought was intimate. The woman turned to Miguel, and at his words, glanced across the room at her.

Lulu was a true politician's daughter. She acknowledged them politely and turned to her mother and Melba. She was about to tell them she was leaving when Rafe approached them.

"Hello, ladies. How did the day of shopping go?"

Lulu's mother beamed at him. "Very well. We're all exhausted."

He laughed. "Guess it was all worthwhile."

"Oh, yes. My mother is a whiz at knowing what to do to fix up the house. It's going to be great."

"Well done, Rosalie," Rafe said, and a broad smile lit her mother's face.

Rafe turned to Melba. "And you? Still standing?"

Melba laughed. "Ready to sit down."

"Can I get you a glass of wine or something else to drink?"

After taking their drink requests, Rafe left, and Becca joined them. "Doesn't Miguel look great? And Valentina is gorgeous. Her father's winery is the one we hope to do some cooperative projects with in the future."

"I see," was the best that Lulu could say as Miguel and Valentina approached. He was as handsome as always. She swallowed hard and tried to push away the memory of his naked body.

"Hi, Lulu!" Miguel said. "I want you to meet Valentina. Her family is hosting my stay in Chile. I wanted to bring her here for a short visit while I take care of some business. This gives her a chance to work briefly with Drew and see what our operation is all about."

"Yes, it is a good opportunity, and so beautiful here," Valentina said, smiling as she gazed at Miguel.

Standing next to her mother, Lulu sensed the stiffening of Rosalie's body. She silently reached over and squeezed her mother's hand, surprised by her protectiveness.

"Valentina, this is my mother Rosalie Kingsley. Miguel, you've been introduced to my mother before, but neither one of you has met our beloved family friend, Melba Milner. My mother and Melba are here visiting for a few days."

"Welcome to Willamette Valley," Miguel said, giving them a broad smile. "Have you seen the Lone Creek Winery yet?"

Her mother smiled happily. "Yes, Rafe showed it to us."

"It's an exciting time for all of us," said Miguel. He turned to Valentina. "We're hoping to do lots of things together with the winery in Chile."

Her smile was as warm as his. "Yes, my father hopes for that to happen too."

"Do you work only at the vineyard?" Lulu's mother asked Miguel.

"At the moment, yes. However, we have plans for expanding the operation, and I'm not sure what role I'll be taking. Maybe as the PR guy. We're not sure yet. I like to travel."

His smile, the way his eyes sparkled with enthusiasm made Lulu sigh inwardly. Careful not to show it, she said, "Excuse me, but I want to speak to Cami."

As Lulu walked away, Rafe came up to her. "How are you doing?"

The meaning behind his words were obvious. She let out a long breath. "Okay, I guess."

He placed a hand on her shoulder. "It'll all work out. Give it time."

"Is Miguel going back to Chile?"

"Yes. That will be a good thing too."

Cheered by the idea she wouldn't have to continue to face him, she went on her way.

"How's it going with the house?" Drew asked her as she approached Cami and him.

"It's great. My mother is adding all kinds of final touches to it, decorating with additional furniture and art objects." She beamed at them. "It looks very nice, and it gives her something to do."

"Sounds good," said Drew. "The house needed it. Abby and Lisa took most of their things with them."

Cami beamed at her. "Rafe said your mother may buy a place here."

"She's selling the house in California and moving to a condo. Then, we'll see."

"That will be nice, especially with ..." Cami stopped talking when Lulu frowned at her.

"Especially with what?" said Drew.

Cami dismissed his question with a wave of her hand. "How unsettled things have been for her."

Lulu's heartbeat steadied. She couldn't wait for Miguel to return to Chile so she could get settled herself before having to face him with the truth.

He appeared at her side. "Hi, Lulu. A couple of us are going to the Green Grape. Want to come?" He gave her a hopeful look.

Heart pounding with mixed emotions, she said, "Thanks, but I can't. Melba, my mother, and I are exhausted from shopping. I'm renting the house where Drew stayed, and we've been fixing it up."

His look of disappointment surprised her and then made her angry. Wasn't it enough that Valentina seemed to be taken with him? Did he need every woman panting after him? She worked to keep an edge out of her voice. "Looks like you have good company anyway."

Miguel shrugged and studied something across the room before turning back to her. "Just thought I'd see if you wanted to join us."

After he walked away, Cami said, "What's the matter? He only asked you to join the group. Aren't you happy about that?" Her puzzled look made Lulu feel bad.

"Sorry. I guess I'm just tired. Mom and Melba said they were going to bed early. I'm going to my house to unload all the stuff my mother bought. She's done a great job of coordinating things to look nice."

"Can't wait to see it! Don't worry about your mother and Melba. They can have an early dinner here and go to bed whenever they want. See you later." Cami hugged her and turned back to Drew.

Lulu waved to her mother and Melba and made a quick escape.

She was almost to her car when Miguel left the house and called to her. "Wait up!"

Lulu reluctantly turned around and watched him trot toward her, willing herself to be strong. She wasn't ready to tell him anything yet. She hadn't reached her first trimester, and she needed to wait to be sure everything was all right.

He stopped in front of her and studied her. "Hey! Did I do something wrong? Why were you upset with me a moment ago?"

"I'm sorry. It's been a long day. I didn't mean to take it out on you. You did nothing wrong." She blinked rapidly, remembering how right everything had seemed in his arms.

"Uh, okay. So we're good?"

"Yeah." She forced a smile. "We're good."

"See you later. Valentina and I are going to be busy for the next couple of days, but maybe we can meet up before I go back to Chile."

"How long are you going to be gone this time?" Lulu asked.

"I hope to be back around the first of April, but it could be a few weeks later."

"Oh, we'll definitely need to get together then," said Lulu.

He grinned. "That's a deal."

Lulu watched him go, her feelings so mixed up she didn't know whether to laugh or cry. Miguel wasn't a jerk; he was every girl's dream. That was the problem.

CHAPTER SEVENTEEN

Lulu stood with her mother and Melba inside the air terminal wishing they didn't have to leave. She was coming to respect her mother in a way that hadn't been possible before, and she'd always relied upon Melba for strength and support. They'd spent the last two days inside Lulu's rental, quietly reading, relaxing, and napping.

"Goodbye," said Melba wrapping her arms around her. "It was wonderful to see you. I have all the faith in the world that everything will turn out right for you. I can see why women are so attracted to Miguel. He's a very handsome man. And charming."

Lulu remained silent. She knew her mother felt the same way as Melba about the man who'd fathered her child. But they all knew very well what living with a man like that could be like.

"Goodbye, sweetheart." Her mother hugged her tight. "I'll be here whenever you need me. Melba has already promised to return with me in the spring."

"Good luck selling the house. If you need me to come to California to help you, let me know."

"Melba and I will do very well on our own, dear. You have enough to worry about."

She gave each of them a last hug and headed out the door to the parking lot. She was truly on her own now with more responsibility than she'd ever had. When the time came to tell Cami and the others the truth, they would, she hoped, support her decision.

###

Back at the inn, Lulu settled into her marketing job. The slower months were perfect for updating the online catalog, gearing it toward spring and summer weddings. Working with Gwen on the inventory of The Barn was fun for Lulu, but she couldn't help worrying over Gwen's lack of color and how tired she seemed to be.

When she could no longer hold back, Lulu said to her, "What is it, Gwen? Are you sick?"

Gwen burst into tears. "After Christmas they found a lump in my breast. They've done a biopsy and I'm waiting for the news. I swear I haven't slept for the past three weeks. One test was inconclusive. Some sort of mix-up or something."

"Oh, I'm sorry. But, Gwen, maybe it's all right, after all."

"My older sister died of breast cancer. That's why I'm so scared."

Lulu hugged Gwen as she began to cry in earnest. "Have you told Cami?"

Gwen shook her head. "No, I haven't told anyone. I didn't want them to worry. I remember hearing stories about the time when Abby's first partner died of cancer. Everyone was devastated, and with all the work for Christmas and New Year's, I didn't dare say anything. It's one of the most important times of the year."

"I think Cami should know. I understand you have no family here."

Gwen shook her head. "Just a brother in New York. We're not close. His wife and I don't get along and, frankly, he's not someone I can count on."

"Well, you can count on your Chandler Hill family," Lulu said with well-founded confidence. "When do you find out the results?"

"At the end of the week." Gwen said, dabbing at her eyes with a tissue.

"Do you want me to go to the doctor visit with you?"

Gwen wiped fresh tears away. "Would you?"

"Sure," said Lulu, pleased to be trusted in this way.

They were sitting misty-eyed in the office when Cami appeared on regular business. At Lulu's prompting, Gwen spilled the whole story.

"Oh, Gwen! I'm so glad you told me," said Cami. "We'll be right beside you. Don't worry about anything here. No matter what the news is, we women will be by your side."

"Thanks. I needed to hear that. I've felt so alone."

"Do you want to take some time off?" Cami asked.

Gwen shook her head emphatically. "I need to keep busy."

"Okay, then. I've got a few catalogs from wholesalers that I want you two to look through. I'm thinking we can offer brides the chance to purchase favors, gifts, everything from us. That way, it's here and ready for them when they arrive—one less thing for them to worry about."

"Good idea," Lulu said. If the time came for her to be married, she wanted something very simple. But she understood how some women had always dreamed of a big, fancy wedding, and she, like her mother, had a good sense of what might be right.

As Lulu was leaving The Barn, Miguel was pulling into the parking lot in his truck. He saw her and waved. She waved back and headed toward her car.

Miguel jumped out of his truck and hurried over to her. "Hey! Glad I caught you in time! I'm leaving tonight to go back to Chile. I was hoping you could join me for a drink."

"Thanks, but I'd better not. I'm on a new diet and trying to stay away from alcohol." She considered it a half-truth, not an outright lie.

He studied her for a moment. "You don't need to lose any weight, You're beautiful. You always look great."

Lulu swallowed hard. "Thanks."

"I know we haven't had a chance to catch up on things on this trip but I hope to make it up to you. Like I've said all along, I want to get to know you better. If I email you, will you promise to answer?" His gaze bored into her.

She nodded before she could stop herself. She owed him that.

He grinned as Valentina headed their way. "Guess I'd better go. See you in the spring after the harvest in Chile."

Lulu returned Valentina's wave and quickly climbed into her car in an attempt to escape further conversation.

Later, alone in her house, Lulu plopped down on the couch in the living area and stared at the flames in the fireplace. Normally a fire soothed her, but tonight her thoughts were too jumbled to relax. The truth was, seeing Miguel and talking with him, remembering their romantic night, she could no longer deny the strong feelings she had for him. She felt a connection to him she'd never experienced with another man. Yet each time she thought of sharing a life with him, she stepped back, certain in her own mind she could never live the way her mother had been forced to exist, knowing other women were in her husband's life. He'd already proved that she couldn't hold his attention for long.

Friday morning Lulu sat with Gwen in her doctor's office, her hands cold with dread. She could only imagine what Gwen must be feeling. It was every woman's hidden worry that each lump discovered meant she had inoperable breast cancer.

The assistant at the desk had greeted them cheerfully as if it was an ordinary day. But Lulu understood that for Gwen, it was a day she'd dreaded. Lulu had tried to reassure her that if it was cancer the doctor would react much more quickly, but Gwen needed his assurance that she was okay.

A nurse called Gwen's name. Lulu rose with Gwen. "No matter what, we'll get through this together."

A smile trembled on Gwen's lips, and then she was gone.

Lulu lifted her phone out of her purse and checked for messages. She and her mother now texted on a fairly regular basis, which reassured Lulu that her mother was continuing to do well. In fact, though the circumstances were far from ideal, her mother was looking forward to having a grandchild.

Gwen emerged into the room crying. Lulu jumped to her feet and hurried over to her.

"Oh, hon!"

"No, no! You don't understand. It was an unusual kind of cyst, not cancer. I'm fine." Her eyes overflowed with fresh tears. "I'm lucky, so very lucky."

They hugged, and quickly left the office well aware of other women sitting there awaiting news of their fate.

"Let's go celebrate!" Lulu suggested.

"I just want to get home," said Gwen. "I need some time alone. I hope you understand."

"I do." Lulu gave Gwen a reassuring smile. She was feeling pretty shaky herself.

Back at the Inn, Lulu gave Cami and Becca the news. They were as relieved as she. Gwen was a dear person and a wonderful asset to the company.

"Dan and I are having a TGIF party tonight. Can you come?" Becca beamed at her.

"Thanks, but I'd better not. The last of the furniture my mother ordered is being delivered tomorrow morning, and I have to get up early. Besides, everyone will begin to wonder why I'm not drinking. I told Miguel it was because I was on a diet, but it's going to be awkward as my pregnancy progresses."

"Everyone is going to know sooner or later," Becca replied. "Why not tell them now?"

"Maybe I'm superstitious, but my mother told me that in her day a woman never announced a pregnancy until she'd completed the first trimester."

"That's almost laughable," said Cami. "Now, everyone knows within a few hours of conception. When one of our waitresses announced it, I asked how far along she was and she said seven days."

The three of them laughed.

"Thanks anyway, Becca. But, like I said, I'll skip this one."

"I understand, but I'm not going to allow you to become a hermit just because you're expecting Will's baby."

Lulu started to explain, but at that moment Imani rushed into the office, her face flushed. "You'd better come. A woman has fallen in the restaurant. She's not badly hurt, but she's already talking about a lawyer."

Cami and Becca took off at a run, leaving Lulu behind with her untold truth.

The next morning, Lulu let out a sigh of relief when the last piece of furniture was delivered and placed in the house. Each one added a nice touch to the room in which it now sat. She and her mother had chosen wisely, selecting pieces that could be moved easily and used in another location.

After the delivery men had gone, she sat on the new chaise lounge in the master bedroom and lay down. She'd been lucky so far that she hadn't suffered morning sickness—just a queasy feeling now and then. She patted her stomach, wondering about the baby. Like her mother, she was getting used to the idea of having this child. Even though they'd probably never marry, she was certain Miguel would be a good father.

On a whim, Lulu called Rafe and asked him to come for dinner.

"I'd be delighted," he replied, a happy lilt to his voice.

"I thought it would be a good way to begin to entertain in my own house. I can't think of anyone else I'd rather ask."

Rafe chuckled. "I can't think of a better evening. Thanks."

They scheduled a time, and Lulu hung up with a smile. Rafe Lopez was her idea of the perfect grandfather. She was pleased that her baby would be related to him even if it was just as a great uncle. Her thoughts flew to Miguel. He looked like she imagined Rafe did at that age. Maybe, if she had a boy, he'd look like the two of them.

Now that she'd scheduled Rafe for dinner, Lulu planned to make an easy chicken and mushroom dish she thought he'd like. That, some rice, green beans, and a crisp lettuce salad would be a nice, simple meal.

Content with her choices, she left to go to the market for fresh mushrooms, vegetables, and, perhaps, a dessert. Rafe, she knew, had a sweet tooth.

Driving into town, Lulu felt like a true native. Gazing at the now familiar scenery, she felt at home in a way that California had never provided her.

Inside her favorite store, Lulu searched for the things she needed for dinner and then paused in front of the baked goods. Strawberry tortes caught her attention. She ordered two, certain Rafe would like them.

She headed home in a cheerful mood as she thought ahead to the dinner. It would feel good to be able to pay back Rafe in a small way for his kindness to her. Even now, with a tough future ahead for her, he was a steady supporter.

When she pulled into the driveway, she gave the house a serious look. It was attractive with a country look, a style she was liking more and more. She parked and got out of the car. As she reached into the back seat to retrieve the bags of groceries, she felt a stab of pain in her abdomen. She stood and clasped her belly. *The baby!* Worry gnawed on her insides. She grabbed the bags of groceries and hurried inside the house.

After dropping the bags on the kitchen table, she rushed into the downstairs bathroom praying she was wrong. But when she saw all the blood, she gripped the edge of the nearby sink feeling faint. Panic froze her and then she raced to the phone to call Cami.

Hearing Cami's cheerful "hello", Lulu tried to catch her breath. "Cami, I need you," she managed to say.

"Lulu? What's wrong? Where are you?"

"At home. I think I'm losing the baby," Lulu said. "I don't know what to do."

"Hang on. I'm on my way. I think we'd better get you to a doctor. Lie down and rest until I get there," Cami said, her voice high with worry.

Lulu clicked off the call, went upstairs to change her clothes and get a pad, then lay down on the bed, squeezing her legs together to try to stop anything more from happening. She hadn't wanted the baby at first, but over the past few weeks she was excited about having it—Miguel's baby. There were complications to overcome with him, but she'd come to realize that like Rafe and others had promised her, everything would work out. Tears slipped down her cheeks.

She heard Cami's car in the driveway and went downstairs to let her in.

White-faced, Cami raced up to the door. She hugged Lulu to her. "Are you sure? What's happening?"

"I've had a lot of bleeding. I'm pretty sure I've lost or am losing the baby," Lulu said, feeling as if she couldn't breathe from holding back sobs.

"Let's get you to the doctor's office now," said Cami, her own eyes misting.

Lulu grabbed her purse and followed Cami to the car in a daze.

Dr. Lauren Lukas was a favorite OB/GYN in the valley. An older woman in her 50's, she'd provided services for years to women of all incomes and backgrounds. She approached each patient like a daughter, as eager to praise as to chide. Babies mattered even more to her. Her patients knew she wouldn't tolerate any behavior that might harm the baby.

Now, she stared down at Lulu with lines of sorrow marring her face.

"It's over?" Lulu's lips trembled.

"I'm afraid so. The ultrasound confirmed what we already suspected. But it doesn't mean you can't go on to have a long-term pregnancy in the future. Sometimes this is nature's way of taking care of an issue that isn't good. You're a healthy young woman, Lulu. You had no problem getting pregnant. I suspect you won't have anything like this in the future."

Holding back fresh tears, Lulu grabbed Dr. Lukas' hand. "It's not my fault, is it? I know I didn't want the baby to begin with, but then I changed my mind. I'd even thought of naming the baby after someone in my new family." She'd liked the name Rafe from the beginning.

Dr. Lukas squeezed Lulu's fingers and handed her a tissue. "No, sweetheart, it isn't your fault. You mustn't worry about it. It's one of those things that can happen. You haven't completed your first trimester. If anything is wrong, this is the time something like this might take place."

"I feel like a failure," Lulu sobbed.

Dr. Lukas patted Lulu's shoulder. "It's all right to grieve. You've lost something precious to you. But there's no sense in blaming yourself or thinking you failed in some way. Support groups are available to help you cope with your loss. I'll ask the nurse at the front desk to give you the information. I suggest giving yourself some time to process this before resuming your normal schedule."

Lulu sat up on the table. "Thank you. I think I'll go to California for a few days."

Sitting in Cami's car on the way home, Lulu stared out the window.

"Lulu, I'm so sorry. Is there anything I can do for you? While you were getting dressed, the doctor spoke to me about the process of grieving any mother goes through in situations like this."

Lulu turned to her with surprise. "She did?"

Cami's expression was sad. "No wonder her patients love her. She's the kindest doctor I know."

"I've been thinking I should take a couple of days off, go to California. My mother is moving into a condo. I can help her."

"Yes, I understand. It's a good idea also because you'll be able to tell Will about the baby. He'll need to know."

"Cami, the baby wasn't Will's. It was Miguel's," said Lulu, relieved to finally get it out in the open.

"Wha-a-at?" Cami pulled the car over to the side of the road and turned to her. "You only went out with him once."

Lulu grimaced. "That's all it takes." She gripped Cami's arm. "You can't tell him or anyone else until I have the chance to talk to him. Only Rafe, my mother, and Melba know."

"Oh my God! What will he think?"

"Rafe said he'd do the right thing and marry me when he learned I was pregnant. Now, he won't have to do that. I wouldn't accept a proposal of marriage like that, anyway. When I marry, it's going to be for true love, not obligation."

"But Lulu, I think Miguel has feelings for you. He asked me about you and Will ..."

Lulu put up a hand to stop her. "I've already decided it would never work. Miguel is too much like my father—a man who draws women to him. Been there, seen that. All it does is lead to trouble."

"Oh, but ..."

"Cami, I'm serious. Now let's go home. I need to call Rafe and postpone my dinner with him."

"He was coming to dinner?"

"Yes, I wanted to try a few things out before inviting the whole gang. And he's been so good to me."

"Sure. I get it. How about coming to dinner at my place? I'll invite Rafe too, so he won't be disappointed."

"Would you? That would be fantastic." Lulu loved that Cami always seemed to know what would make her happy.

"Right now, you need to go home and rest," said Cami. "And don't worry, I won't let anyone else know about Miguel's being the father of your baby. That's your news, but I think you're going to be far better off telling him as soon as possible."

"How can I? He's in Chile for the next few months."

Cami's brow lined with creases of worry as she studied her. "Nonnee always used to say, 'Sitting on the truth will hurt you most of all'. You need to tell him before he finds out in any other way."

"Maybe you're right. Promise you won't say a word to anyone else?"

"I promise," Cami said solemnly.

Cami delivered Lulu to her house and said, "Why don't you come at six o'clock? Drew has a guys' night out, so it'll be just the three of us—you, Rafe, and me. If you want, I'll call him for you."

"Thanks. That would be great. See you then."

Lulu got out of the car, walked into the house, and collapsed on the couch. Her life as she'd known it was suddenly gone. Her ruined plans and tumbled feelings sent fresh tears down her cheeks. If someone were to ask her how she felt, she'd say she felt empty, so empty.

After another good cry, Lulu got up from the couch and headed into the kitchen. She put all her fresh groceries in a bag to take to Cami and stored the rest away. Then she called an airline and made plans to leave the next day. She couldn't wait to leave Chandler Hill.

Later, after a good rest, Lulu headed over to Cami's with the bag of groceries she'd set aside for her.

Cami greeted her with an extra-long hug. "Rafe's already here."

When Lulu entered the kitchen, Rafe got up out of his seat at the table and came over to her.

Hugging her close, he said softly, "I'm sorry, sweetheart. I know how much it hurts. My wife, Maria, and I went through the same thing many times before she died.

Misty-eyed, Lulu looked up into Rafe's weathered face. "I wanted this baby, Rafe. I wanted Miguel's baby."

He stroked a wisp of hair away from her face. "What are you going to do now?"

"I'm leaving for California tomorrow. I need some time away from here, and Mom has bought a condo. I'm going to help her for a few days until I'm ready to come back to Chandler Hill."

Cami approached them. "I heard that, Lulu, and I want you to take as much time as you need."

"And Miguel?" Rafe prompted. "What are you going to say to him?"

"I don't know," Lulu said. "I suppose it's something that isn't important to him now. It's done. It's over."

Rafe cupped her face in his hands. "*Cariño,* you know that's not true. It would matter to Miguel. He's not the kind of man who wouldn't care."

Lulu's vision blurred. "I know. But I don't want to ruin his plans to marry Valentina."

Rafe leaned back and frowned at her. "Why would you say such a thing? I don't think that's the case at all."

"I spoke to him before he left. He wanted me to go out with Valentina and him. Then she came over to him, and I saw the look they exchanged."

"A business friendship. Nothing more. Trust me."

Lulu nodded, but knew it was only Rafe's way of trying to make her feel better.

CHAPTER EIGHTEEN

Lulu breathed in the warm air of Southern California and vowed to herself that she would shake off the pain and guilt she felt over losing the baby. Guilt because she hadn't wanted the baby at first and the pain of never having the opportunity to tell that baby how much she'd grown to love him or her.

Melba and her mother met her in the baggage claim area as promised.

Upon seeing Lulu, her mother rushed over to her and swept her into a warm embrace. "Oh, darling, I'm so, so sorry about what happened. I know how you feel. I lost several babies myself. You never forget." Shaking her head, she dabbed at her eyes.

Melba stood by wearing a look of concern usually reserved for Lulu's mother. Lulu turned to her and sighed with relief when Melba's arms wrapped around her. "It's going to be all right," Melba said to them both. "Right, Rosalie? We're going to be strong for Lulu."

"Oh yes," Lulu's mother said, giving her a shaky smile.

"And I hope you will discover that, for whatever reason, nature had other plans for you. And while it isn't easy, you are not to blame yourself. You are loved, child, and that love will help you through it."

Lulu snuggled closer and then stepped away feeling better. Women helping women. It was something she'd always admired. .

"I'm glad you're here," her mother said, and Lulu felt a new sense of homecoming. "I hope to get some ideas of what I should keep and what I should sell or give away when I make this move. Please take whatever you want from the house. I intend to start mostly with new things in the condo."

Lulu loved hearing the excitement in her mother's voice and realized how little the expensive, fancy things in her mother's house meant to both of them, especially when they were eager to make a fresh start.

"We'll go through everything, and then you can hire someone to run an estate sale for you," Lulu suggested.

"One of the couples interested in buying the house has indicated they were willing to buy some of the furnishings. My real estate agent thinks it might make the offer more enticing, if I were willing to make it part of a deal. I told her I'd give her an answer soon." Her mother beamed at her. "Now, with you here, I'll be able to do so."

At the thought of keeping busy this way, Lulu was glad she'd come home.

When her mother drove into the driveway, Lulu stared at the house. It's size, its Mediterranean style were impressive. But Lulu knew a beautiful house didn't make a loving home. She was ready to move on with her life.

Inside the house, Lulu stood with her mother and Melba.

"I've already marked a few pieces I'll take with me to the condo. Melba has decided on a few pieces herself. Now, you can tag anything you want."

"I don't want any furniture. I might want to take a couple of paintings and a few knick-knacks, but that's it."

Her mother nodded. "I understand. We'll need to go through personal papers and such. I'd like to do that together."

"Okay," said Lulu.

"I've made a nice lunch," said Melba. "Why don't we give

you a few minutes to get settled, Lulu, and sit down. I know how much you like my chicken noodle soup."

Lulu chuckled. "I'm not sick, but what a sweet thought." Tears suddenly filled her eyes. "I'm sorry. I guess I'm going to be weepy for a while. Hormones and heartbreak and all those things I'm dealing with."

"Honey, you can cry as much as you want to." Her mother's eyes filled. "We'll give you all the time you need. I know what it's like to have the opportunity to grieve taken away from you and having to put on a brave front when you just want to curl up into a ball of misery."

Lulu studied her mother. "Maybe I should start seeing your therapist. You sound so different."

"Anytime you feel the need to talk to one, I'll give him a call," her mother replied with pride.

"Let's get you settled, sweetheart." Melba lifted her suitcase and led Lulu up to her old bedroom.

Stepping into the bedroom as pretty as any room one would find in a magazine, Lulu drew a deep breath. The queen-sized bed hosting a handsome, gray-patterned duvet and multiple pillows seemed stifling to her. She knew it wasn't the furniture, but the memories that still tainted the air like the smell of a dying rose. The press had accused her of being a spoiled little rich girl, but they didn't understand the price that went with being the daughter of someone like Congressman Edward Kingsley. As nicely as the room was furnished, she wanted none of it.

Melba placed Lulu's small suitcase on a rack. "Come down when you're ready. I've made some of your favorite biscuits to go with the soup."

Lulu unpacked. As she placed pieces of clothing in drawers or hung them in the closet, she realized she'd have to go through her wardrobe and make decisions of her own. She'd choose carefully what things to keep and give the rest to charity.

Moments later, she was sitting at the kitchen table with her mother and Melba.

"Will has kept in touch with me," her mother announced. "Such a fine, young man. I hope you don't mind, but when he called this morning I told him you were coming home for a few days."

"I don't know if I should see him or not," Lulu said. "I'm still feeling pretty shaky and very mixed-up at the moment."

"Do what your heart tells you to do," said Melba.

After Lulu had eaten the last of her soup and swallowed the final piece of her biscuit, she sat back in her chair. "That was delicious. Thank you so much, Melba. If you two don't mind, I'm going to lie down for a little while."

"Not at all," said her mother. "Rest will be good for you."

As Lulu left the kitchen, she overheard Melba say to her mother, "You did a good job of keeping bad thoughts away. I know how worried you are about Lulu."

They were such wonderful friends, thought Lulu. She knew from helping her mother with her father's estate that Melba had been well taken care of as the beneficiary of a large insurance policy of his. He'd had several other policies designating her mother and her, but none pleased her more than the one indicating her father had recognized Melba's contribution to the family.

Lulu climbed the stairs and stopped in the upstairs hallway to view the family photos mounted there. Pain stabbed her when she saw a picture of her and her brother standing on a sandy beach. Her brother should not have drowned. He was a healthy boy, a good swimmer. Even though everyone told her it was an accident she couldn't have prevented, she always wondered if he'd be alive today if she'd been there with him.

She studied the picture of her father and her standing on a dais together, his right fist raised in triumph. Oh, but he was a good-looking man adored by everyone—the expression on her face as she looked up at him said it all.

She moved along to study other family photos. As she stared at the photos of the four of them, then the three of them standing together, she thought what a façade it was. The smiles on their faces failed to reach their eyes. *Were all political families like this?*

Saddened, she went into her bedroom. Exhaustion softened her limbs. Too weak to stand, she lay down on her bed and closed her eyes.

The blue skies were turning gray when she awoke and lay staring up at the ceiling. She told herself to get up and get moving before the hopelessness she felt overwhelmed her. After a minute or two, she forced herself to her feet.

When she went downstairs, she found Melba and her mother sitting in front of a computer.

Her mother looked up at her. "We're making a list of the furnishings so any dealer who comes in will know exactly what I have."

"Good idea. The only two things I want are the oil painting over the fireplace and the watercolor in the den."

"You've got it," her mother said. "I was going to take the oil painting, but I can envision how nice the landscape will look in your house, and I want you to have it. You can also take the watercolor. It's a nice, woodsy scene that reminds me of Chandler Hill. I bought it right after your father and I were married. There's another painting you might want. It's the abstract in the front hall. Check it out."

Lulu went into the front hall and studied it. The blues and

purples along with the other colors of reds and oranges reminded her of sunsets at Chandler Hill. She promptly decided to accept it.

She told her mother she'd take all three and said, "What can I do to help?"

Melba handed her a sheet of paper entitled 'Dining Room.' "The top listings are things your mother is keeping. Anything else needs to be listed."

Lulu was in the dining room sorting through dishes and linens when her mother rushed into the room. "The house has been sold! I have thirty days to get out. Oh, Lulu, I'm so glad you're here! Now I can move everything I want into the condo and leave the rest behind. You're going to have to take anything you want when you drive back to Oregon."

"How? My car is there."

Her mother grinned. "I was saving it as a surprise, but I'm buying you a new car! An SUV that's more suitable than your small convertible. A Lexus—something like Cami has."

Lulu's eyes widened with surprise. "Really? That would be wonderful and much more useful."

"All you have to do is pick the color. Guess you shouldn't wait too long. It looks like you'll be needing it. We have a lot of work to do to get everything you want into the car. Remember, you can have anything you want that Melba and I haven't already chosen." Her mother all but danced out of the room.

Watching her leave, Lulu shook her head. Maybe, like her mother, it was time to leave all the bad memories here and move ahead. But, like her mother, she'd take some practical things with her.

After she finished doing an inventory of the dining room, Lulu taped together one of the boxes Melba had picked up at the store and labeled it hers. She carried it into the dining room and carefully wrapped a few serving pieces, candlesticks, and other things she'd decided to keep and placed them in the box.

The living room was next on her list. Lulu noted that her mother had chosen few pieces from that room and none of the furniture she'd disliked. As for herself, Lulu chose a small sculpture that had always sat next to a decorative vase on the mantlepiece. She listed everything else carefully on the sheet of paper.

Melba came into the room as she finished. "I've fixed dinner for you. I'm going home to Jerome. See you tomorrow."

"Thanks for everything," Lulu said, meaning more than her physical help today.

"You're going to be just fine," Melba said quietly, and hugged her close.

Dinner that night was pleasant. Pot roast had always been one of her mother's favorites. Especially the way Melba cooked it with fresh carrots and pearl onions. A comfort food, for sure.

"Are you going to miss any part of this house?" Lulu asked her mother.

"Only the sun room," she replied. "Your father allowed me to decorate it the way I wanted with lots of clean-lined furniture and plenty of plants. I always felt as if I could breathe easily there. Of course, things are different now. I'm much freer to do as I wish without seeking approval from your father. He very much enjoyed having control over things."

Lulu set down her fork and leaned toward her mother. "Why didn't you fight him on this and everything else? Many women today wouldn't put up with that kind of crap."

"I don't know," her mother said. "Maybe because like so many of his believers, I thought I'd help him do good for others by keeping things the way he wanted them at home. Especially because I couldn't give him all that he wanted."

"More children?"

Her mother's cheeks grew pink. "And other more intimate things. Especially after I learned of his affairs."

Lulu sighed and shook her head. "I always feel conflicted when I think of Dad. I loved him, but I hated what he did to you and how he thought he could have anything or anybody he wanted."

"He was trained from an early age to believe that," Lulu's mother said. "His father was a driven man living vicariously through his son. Edward was born to fulfill his father's dream. He believed all he'd been told through the years, and having money and his good looks helped. I thought I was going to be his helpmate. But I learned early on I was only a prop. By then I'd started to have real issues with depression which, I'm sure, I inherited from my mother. It became clear that I couldn't do everything he or I wanted."

"But you're doing so well now," said Lulu.

"I am, but I'm working on it in a way I never did before. Therapy, new medications, staying away from alcohol and pain killers are all helping me."

"And having Dad gone," said Lulu.

"Yes, that too, as awful as it sounds."

"I love you, Mom. I feel much closer to you than I ever have."

Her mother reached across the table and squeezed her hand. "Me too."

They sat discussing various topics. And when they both began to yawn, they worked together to rinse the dishes and put away the food.

"Tomorrow is another busy day. I want to show you the condo, and we have to choose the color of your car."

"I'll need to pick up more boxes for all my stuff. After working on the inventory, I think I'd like a few more things than I'd thought. Nothing big, just things that mean something to me and to keep for the family I hope to have one day." Lulu's voice broke.

"Aw, honey, it's going to happen. You'll meet the right man, and everything will fall into place."

Lulu sighed. "I guess so."

"C'mon, let's get to bed."

Lulu followed her mother up the stairs, trying not to think of the man that she might have found already. It would never work between them.

CHAPTER NINETEEN

After meeting with the car dealership and selecting the car she wanted, Lulu rode with her mother to Rosalie's new condo, curious to see what it would be like. Situated in the Hollywood area, which was enjoying rejuvenation, the complex was touted as something unique. Still, Lulu was unprepared for the contemporary elegance in her mother's condo, the expanse of glass, and the flow of space in the large, three-bedroom, four-bath home.

"It's gorgeous! I feel like a bird sitting on a tree limb high above the ground," gushed Lulu. At the smile on her mother's face, she knew she'd said the right thing.

"I feel free here," her mother said. "Your father made this possible, for which I'll always be grateful."

"You've earned it, Mom," said Lulu, gazing out the window at the views all around her. "I'm happy for you."

"You can understand now why I have no need of anything from the house. Better to give it to someone we know or to charity."

"Absolutely."

After taking a second, longer tour of the property, Lulu was more convinced that this was the right place for her mother. And when a neighbor rang the bell to welcome her, Lulu was even happier with her mother's decision.

"How does Melba like it?" Lulu asked on their way back to the house.

"She loves it. I thought she might like to retire, do more traveling, but she said she loves being free to come and go as she wishes and have a life separate from her own with Jerome. They deeply love one another, but since he's retired they need a break from one another. Retirement is something all my friends tell me can be a very difficult position for many."

"This will give you the chance to do some of the projects I remember you used to like," said Lulu. "Everything will be convenient for you."

"Yes, but I intend to come to Chandler Hill too. It will be a nice break, and I love being part of the family there with you."

"Me too," said Lulu, realizing that though she'd been anxious to leave it, she was now eager to get back there.

She was working at her mother's house when she received a call from Will. "Heard you were back in town. Can we get together? It's important."

"I'm sorry, but I'm very busy helping my mother move. Is it something we can take care of over the phone?"

"Lulu, I need to talk to you. In person. Can you do that for me?"

"Okay. How about later today? I can meet you then. Shall we say Giardi's at five?"

"Sounds good. See you there."

The minute Lulu walked into the bar she saw Will talking to a gentleman she didn't know. When he saw her standing there, Will hurried over to her. "Glad you're here. I want you to meet Mike Sanchez. He's a generous supporter of mine."

Lulu frowned and tried to hide her annoyance. "I thought you wanted to discuss something personal. This is business."

"You got it. Big Business. You have to help me here."

Lulu sighed and walked with Will across the room to the man openly surveying her.

"Mike, here she is. Louise Kingsley, Edward's daughter.

Following in her father's footsteps, she's as savvy as they come. I'm sure she can provide the kind of impact we're trying to create, if you're willing to lend a hand."

Lulu clenched her jaw to keep from screaming at Will. *He was using her to get donations for his campaign? The ass!*

"How do you do, Louise," Mike said, giving her a smile Lulu thought was a bit sly. "I'm an old friend of your father's and remember seeing you on a couple of his campaign trails. Once a politician, always a politician, eh?"

"Not always," Lulu cautioned him. "In fact, you might not have heard, but I'm no longer living and working in California and have no desire to return."

"Having you live out-of-town doesn't prevent you from endorsing my campaign and helping out from time to time," said Will smoothly. "That's the beauty of it. It's the best of both worlds." When she didn't reply, Mike turned to Will. "We'll talk later. I'm on my way to another meeting. Nice to meet you, Louise."

Lulu shook hands with him and then excused herself to go to the ladies' room. She hated being used by Will and wanted to wash the sleazy feeling off her fingers before attacking Will for putting her on the spot like that.

When she returned to him, he said, "I'd offer to buy you a drink, but I guess that's inappropriate in your condition."

Lulu blinked rapidly at the sting of tears in her eyes. "I lost the baby."

"Well, then, let's take a booth and we can talk there. Red wine sound okay?"

She nodded and went to the booth farthest from the door. She didn't want to be seen with Will.

He brought back a glass of wine for her and a glass of what she knew would be expensive Scotch for himself. "Sorry, I couldn't give you an earlier warning, but I had to take the chance for you to meet Mike when the opportunity arose," he said, sliding into the booth.

He raised his glass. "Here's to you! Are you okay? I'm sorry about the baby."

"Thanks. It's a big disappointment to me."

"Oh, but ..."

At the warning look she shot him, he stopped talking.

"I'm sorry, Lulu. I really am. However, this should make it easier for you to help me out. Even from a distance you can do things for the campaign."

Lulu set down her wine glass. "I didn't lie to you, Will, when I said I love my new family and want to stay there to help them. I'd be willing to endorse you, but that's it. I'm done with politics. You of all people should understand. As we speak, you're already filling my father's shoes. For all the good he planned, I'll do what I said, but nothing more."

"I'll give you more time to think it over," said Will. "I shouldn't have pushed this on you without warning."

A flash of light suddenly went off, stopping their conversation.

"What the ..." said Will, rising to his feet and facing a photographer.

"Compliments of Mike Sanchez," said the photographer. "For future use."

Lulu's stomach twisted with disbelief. She felt sicker than she had in the last weeks. What a dirty, slime ball trick. One she wouldn't fall for.

When their picture hit the papers and the online networks picked it up, Lulu was once more caught in a vise of unwanted publicity. She swore, then cried as she vowed to leave California forever.

"I'm furious with Will for putting you through this," said her mother. "He should know better than to make you a target of the media. He's aware of what we've gone through."

"It's so unfair," said Lulu. "I'm so done with public life. As soon as I can, I'm going back to Chandler Hill where I'm safe."

Two days later, her "cashmere tan" SUV was packed to the top with clothing, shoes, boxes, a couple of lamps, and the three large paintings she loved.

She glanced at the rear-view mirror and saw her mother and Melba standing side by side waving goodbye. A lump filled her throat. They were two incredible women, and she was glad to have them in her life.

When she finally drove up the driveway to the house she'd rented, Lulu couldn't help but compare it to the glamorous, high-end condo her mother now owned. As different as they were, Lulu felt they were the right choices for each of them. It pleased her that she'd be able to dress up the house with things that were special to her. If necessary, she'd ask Rafe to help her hang the artwork.

Thinking of him, she wondered about Rafe and his wife, Maria. She'd been told their marriage hadn't been all that happy, but the sadness in his eyes when he'd talked about the babies they'd lost gave her a better understanding of how much he treasured Cami and now her. He was definitely a family man. She'd thought at one time that if her baby was a boy, she'd name him Rafe.

Lulu called Cami to say she was back in town and would be available for work tomorrow.

"Wonderful!" Cami said. "You're just in time for the Valentine Dinner Dance this weekend. We need all of our family and top staff to be present."

"I'll be there to help," said Lulu, grateful to be considered family. "Have the things I ordered for the spring catalog come in?"

"Gwen said only a few are outstanding, but you'll want to check in with her."

Lulu spent the day unpacking her car and organizing everything in the house. After two different trips to the hardware store, all three paintings were hung in what she considered perfect spots. With a few additional touches to the living areas, more utensils in the kitchen and serving pieces stored in the dining area, Lulu was much more comfortable in the house.

Later, Cami stopped by with two large, indoor plants in lovely, rustic pots. "Glad to have you home. Thought this bit of greenery might cheer you up."

They hugged and placed one plant by one of the front windows and the other by the sliding door leading outdoors in the back.

"Perfect!" said Cami, looking around. "You've really fixed up the place. I love the new additions to the décor."

"Thanks. I hope to be able to talk Abby and Lisa into selling this house to me one day. I don't plan to go back to California except to visit my mother."

"How're your mom and her new digs?"

"Great! The condo is open and airy, with 180-degree views. For once, my mother created an environment that pleases her. The changes in her are amazing."

"Do you think it has to do with her being alone now and taking control of her own life?"

"Definitely. Another reason for me to think carefully about getting serious with anyone. You and Drew seem such a good match. I hope I can find someone as easygoing as he."

Cami's sigh spoke volumes. "He's pretty wonderful."

"As soon as I'm ready, I'll make an effort to meet people here in the valley."

"Ross Coughlin was asking about you." Cami grinned. "He's a doll."

Lulu laughed. "Don't try to play matchmaker. I'm still sorting things out."

"Okay. Just saying ..." A look of determination crossed her face—a look Lulu recognized as her own.

"You'll be the first to know if anything comes up."

"Good. Now that it's settled, I have to go." Cami patted her on the shoulder and gazed tenderly into Lulu's eyes. "Everything is going to be fine. You'll see." After giving her a cheerful wave, she left.

Lulu walked over to the sliding-glass door leading to the garden and stared out at the gray, rainy weather and reminded herself that the ache in her heart would soften over time. But at the moment she didn't know if she'd ever feel fine again.

Keeping busy helped Lulu recover some of her usual optimism. In addition to creating online marketing plans, she loved working on sales catalogs for The Barn and going over the inventory with Gwen.

Valentine's Day would signify the beginning of the end of winter in retail. It would be Lulu's first spring at Chandler Hill, and she was looking forward to the sight of the sleeping vines growing green with life. But now, everything was about the annual dinner-dance Chandler Hill held for inn guests and other winemakers in the valley. She'd been warned that reservations for the Valentine's event would quickly be filled. Becca, Imani, Gwen, and a few other long-time employees had been invited, filling all spots.

As the time grew closer, a buzz of excitement filled the inn. Those employees who worked the event would be rewarded with a party of their own at the close of the evening.

"What are you going to wear?" Becca asked Lulu the morning of the party.

"I guess a cocktail dress. How about you?"

Becca clasped her hands with excitement. "I bought a long, red dress. It will be a good addition to my trousseau."

"Should I wear something dressier?" Lulu asked, surprised by how fancy the party was.

"Yes, I think so. I talked Dan into wearing a tuxedo." Her eyes sparkled with excitement. "I told him it was practice for our wedding. We got engaged right after the party last year."

"Sweet," Lulu commented. She'd heard the details of Becca's engagement more than once. "Thanks for the input. I'll choose something different." Lulu filled with excitement. She hadn't been to a party like this in a long time. She hoped no politicians would be there to spoil the fun.

Later, as she stood in front of the full-length mirror, Lulu was glad she'd decided to hang onto some of her dressier clothes. The long-sleeved, scooped neck, winter-white dress met her ankles in silky folds that flattered her body. Her dark hair fell to her shoulders in shiny waves, and the new mascara she'd bought in California thickened her lashes, giving her eyes a new dimension. The diamond pendant her father had given her nestled against her chest. Dangling diamond earrings added sparkles.

She thought of Will. He'd approve of her appearance. She'd once worn this outfit to a political function. She sighed at the memory. He'd turned out to be such a disappointment. Better to discover it now, Lulu told herself. For all the sophistication people thought she had, she hadn't done that much dating. And growing up, fooling around was out of the question. Her father had made that very clear to her and any young man who might be interested in her. Wrapping a warm, black cloak around her shoulders, Lulu headed out.

When Lulu arrived at Chandler Hall, she stood a moment admiring the tiny red and white lights strung among the foliage lining the base of the building. Shiny red hearts had been attached to some of the branches, adding a nice touch to the occasion. Inside, lights twinkled, soft music played, and staff members lined the back hall, waiting to go into service. Cami, Drew, Rafe, Adam, and Dan stood together by the small stage against one wall of the room. Becca and Imani stood laughing at something one of them had said. When they saw her, they waved and she hurried over to greet them.

A staff member took her cloak.

"Wow! You look gorgeous!" Becca exclaimed.

"As do the two of you," Lulu said. Becca's dress was a simple, classic red one that was stunning on her. Imani was wearing a silk, red-and-gold sari that accented her classic features. Even as she stood talking to them, Imani's date, Hank Danvers, was gazing at her with a dazed smile.

Cami, dressed in a black, sleeveless, ankle-length dress, joined them. "I must say, Chandler Hill has the most beautiful women of all. Remember, it's important for us to interact with everyone, especially the other winemakers. We want to showcase all three wineries tonight. I'll do Chandler Hill, Drew and Rafe will do Taunton Estates, and Dan and Adam are representing Lone Creek Winery."

"What about me?" said Miguel. "I'm here for Lone Creek too."

Cami gasped and hugged him. "You're back! For how long this time?"

"Just a couple of days. I know how important this party is as a way to tout our wineries and thought I should be a part of it. Rafe agreed."

Lulu felt as if she'd turned to stone. Miguel's tuxedo-covered body she'd once made love to was ... delicious. As sexy as he was in blue jeans and a plaid shirt, his presence was even more dynamic dressed like a highly paid model for one of the menswear magazines.

His smile left Cami and landed on her.

A shiver went through Lulu. She remembered that same smile after they'd made love.

"How are you, Lulu?" he asked, sending more shivers through her. His brown-eyed gaze remained on her.

Like someone whose tongue had been removed, she simply nodded.

"Save a dance for me," said Miguel, grinning.

"Okay," Lulu said, hoping she didn't sound as nervous as she felt.

He greeted the other women, then walked over to Rafe, Dan, and Drew, where handshakes and man-hugs were exchanged.

"I swear," said Becca a little breathlessly. "He's one gorgeous hunk of man."

"Oh, yes. I think so, too," Imani said, shooting Hank an apologetic look.

When Lulu remained quiet, Becca nudged her. "What do you think? Isn't he something?"

"He's good-looking, but not much more than that," she said, lying to herself and them.

Becca frowned. "Miguel's a good guy. He's just not ready to settle down. Who can blame him? He has a lot of women falling all over him."

"But he wants to dance with Lulu," said Imani, giving her

an encouraging smile.

Afraid to show her emotions, Lulu said, "Excuse me. I need to talk to Cami." She knew she was being rude, but the thought of standing with her friends talking about the man who made her insides burn was unnerving. She didn't want anyone to suspect her true feelings for him. Especially when she knew how bad a choice he was for her.

When she saw Lulu approach, Cami stepped aside from the group she was with. "What a surprise, huh?"

"You didn't know he was coming?"

Cami shook her head. "Apparently, Rafe did. I honestly didn't. But this is a good opportunity for you to talk to him about everything."

"I wish I didn't have to." Lulu was well aware she sounded like a reluctant child, but couldn't help herself. Still, she'd never run from her responsibilities and wouldn't start now. Tomorrow, she'd speak to him. But she wouldn't, couldn't ruin tonight's party.

CHAPTER TWENTY

Though the unnerving thought of having the upcoming conversation she owed Miguel stayed on her mind, Lulu forced herself to go through the motions of introducing herself to guests and making sure they were taken care of. Most people in the valley already knew she and Cami were related and how. When Cami teasingly introduced her as Weezie Lopez everyone took it in stride.

Cami and Rafe stood side by side on the stage and welcomed everyone to the party. Standing behind them, the new owners of Lone Creek Winery beamed at the crowd.

"This year, we are especially pleased to announce that the hosts for the party are not only Chandler Hill and Taunton Estates, but Lone Creek Winery," said Cami.

Rafe said, "As most of you know, after a not-so-good year and with a fire there, Rod Mitchell put the property up for sale. Let me introduce the four new owners of the property—Dan Thurston, Miguel Lopez, Adam Kurey, and Drew Farley."

Loud applause rang out. Lulu had been told that Rod Mitchell had never fit into the community. The man apparently had a nasty superiority complex.

Rafe handed the microphone to Adam.

Adam grinned at the audience. "Hang onto your hats, people. Lone Creek is going to give all of you a run for your money." When the hooting and hollering died down, Adam continued. "Seriously, the four of us are committed to making the Lone Creek Winery what it was meant to be all along—a winery equal to the best in the valley."

Watching and listening, Lulu's gaze traveled to Miguel. The pride on his face was touching. She knew he, like the others, would put in his best effort to succeed. For a brief moment, tenderness brought the hint of tears to her eyes. They were all such good people.

Becca came over to her and put an arm around her. "I'm so proud of Dan and the other guys."

Lulu smiled at her. "They're a wonderful team. And you've changed the house there into something very special."

"Yes, now we have to get the house at Taunton Estates finished."

Uncomfortable from the memory of the house as she'd seen it, she made no comment. She turned her attention back to the announcement that the dance floor was open while food was being set up at the buffet table.

Dan came over to Becca. "Dance?"

Becca all but ran into his arms, leaving Lulu awkwardly standing alone.

"Ah, there's my dance partner," Miguel said, smiling as he approached her.

She told herself to remain cool, but her racing pulse gave her away. Heat rushed to her cheeks.

Miguel bowed before her with mock formality. "May I have this dance?"

She played along and curtseyed. "Of course, kind sir."

His fingers wrapped around her hand, sending warmth through her. She followed him to the dance floor and held her breath as his arms came around her.

For a moment they simply stared at one another. Miguel's eyes darkened until they were pools of mystery drilling into her.

A couple accidentally bumped into them, and the magic disappeared, leaving Lulu to wonder if it had happened at all.

They moved together effortlessly to the rhythm of the slow song the musicians were playing. Miguel began to hum softly to the music—lovely muffled notes.

She pulled away and looked at him with surprise. "You sing too?"

"I'm not the greatest singer in the group, but I do my best," Miguel replied. The tips of his ears turned pink.

At that moment, a stunning blonde walked over to them. "May I cut in? I need to talk to you, Miguel."

Miguel clasped Lulu's hand tighter. "Maybe later." He deftly moved Lulu away from her.

"What's that all about?" asked Lulu, observing the way Miguel's nostrils flared. He was pissed.

"We were supposed to go out, but I had to cancel. I left a message for her. I didn't just leave for Chile without bowing out of our date. My mother taught me better than that."

"Your mother and Rafe ... How are they related?"

"My father was Rafe's nephew. The Lopez men make damn sure their sons are gentlemen."

Lulu realized how proud all the Lopez men must be and imagined how difficult life could sometimes be for Miguel. She'd always thought he loved the attention, but maybe she was wrong.

The dance ended.

"Thank you," said Miguel, still holding her in his arms. "Maybe we can do some more dancing after dinner?"

"Yes, we need to talk. But not tonight. Do you have free time tomorrow?"

His grin brightened his dark eyes and exposed white teeth in a heartwarming moment. "I always have time for you."

She wondered if Miguel knew that it was this kind of banter that drove every woman around to fall a little bit in love with him.

Before Lulu left the floor, Rafe came over to her. "Care to dance?"

Pleased, she replied, "That would be lovely."

For someone who'd worked hard tromping his land overseeing his vines, Rafe was a very smooth dancer. Lulu smiled up at him.

"You look beautiful tonight, *Cariño*." Rafe gazed down at her with admiration. "Like a star among planets."

"A star among planets?

"Whatever the hell that means," he replied, chuckling.

Suddenly they were both laughing.

Lulu loved this sweet man.

After the dance ended, Lulu went to find Cami. She was standing by the buffet table chatting with people as they lined up for food. Observing her from a distance, Lulu was still amazed that after all the years growing up and wishing for a sibling, she'd had one all along.

"Hi, Weezie," said Cami, giving her a devilish grin.

"Hey there," Lulu replied, pleased by the nickname. It lent her a sense of moving on with her life in a place where she was her own person, not the daughter of someone infamous for his misdeeds.

After being introduced to several people, Lulu checked the wine table. As they did each year, local vintners supplied bottles of wine to be shared by all. This year, the bottle with a hummingbird label was a new addition—Lettie's Creek wine from Taunton Estates. It was a young wine, but something that would age nicely.

"I'm real proud of this bottle," said Drew showing it to her. "It's a tribute to a great lady and my first year to be able to bring it out."

"Cami says it's going to be very good."

"Yeah, she wanted to serve it at our wedding."

"When are the two of you going to get married?"

Drew let out a sigh. "I'm not sure. It'll probably be something on short notice, depending on how things are going at the inn. We're going to France on our honeymoon. That much is certain."

"Sounds wonderful. I'm happy for you both."

"I'm a pretty lucky guy," said Drew looking across the room at Cami.

Lulu felt a pang of jealousy. Life seemed so planned for them while she was still struggling to find herself. She walked to the end of the buffet line.

Darren and Liz and the kitchen crew had been working for days to prepare for the party. The roast steamship round of beef, stuffed chicken breasts, and baked salmon entrées looked delicious. The side dishes too—potatoes au gratin, three different kinds of vegetables, two variations on tossed green salad, and a favorite rice casserole. Rolls and all the accompanying sauces were tasty additions.

"The food is always so good here," said one of the women standing in front of her.

The woman's companion said, "Yes, and the desserts are to die for. I eat almost nothing before coming to the party so I can have a taste of everything."

Lulu thought back to her days in California. Many women in Los Angeles would seldom talk about eating this way. So many of them hardly ate a decent meal. And for what? Lulu had been caught in the trap of thinking she had to be skinny to be beautiful, but since coming to Chandler Hill, she no longer felt that way. In fact, Darren had allowed her to sneak a piece of pastry from the kitchen earlier that day.

Lulu filled her plate and then looked for a place to sit. Becca waved her over to a table where she sat with Dan and a pleasant couple that she introduced as Dan's parents. Hearing them talk to one another, Lulu was happy that Becca had found such a wonderful guy with parents who seemed excited to have her join the family.

As the music continued to play, she turned to watch the dancers. An older gentleman from the next table rose and came over to her. "May I have this dance?"

Surprised but pleased, Lulu rose.

"I'm Mark Pierce, one of Lettie's old friends. Rafe's too. My wife, Jean, can't dance anymore. Bum hip. She suggested I ask you."

An older, pleasant-faced woman waved to them.

"Well, then, I'll dance for Jean," Lulu said, touched by the obvious show of affection between them.

While Mark wasn't a great dancer, he was easy to talk to. After she explained how she was renting the house that Abby and Lisa owned and mentioned she'd love to be able to buy it one day, he said, "It's a beauty. I know the original owner, and it was built right. Not like today when houses and apartments seem to be built in a day."

Lulu made note of his remark and decided not to wait to let Abby know how serious she was about purchasing the house.

After the dance ended, dessert was announced and everyone made a dash for the display of pies, cakes, and pastries that were laid out.

Lulu stood with Becca and Imani, making sure the buffet line moved well.

"Looks delicious," said Becca. "I hope there's still some left by the time we can help ourselves."

"Me too," said Imani. Her eyes twinkled with amusement. "This sari can cover a lot of sins."

Lulu laughed. Imani had a well-known craving for sweets.

"Not standing in line?" said Miguel.

The three of them shook their heads.

"Ah, I see. You're supposed to wait. Should I get anything special, Lulu? Something to share?"

Becca and Imani turned to her.

Hating the heat filling her cheeks, Lulu said, "No, thanks."

After Miguel moved on, Becca elbowed Lulu. "Are you crazy?"

Lulu knew Becca thought there was a lot more to Miguel's invitation, but after talking to him earlier, she was well aware he was making the offer simply to be polite. Besides, the thought of making her confession to him tomorrow made her feel a little sick.

At the end of the evening, Lulu shook hands with the guests who were leaving. She'd met some very nice, hard-working people. Mark and Jean Pierce headed her way. Lulu had learned from Cami that every year so far, they'd won two first-class airline tickets in a contest for being married the longest and then given them away to a much younger couple. It was all part of a scheme Lettie and Jean had cooked up several years ago. Fear of flying had kept Lettie at home. This was just a sweet way of giving someone else wings.

After the last guests had left, the staff gathered in the kitchen.

"Help yourselves to whatever you want, ladies and gentlemen," Darren announced. "Happy Valentine's Day to all of you."

"Yes," said Cami. "Thank you for a job well done."

Exhausted, Lulu told Cami that as long as she wasn't needed, she was going home.

"See you tomorrow," Cami said. "Though the inn is packed with guests, it should be a quiet Sunday morning. As part of the weekend package, we serve a late brunch so people can sleep in."

"If you need me, call," Lulu said, wrapping the fur around

her and stepping outside.

"There you are," said Miguel as he walked over to her. "I've been waiting to give you a ride to Cami's house."

"Oh, that's kind of you, but I don't live there anymore. I've moved. Besides, I have my car." The last thing she wanted to do was to be with Miguel when her defenses were low.

"Okay, just thought I'd ask. What time do you want to meet tomorrow?"

"Why don't you come to Abby and Lisa's old house at ten? That's where I live now."

"I'll be there." Miguel gave her a little salute and went on his way.

Lulu watched him go, wondering if he had any idea of how difficult it had been for her to turn down his offer.

CHAPTER TWENTY-ONE

The next morning Lulu lay in bed staring at the rosy fingers of light reaching through the blinds in her bedroom window, beckoning to her. It promised to be a bright, sunny February morning. But Lulu could think of nothing else but how her day was likely to evolve into a stormy, gray existence. She knew now, as Rafe had told her, Miguel would have done what was required, would have asked her to marry him rather than leave his baby without a father. But that wasn't something she'd wanted.

Wishing she could renege on her invitation and send him a text instead, she got out of the bed to face a day she was dreading. The house she thought of as a nice place to raise a baby alone now seemed large and empty.

After a hot shower, Lulu dressed in jeans and a warm sweater and headed downstairs to the kitchen. Cami always served something sweet in the morning. Maybe, Lulu thought, it would make things easier if she had a treat of some kind for Miguel.

She fixed herself a cup of coffee, and following a basic recipe she found online, she began putting together the ingredients for buttery sugar cookies. Melba made some similar to this recipe, and she'd always loved them.

As she scooped the last batch off the baking sheet, she heard the sound of Miguel's truck. She quickly placed warm cookies on a plate, set it by the coffee maker, and put the pan in the sink.

The sound of the doorbell broke through the tension that

had stiffened her shoulders. *I can do this,* she told herself.

Her heart skipped a beat at the smile on Miguel's face when she opened the door.

"I smell something wonderful." He entered the house as she stood by nervously holding the door.

"I thought we could sit in the kitchen and have coffee," Lulu said, her stomach whirling.

"Okay," Miguel said giving her a questioning look.

"Then we can talk." The firmness in Lulu's voice didn't reflect the quivering inside her body. She had no idea how one went about telling someone her kind of news.

"Great party last night, huh?" Miguel commented, following her into the kitchen.

"Very nice. A great way to break up the winter months."

"You looked beautiful. I noticed you laughing with Rafe on the dance floor."

Lulu smiled at the memory. "He said something silly. Honestly, he's such a wonderful man. I love to think he's my adopted grandfather. I never knew my own. How's it going in Chile?"

"It's very interesting. Though it would seem the process is the same, every operation is unique. The grapes, the climates, and varying techniques all make a difference. Adam and Drew are thinking of working together on producing something new to the area. We'll see if my research helps or not."

"I think the four of you are going to be a big success," Lulu said, admiring the earnest expression on Miguel's face when he discussed wines.

Miguel walked over to the sliding-glass door and looked out at the garden. "Abby and Lisa did such a good job with this. I remember how rundown the place looked until they took it over. The renovations they made are great." He turned to her. "I can't wait for you to see the addition to my house after the changes are complete. You're one of the few who understood how much I liked the idea of sleeping in the open while being inside."

He studied her, his look reaching inside her. "You remember that night?"

Lulu pressed her lips together and nodded. When she could catch her breath, she said, "That's what I have to talk to you about. Rafe said I owed it to you."

Miguel frowned. "Owed me what?"

"You'd better sit down," Lulu told him. Her knees were wobbling and her mouth was dry.

They sat at the kitchen table, facing one another.

His look grew suspicious. "What aren't you telling me?"

"That night ... I got pregnant. I lost the baby thirteen days ago."

The blood drained from Miguel's face. "What? You were going to have my baby? Are you all right?"

Miserable, she nodded.

Color raced back to Miguel's cheeks. "Wait! You were going to have my baby and didn't even tell me?"

"You were in Chile ..." her voice trailed away.

He stared at her with suspicion. "When I came back to Oregon with Valentina, did you know then?"

Tears filled Lulu's eyes. "Yes, but I didn't know how you'd feel about it. You can have any woman you choose. They all want you. Why would you choose me or the baby you didn't plan on?"

His lips drawn into a thin line, Miguel shook his head.

She forced herself to continue. "I was going to raise your baby alone ... and then I lost it—the baby I already loved." Tears, warm and wet, slid down her cheeks.

"Am I to understand that when you had the decency to tell me, you would also announce that you were going to bring up my child alone? Do I have everything straight?" Miguel's voice shook with anger. His eyes darkened as he stared at her. "To you, I was just the sperm donor."

She fought to find the right words. "Rafe told me you'd do the honorable thing and ask me to marry you. But as I told him, I won't be married to someone who is acting only out of a sense of duty."

Miguel got up out of his chair and marched over to the sliding-glass door.

Lulu clutched her hands and remained seated as he continued to stare out through the glass. When he turned around, the sadness in his eyes tore at her heart.

"You have no idea who I am. Not at all. But I know you better now. You're just like your father, making people believe in you until they discover that everything about you is untrue."

Nauseous, Lulu clasped her stomach. "That's so unfair! You know I'm not like my father."

"Do I? Think about it." He headed for the door.

Lulu jumped to her feet. "Wait! I was scared and confused. I thought I was doing the right thing. I didn't want to put you in that kind of situation. You'd be able to have your freedom and be able to choose anyone you want to share your life with .... I never thought ..."

His eyes widened with surprise, then grew moist with hurt. "My God! Is that what you think of me? I'm out of here," Miguel announced, cutting her off.

His shoulders slumped as he hurried out of the house.

The roar of the truck's engine indicated his anger.

Lulu covered her mouth and doubled over.

Later, she was curled up on the couch when Cami knocked on her door and entered.

"What in the world happened between you and Miguel? He's furious that I knew about the baby and didn't mention it to him. And Rafe called me. He and Miguel had words."

"I tried to explain that I didn't want to pin him down to a wife and a child he may not want. But I screwed up. He thinks I don't respect him at all. I never got the chance to tell him how much I like him. He walked out before I could say it."

Cami gave her an incredulous look. "Whoa! You said all that?"

Sobbing miserably, Lulu could only nod.

Cami sat down on the couch and hugged Lulu. "Girl, you've really messed up this time. The Lopez pride is well-known."

"What am I going to do?"

Cami sighed. "As Nonnee would say, 'Time will help, even if it doesn't heal all things.' Maybe, it's a good thing Miguel's going back to Chile."

"Going back to Valentina, you mean," Lulu countered, as fresh tears filled her eyes.

"We'll see. We'll see." Cami gave her a squeeze that did nothing to make Lulu feel better.

CHAPTER TWENTY-TWO

Lulu wasn't surprised when Rafe showed up at her house a little later. They sat together in the kitchen, sharing coffee and the sugar cookies that now seemed a foolish gesture for Miguel.

Trying hard to keep herself together, Lulu repeated what she'd told Cami.

Rafe's dark-eyed gaze settled on her. "Miguel is very angry right now, thinking we coordinated an effort to keep him from finding out. More than that, his feelings are hurt by how you view him as a person, a man."

"But I didn't want him to feel any responsibility toward me. I thought he'd be relieved that he wouldn't have to face the circumstances."

Rafe shook his head. "Ah, Lulu, you're so young, too honest, and very foolish. A man doesn't want to be judged that way. Lopez men most of all."

"I want the real deal. And if that's being too honest, I'm sorry. The man I marry is going to be crazy about me, not because he's doing what he considers the right thing."

"What about Will? He was crazy about you." Rafe's steady look made Lulu feel very uncomfortable.

"Well, I wasn't crazy about him," Lulu said lamely. Her thoughts flew to the memory of her dancing with Miguel. It had felt so right to be in his arms. There was no comparison between the two men.

Rafe's eyes widened. "*Ay, Dio mio!* You really care for Miguel."

Lulu's sigh was painful. "It doesn't matter. I've ruined every chance I had with him. I could never get him to understand."

Rafe reached over and squeezed her hand. "It was a shock to Miguel. Let things settle for a while."

Lulu acknowledged his comment with another sigh. "I guess I have no choice but to wait." The next few weeks would seem unending. But, she acknowledged to herself, whose fault was that?

The dreary months of January and February over, March entered like a lamb, bringing a lighter step to feet and more frequent smiles to the faces of their guests. Though they'd hosted a couple of sweet, small winter weddings, the official wedding season at the Chandler Hill Inn opened with the advent of spring.

One morning, Lulu walked into her office to see a bouquet of pink roses sitting on her desk. An envelope with her name on it lay at the base of the crystal vase. With trembling fingers, she opened it and read writing on the card:

"I'm sorry about everything, Lulu. You and I need to get to know each other better. I'll begin with the first email. You once promised to answer them. I hope you do. Miguel."

Lulu slumped in her desk chair and, taking deep breaths, she covered her face. Hope broke through the pain she carried inside her. Maybe they could at least form a friendship.

Miguel's first email was short, but it was a beginning. It simply said:

"I'm sorry for running out on you because I was so angry. I realized we don't know each other at all, and I want to know everything about you. I wish there was something I could do for you to make you feel better. As I hope you understand by now, I would have welcomed our baby with more than a sense of responsibility. Family is important to me."

Touched by his message, she quickly wrote back:

"Thanks. It was good to hear from you. I'm sorry too. Family is important to me, but I haven't had the best example of one. I've seen so many people hurt by making the wrong choices—each of my parents, for instance. And, Miguel, thank you for the roses. It was sweet of you to remember that they're my favorite. I hope things are going well for you there. Spring has arrived here and, with it, all the activity of new beginnings. 'Bye for now."

While she waited to hear from him again, Lulu threw herself into keeping busy with marketing, planning merchandising events at The Barn, building catalog sales, and helping with weddings. She knew Miguel would have done the right thing by her, but only because of his upbringing and the nice person he was. A good friend.

When his next email came, she closed the door to her office and took a few moments in the quiet to read it.

"I'm glad to hear from you. In the past, I haven't had many women I could really talk to about things. I like the idea of us emailing back and forth. It's a good way to get to know one another. I guess that's what's been missing for me in the past. I've got lots of guys to hang out with, but no women to talk to like a friend, you know? Sisters are sisters. Anyway, I've decided in spite of all the good things about a winery in Chile, I like it best in Oregon. Even though my father wasn't around much, Uncle Rafe and other relatives gave me a love of winemaking and the Valley. You wrote it was spring there. Are the buds coming out? I'll write later. I've gotta go"

Lulu let out a sigh of happiness. She was so glad Miguel genuinely wanted to stay in communication. It meant so much to her. She sat at her computer and began typing.

"Good to hear from you again so soon." She told him all about the status of things at the wineries and then described a wedding where the father of the bride had almost refused to give his daughter away. "I swear, he was crying so hard we weren't sure he could say the words, 'Her mother and I do' when the minister asked who was giving the bride away. It was so touching. I think I caught the emotion in the photographs I took. Traveling with my father, being with him, made me see people in a whole new way. In politics, it's hard to find someone you can trust."

He quickly wrote back.

"Be careful that your time in politics didn't make you too jaded. People like the Chandlers are real, and you're lucky to be a part of that family. Speaking of family, any wedding news from either Cami or Becca? I'll need to be around when that's happening. Drew told me he and Cami are planning on a Paris honeymoon. How about you? Are you off to California anytime soon?"

Cami knocked on Lulu's office door. "Can I get your help? I have some ideas for a marketing campaign on the website to discuss with you."

"Sure," said Lulu, her heart still warm from the online conversation she was having with Miguel.

That night, after she was tucked in bed, she answered Miguel's email.

"It's so busy at the inn that neither Cami nor Becca have announced wedding plans. I'm not going to California in the foreseeable future. My mother is doing so much better these days. She loves it here at Chandler Hill and thinks that someday she might spend more time here. It's nice for me to have her here. We weren't that close when I was growing up. So tell me about your family. I heard they live in California. And tell me what some of your favorite things are. You know two of mine."

Exchanging emails became a daily thing. For Lulu it was the best ending of any day, telling Miguel everything she'd done that day, answering questions he had for her, and writing down questions for him to answer. She learned he loved his mother's cooking, hated broccoli, loved a hoppy beer, and was thinking of taking more courses at college so he could prepare for the sales position for all three wineries.

In exchange she told him about her love of photography, that she was learning to cook, and how she cried at the few movies she got to see. She asked about his musical ability and learned he'd inherited it from his father. She learned his mother and sisters lived near one another in a small community outside of San Francisco and had no interest in coming back to Willamette Valley.

Satisfied that her friendship with Miguel was growing, when Ross Coughlin called and asked her out, she accepted.

Sitting in the Green Grape, having a drink and an early dinner one Thursday evening, Lulu and Ross talked easily with one another. She found him to be interested in many things, which stimulated their conversation. Before they knew it, the band arrived and the evening turned into a party.

After they'd danced a time or two, Ross gave her an apologetic look. "Sorry. But I have to get up early tomorrow. It's a school day."

"No problem, we have our first wedding weekend of the spring. Guests will start arriving tomorrow. I promised Cami I'd be on board to take pictures of the group. I'll be busy doing that most of the weekend."

"Maybe we can catch up sometime next week," said Ross, as he led her to his car. "I'd like to see you again."

He pulled his car into her driveway and turned to her. "Thanks for a great evening. I meant what I said. I'd like to see you again." His smile softened his features and brought a light to his blue eyes. "And again."

"Thanks, but I have to be honest. I'm not ready for anything serious. All I can offer is friendship."

"I'll take it." He studied her for a moment and then said, "I'll call sometime. May I walk you to the door?"

"No, thanks anyway. It was a fun evening. See you soon."

He waited until she reached the front door, then beeped his horn to signal goodbye.

Lulu entered the house and plopped down on the couch. She'd tried her best to put magic into their evening. But the whole time she'd been thinking about Miguel.

When she went inside, she checked her computer for a message from him.

He'd sent a whole bunch of photographs with the message:

> "Thought you'd like a look at the vineyard here in Chile. Maybe you will see it someday. It's fall here, and the thought of spring in Oregon is making me homesick. Hope you're enjoying it."

She studied the photographs. In one he was standing next to vines holding up a beautiful cluster of grapes. Gazing at it, Lulu clasped her hands to her chest. He looked so healthy, so wonderful. She quickly wrote back:

> "Thanks for the photos. It looks like beautiful country. And you look as if you're enjoying it. We all miss you here in Oregon. Drew, Adam, and Dan are busy with the vines. By the time you are home, the growing season will be underway. My first spring in the Valley. So exciting!"

There was so much more she wanted to say, but couldn't.

Miguel was opening up to her as a friend. It was a very nice beginning, but she needed a lot more than that before she was comfortable about building a stronger relationship with him. It was, she knew, a trust issue. One she was trying to work on. And though they emailed back and forth, they stayed away from the subject that was still painful to them.

Flowers began to bloom in the back of the house she was renting, opening to spring days at first shyly and then with bursts of yellows and purples and pinks. Sitting outside in the late afternoon sun, Lulu decided to call Abby and Lisa hoping to convince them to sell the house to her. It had become a peaceful, pleasant home.

When Lulu finally reached Abby and Lisa, Abby explained that they had been out of the country on a European trip and apologized for not getting back to her.

"Sounds lovely. Where did you go?"

"As boring as it may sound to some, we toured museums and cathedrals in a number of cities from London to Paris to Rome. It was glorious!" Abby gushed. "What can we help you with, Lulu?"

"I want to buy the house. I'm connected to the area now and love being here in your home. It's become mine, and I'm willing to pay you fair market value with no bickering back and forth."

"I thought you would have heard from the new owner." Abby's voice was high with surprise. "We sold the house last month."

Disappointment speared Lulu's body. "Oh, no! Am I going to have to move out?"

"I wouldn't think so. Your lease doesn't expire for several more months."

"May I ask who the new owner is?"

"Hold on a minute. I need to talk to Lisa."

Lulu could hear whispering in the background and then Abby said, "We think there must be a reason you haven't been notified. We'll follow up at this end, but we don't feel we have the liberty to give you the name. We hope you understand."

"I'm not sure I do. If I don't hear shortly, I'll call you back. I have to know where to send the rent check."

"Of course. We'll make that clear." After chatting about non-consequential things, Lulu ended the conversation with a sigh, annoyed with herself for waiting too long to ask.

That night, when her mother called, Lulu told her about it. "I just don't understand. It seems strange. Who could it be?"

"How about me?" her mother said, and became quiet.

It took Lulu a few seconds to register what her mother had said. "You? Why would you buy the house I'm renting?"

"Because I love it, and I need to know you have a nice, safe place to live. I intend to come visit, and should you decide to rent or buy something else, I'm happy to have it for myself."

Lulu started to giggle and found she couldn't stop. Her mother had gone from a cold, secluded stranger in the shadow of her husband to a warm, wonderful woman—a person she was proud to call her mother.

"Good thing you bought all the furniture you loved. I promise to take care of it. And, Mom, I'm going to pay you the monthly rent just as I would otherwise. Deal?"

"Yes," her mother said. "My accountant insisted it remain a business arrangement until you make a decision one way or another."

"Would you mind if I get a dog? Sophie's breeders have a new litter of dachshunds, and I'd love to have one. Cami is thinking of getting a second one to keep Sophie company, and they could all play together."

"It would be fine with me. Sophie's a darling dog and quite the charmer."

"And a good hunter and watch dog," said Lulu, thrilled with the idea of having one like her. "I'll pay for any damage that might happen," said Lulu.

"Of course," her mother said. "I would expect that of you."

If Lulu wasn't mistaken, her mother sounded a lot like her father at that moment. She hung up the call wondering what other changes were coming her way.

That night she wrote to Miguel about what her mother had done.

"Are you happy about it?" he asked.

Lulu smiled as she typed her answer:

"Yes, I'm thrilled. And she's given me permission to get a puppy. A new litter of dachshunds is available at the breeders where Cami got Sophie."

Miguel wrote back:

"Sophie is a good dog. It'll be nice for you to have some company. I'm happy for you."

"Me too," Lulu typed, realizing it was more than the thought of a puppy that pleased her. Miguel was becoming a real friend.

A week later Lulu experienced the unexpected challenges of being a mother to a dachshund puppy. Barely ten weeks old, Dolly was a blur of black-and-tan activity. Bright-eyed, the dog moved from one spot of trouble to the next, wagging her tail, making it almost impossible for Lulu to keep up. But warm, pink-tongued licks and snuggles melted away Lulu's frustration in a hurry. She couldn't resist sending a picture of Dolly to Miguel:

"Isn't she the cutest?"

He quickly wrote back.

"Like her owner."

Reading his brief but meaningful message, her vision blurred with tears. It was such a sweet thing for him to say.

As she went about preparing three puppy meals a day, cleaning up messes, and encouraging Dolly to sleep, Lulu wondered if this is what it would be like raising a human baby alone. Understandably, it was easier for two people to handle it. Still, if she hadn't lost the baby, she would have gone ahead on her own. Or tried to. Now, she knew she'd been wrong to think that way

The month of April ended in a blur of activity, and then the May weddings began, making life even busier for Lulu. Though they now had a local professional photographer on hand for Chandler Hill weddings, every once in a while, Lulu's services were requested. Photographing happy wedding couples was both a pleasure for her and painful. On the surface, her life was busy, fulfilling, and focused on the moment. But observing couples vowing to have a future together made her aware of an emptiness that wouldn't go away. Evenings spent exchanging emails with Miguel became very precious to her.

On this day, she, as Cami and Rafe often did, found her way

to the stone bench among the grove of trees to try and get a better sense of herself and her future.

The bud break had come and gone, and as they did most days in May, workers were managing the canopy to make sure when bloom time came, grapes could ripen evenly and sunburn could be avoided. This was also the time when extra shoots were thinned out. The bloom would happen at the end of the month or early in June.

Sitting quietly, thinking of the time when Miguel would be home for good, Lulu wondered if he would bring Valentina with him. The last time she'd seen them, they'd acted like a couple. In all their conversations about his life in Chile, he hadn't mentioned her and she hadn't dared to ask.

She turned at the sound of someone walking toward her and waved at Rafe.

He waved back, hobbled over to her, and sat down beside her with an uncharacteristic groan.

"What's wrong?" Lulu asked, immediately concerned.

"These ... old bones ... are tired," he mumbled. He tried to smile, but only one side of his lips curved. "Left arm, leg numb," he managed to say brokenly.

Lulu watched in horror as his whole body sagged, and he slid to the ground.

"Rafe! Rafe! Can you hear me?" Lulu cried, kneeling on the ground beside him, fighting tears. "Do you understand what I'm saying?"

He opened one eye. His words were a jumble of confusion.

Lulu whipped the phone out of her back pocket and called 911. Cold seeped through her body making her shiver. *A stroke* she thought. *Maybe more.*

As calmly as she could while her pulse raced, Lulu gave the person on the other end of the phone as much information as possible. "His granddaughter is at the inn. She will know how to find us. Hurry. Dear God, please hurry!"

"Stay right there with him, and stay on the line until I'm sure help has reached you. Speak calmly to the patient and reassure him help is on the way."

"I will." Lulu looked for Rafe's phone where he usually kept it in his jacket and pulled it out. She searched and found Cami's number and pressed it.

"Hello, Rafe. How are you?" Cami's cheerful voice brought tears to Lulu's eyes.

"Cami, it's me, Lulu. I'm with Rafe at Lettie's bench. I think he's had a stroke. I've called 911. You need to lead them to this spot. They're on their way! Hurry!"

"Oh my God! Oh my God! Is he going to be all right?"

"I hear the sirens now. Go outside, Cami, and show them how to get to us."

Lulu clicked off the call and turned to Rafe. "Hang on, Rafe. Help is here."

The moments ticked away, one crawling second after another.

Lulu clung to Rafe's hand, and realized how frail his frame had become. She'd never thought of him as old because of the energy that usually surrounded him and the smile that made him seem so young and alive.

Silently she prayed. *"Please, God, don't let him die. We need him here too much to let him go."*

Cami came running into the clearing followed by two men hauling a gurney and medical equipment. Cami threw herself down on the ground next to Rafe. Hugging him carefully, she said, "Rafe, please don't die. I couldn't bear it!"

"Excuse me, Miss, but you'll have to move. Both of you," said one of the EMTs gently.

Cami moved away, and arms around each other, Cami and Lulu watched as the men began the job of evaluating the medical issues. In moments, they had oxygen hooked up to Rafe, an IV inserted in his arm, and were carrying him on the gurney across the ground.

Cami and Lulu kept pace, guiding them to a path and then a driveway that would allow them to roll the gurney to the waiting ambulance.

"I'll go with him," Cami said. "I'm his granddaughter, his closest living relative."

"Why don't the two of you follow in a car," said the smaller of the two men, giving them both a sympathetic look. "We'll meet you at the Medical Center in town to make sure he's stable, and then we'll talk about what steps we'll take from there. There are two well-known stroke centers in Portland."

Cami grabbed Lulu's hand, and they ran to get her car.

Standing outside her car, Cami fumbled with the fob. "I'm so nervous," she muttered, then opened the door and slid behind the wheel. As Cami started the engine, Lulu settled in the passenger seat and buckled her seat belt.

Tears streamed down Cami's cheeks. "I don't know if I can drive. I'm too upset."

Lulu drummed up every bit of calm she could muster. "We'll do it together. You drive and I'll talk."

As Cami headed away from the inn, Lulu talked quietly to her. "I was just sitting there when Rafe approached. He waved and managed to sit for a few seconds before it happened. I knew what it was right away."

"I'm very glad you were with him. He's been going there alone more and more often. It's such a peaceful place for him." Cami hiccupped and began to cry softly.

"Hang on, sis," Lulu said, trying to keep Cami focused. "We're almost there."

"I'm so relieved you're with me, Lulu. You're such a good sister."

Lulu didn't answer. She couldn't. The lump in her throat blocked any words.

When they rushed inside the hospital, they were reassured Rafe was being well taken care of. A nurse explained his vitals and other information had already been provided to the Oregon Health & Science University Telemedicine Network.

"It makes a huge difference in handling emergencies like this. Doctors will confer on the case and work on the outcome together," the nurse continued. "As soon as the doctor working on your family member is able, he'll fill you in on the details."

Lulu settled in a chair next to Cami and tried to think healing thoughts.

A doctor soon appeared. "Are you the next of kin for Rafael Lopez.?"

Cami stood. "I am. How is he?"

"We are preparing to send him by helicopter to the OHSU Hospital in Portland. A vascular neurologist is waiting for him there. Mr. Lopez has been given what we call 'clot-busting' medication to help prevent any further damage, but we need to have him evaluated there to make sure we've done all we can do to save brain tissue and function."

"Can we see him?" Lulu asked her voice wobbling.

"For only a few minutes. In cases like this, the faster we move, the better."

Cami and Lulu followed the doctor to a room where Rafe was being monitored. His eyes showed recognition at the sight of them.

They each gave him a kiss on the cheek.

"I love you, Rafe. Get well soon. We'll see you in Portland," Lulu said, trying to hold herself together. She left the room so that Cami could have some time alone with him.

When Cami joined Lulu, her face displayed silvery tracks of tears. "I have directions on how to get to the hospital. He's going to the Brain Institute first."

"Okay, good. While I was waiting for you, I called Becca and told her what was happening. She told us not to worry. She and Imani will handle things at the inn."

"Oh, thanks," said Cami. "I can't even think of that now. The doctor told me he's encouraged by how quickly things have been done for Rafe, but I have to know he'll be all right." Cami turned to her. "How did you even know about strokes and what to do?"

"I just saw something on television about it. Thank God!"

As they were driving to Portland, a helicopter flew over them. Aware of the special passenger it carried, silence filled the car.

"You know, strokes are a part of my family history," Cami said. "In the 1970s, Rex Chandler, the original owner of the land, died of a stroke right after my grandmother married Kenton Chandler, leaving them the land and the inn."

"I didn't know that," said Lulu.

"Yes, and then Kenton was killed in a car accident, leaving my grandmother to raise my mother alone. I hope this isn't going to be one of life's circles," said Cami. "You know, where the beginning and end meet."

"I don't think that's going to happen, Cami. Medicine has come such a long way since then. And as you said earlier, the doctor is encouraged by the way Rafe is responding to quick treatment."

"What if something more happens to him, and Rafe becomes totally paralyzed?"

Lulu put a hand on Cami's arm. "Don't even go there. Rafe has a lot to live for, and he's always been a strong man."

CHAPTER TWENTY-THREE

The news, when they finally got it, was much better than Lulu and Cami had hoped. The doctor explained that the drugs seemed to have cleared the problem, and no new clots or blockages were found. "He's a very lucky man," the doctor said. "A quick response not only saved his life, but made for a much better recovery. He'll be on blood-thinning meds, will have to watch his diet, and will need physical therapy to strengthen his left leg and arm."

"Thank you! Thank you!" Cami cried, clasping her hands in front of her in a prayerful pose.

The doctor beamed at the two of them. "We like outcomes like this. You can thank the young lady who acted so quickly."

Cami threw herself at Lulu, and crying softly, they hugged.

When Lulu saw Rafe sitting up in bed, her eyes filled. Everyone was thinking of her as some kind of hero, but she'd been scared silly by Rafe's collapse.

"Come here. Both of you," said Rafe. Lulu and Cami rushed to his side.

"I'm so glad you're going to be all right," said Lulu, hugging him.

"Me too. You scared us to death, Rafe, I can't get along without you," said Cami. Her voice trembled.

"Ah, *Cariño*, someday you will have to get along without me, and you'll be fine. But I'm not leaving you now." He gave them each a steady look. "I saw Lettie. She told me my time on earth was not up." Tears filled his eyes. "She said she's waiting for me."

Lulu glanced at Cami and then studied Rafe. He was a sweet, gentle man, but not one for fanciful ideas like this.

"It's true," he said, and Lulu believed him.

"What did Nonnee look like?" Cami said.

Rafe's smile reached his eyes. "Like the young woman I fell in love with so many years ago."

A nurse interrupted the emotional silence that followed. "Just checking your vitals. You should get some rest, Mr. Lopez." She eyed Cami and Lulu meaningfully.

"Okay, we'll go," said Cami. "We'll see you tomorrow. The doctor said if all continues to go well, you should be able to leave the hospital tomorrow afternoon."

"I'm going to be fine," Rafe said with such conviction Lulu knew he was referring to his meeting with Lettie. Such a strange story. She'd heard others like it before. Some people attributed these kinds of moments to simply the activity of the brain, but Lulu thought of them as spiritual.

That night she told Miguel everything, including Rafe's vision. "Do you believe in such a thing?" she asked Miguel, aware of how important his answer would be to her.

Miguel answered. After quizzing her on more details of Rafe's health, he wrote:

"If Rafe says he saw Lettie, then I say he did.
He loved her so much, it's possible."

Though she didn't completely understand it, when she read his words, tears came to her eyes.

The next afternoon Lulu accompanied Cami to Portland to

pick up Rafe from the hospital. They'd waited all day to hear from the doctor and both were relieved when he gave the go-ahead for Rafe's release.

"Rafe isn't going to like it, but I'm going to insist he stay with me for a few days until we all feel better about his condition," said Cami.

"Good idea," Lulu said. "We can take turns checking on him throughout the day." Lulu grinned at Cami. "He'll hate knowing that, so we'll have to be very subtle about it."

Cami returned her smile. "I'm glad we can laugh about it now. I was really worried he'd die."

"Me, too," Lulu admitted. "I think of him as my grandfather, too."

The conversation during the rest of the ride into Portland consisted of discussing business at Chandler Hill Inn.

"You're okay covering the Welles wedding?" Cami asked her. "Bethany Welles is a friend of Justine Devon Dickinson, my favorite bride at the inn. She's sent a lot of business our way, and I want everything to be perfect for Bethany and her groom, Jason Sands."

"Yes," said Lulu. "I've explained to them that I take only candid shots, nothing formal, and suggested they use our regular photographer too."

"It's nice that you provide your services for such a low fee. I know you could charge more. Why do you do it?"

Lulu's smile was genuine. "For me, it's a matter of keeping in touch with my inner self, the one who loves people, flaws and all. That feeling for individuals has been so tarnished by my experiences with the media that I need reminders of it. We can't afford to lose love of humanity. That binds all of us together."

Cami looked at her and nodded. "You're right. My mother felt that way, which is why she spent many years in Africa."

"My father, too. Funny, isn't it, how that love of humanity brought us together."

"Yes, I've thought of that many times," said Cami. She reached over and patted Lulu's hand. "You're a good person, someone others can trust to do the right thing."

Lulu remained quiet as she thought of Miguel and their baby. She hadn't considered his feelings. She was very relieved they were exchanging emails on an almost nightly basis. It was a chance for each of them to reach out to one another and heal from a loss that had hurt them both.

"Ah, here we are," said Cami. "Let's see if we can find a parking spot."

After parking, the two of them headed inside. Cami carried a bag holding the fresh clothes Rafe had requested.

At the sight of them, Rafe's eyes lit. "My guardian angels," he said, attempting humor.

Lulu chuckled with Cami and hid her shock at Rafe's appearance. In a hospital gown, Rafe's body seemed withered by age. She quickly blinked back tears. Life was so uncertain. She'd almost lost him. They waited while Rafe went into the bathroom and changed into his fresh clothes. Cami read the discharge papers and gathered his personal items, which had been packaged in a bag to take home.

When Rafe appeared wearing jeans and one of his favorite, plaid flannel shirts, he looked ten years younger. Lulu whispered a soft prayer of thanks. Maybe, as Cami's grandmother had told him, he had more years left on earth.

She snapped a photo of him to send to Miguel. He'd want to see Rafe like this.

As they had expected, Rafe fought Cami's idea of his spending time at her house. But Cami remained firm. "Just for a few days, Rafe. I know you don't want to wear one of those emergency buttons, so we'll keep you close to make sure nothing goes wrong. Then you can go back to the cabin."

"Okay, but for a few days only. And I'm not staying in bed or lying on the couch to make you feel better."

"Deal," said Cami.

"My mother is arriving for a visit tomorrow," Lulu said. "Maybe the two of you can spend time together. She thinks the world of you, Rafe. You're one of the few people she feels comfortable enough with to be herself."

Rafe's lips curved, smoothing out the worry lines that had creased his brow. "I admire her, too. Time together will be good. I understand she bought Abby and Lisa's house."

"Whaaat! I didn't know that," exclaimed Cami.

"I haven't told anyone. She must have talked to you, Rafe," said Lulu.

He gave them a knowing smile. "I thought it would be good for her and all of us if she knew she had a safe place to come to. And with you living here, Lulu, it means the world to her to be close by."

Lulu nodded but wondered what other things her mother had discussed with Rafe. She wrote to Miguel to assure him Rafe was fine and that her mother was arriving for a few days:

"It's always nice when they are together. It makes my heart sing."

He wrote back:

"Two good people. Thanks for keeping me informed. I've come to count on hearing from you."

Home At Last

Reading the words, she felt her lips curve. She counted on his emails too.

The next afternoon, Lulu picked up her mother at the airport, dropped her off at the house, and headed to the Inn, hoping she wouldn't be late. Bethany and Jason were due to arrive any minute, and she wanted to capture their arrival.

She'd just grabbed her cameras and entered the reception area when two people walked into the lobby. She knew from Facebook photos they were Bethany Welles and Jason Sands. Lulu snapped a shot of them and then a couple more.

The bride was a tall, willowy, African-American woman. Her groom was a tall, broad-shouldered, robust white male sporting a buzz cut and a lot of muscle. She knew from their wedding information sheet that Jason was a former football player for the Seattle Seahawks. He was now acting as coach for a college program in Washington state.

When she'd taken enough shots, Lulu approached them. "Welcome to the Chandler Hill Inn," she said, and turned as Cami and Becca approached. Greetings and handshakes were exchanged, and then Laurel entered the room.

Cami introduced the bride and groom to Laurel.

"I'm overseeing your wedding here at the Chandler Hill Inn," Laurel said smoothly. "If you or any of your family members need anything done, please don't hesitate to call me. I'm here to serve you."

"Very nice," said Bethany. "My mother and stepfather will be arriving soon. My father and his wife will come tomorrow." Her smile was thin. "It's best to keep them apart as much as possible."

"My parents will arrive tomorrow too," said Jason. "My football buddy, Stan Young and his wife, Caren, are serving as best man and matron of honor. They'll arrive late tonight."

"Am I correct then, that the only other members of the wedding party who will be here in time for dinner are your mother and stepfather?" Laurel said to Bethany.

"Yes. We're going to keep it low-key by staying right here at the hotel for dinner, like we planned."

"Okay, we'll make sure you're seated at a private table in the dining room," said Laurel.

"And I'll make sure I'm there for photographs," Lulu added. "Do you want photos of either set of parents arriving at the hotel?"

"No, thanks," Bethany said with such firmness, Lulu couldn't help wondering about them. "I appreciate all you're doing for us. It's such a small wedding."

Jason clasped Bethany's hand. "But important to the two of us."

"Yes," she replied, beaming at him with such love that Lulu's breath caught. "It's been a struggle, but we finally convinced all the parents we truly love one another."

"And we didn't want a big wedding and were actually planning to elope. Being here with them is the compromise we made," said Jason.

"We're very pleased we can hold the wedding here," Bethany quickly added. "Justine told me all about her wedding, and though ours won't be anything like it, she assured me that everything would be perfect for what we want."

"It's a wonderful time of year for an outdoor wedding in the woods," said Laurel. "I know you'll be pleased."

After saying goodbye, Lulu went home to her mother. She wouldn't be needed until that evening.

As she approached her rental house, Lulu saw her mother holding Dolly while standing outside talking to Rafe. Such an interesting pair, she thought, feeling a rush of tenderness for these two adults. In the last year, her life had been turned upside down by her father's unsavory actions. But it had given her a chance to know her mother and meet the man who headed the Chandler Hill family. Both, priceless opportunities.

She pulled the car up to the house, got out, and went over to them.

"Hi, Mom! Hi, Rafe! How are you feeling today?"

He grimaced. "If one more person asks me that, I don't know what I'll do. But, thank you, I'm fine."

"We were just discussing the landscaping," said her mother. "I may take out some of the bushes that are becoming overgrown here in front and replace them with something different. What do you think?"

Lulu shrugged. "It's your house. I say do whatever you want."

"You aren't angry I bought the house, instead of you?" Her mother sent her a worried look.

"Not at all. When the time comes, I'll find a place of my own. But, don't worry, I'll be a very good renter until then."

Her mother's face brightened. "If Rafe hadn't encouraged me, I might never have bought here. I'm so glad I did. I feel much more at ease here than in California."

"Me, too," said Lulu. "See you later. I'm going to work on a couple of projects for the inn here in my office, have an early dinner, then go back to the inn to take some pictures for a new wedding in the house."

"She has such a talent," said Rafe to Rosalie.

"I know. I'd like to think Lulu gets her artistic side from me. I never had the chance to do anything with my painting, but I might try to dabble with some projects here."

"That would be wonderful," Lulu said, surprised as usual

by all she hadn't known about her mother.

Inside, sitting in front of her computer, Lulu worked on ideas for a Christmas catalog. In the catalog game, you had to be working at least six months in advance in order to promote it and have the merchandise on hand.

Her mother knocked on the door and entered. "Rafe's gone home to take a nap. I think I will too. I'm tired."

"Okay," Lulu said, wondering if her mother was headed for a low period.

She called to Dolly and went outside. Tossing a ball to the puppy, Lulu felt herself relax. She decided not to worry about her mother or other things that might never happen, and after playing with the puppy, sat in the sun reveling in its warmth.

When she went inside, her mother was up and wandering around the kitchen.

"Awake so early?" Lulu asked.

"Too excited to stay still. This place invigorates me."

Lulu let out a happy sigh, relieved to see her mother so happy.

As she walked into the inn's library, Lulu observed Bethany's stiff posture and the way Jason's feet were firmly planted on the ground, and had the impression a verbal battle was taking place between them and Bethany's parents.

Bethany's mother, Jarinda Baxter-Welles, was an attractive, heavy-set, African-American woman who enjoyed some notoriety in her home state of California by serving as a vocal mayor of a high-profile resort town in the mountains. She sought publicity whenever she could to get people to support her cause of paying all workers a living wage and giving them the same benefits higher-paid employees automatically received. A shiver traveled down Lulu's spine.

She'd met so many political people like her.

Lulu studied Bethany's stepfather. As tall as his wife, he seemed smaller as he stood by and quietly listened to Jarinda talk about her disappointment that this wedding wasn't the lavish event she'd envisioned. As she spoke, she directed her words to Bethany, ignoring Jason.

"Hello," Lulu said, noting Bethany's relief at her arrival. "I'll be taking some candid photographs throughout your stay."

Jarinda narrowed her eyes at Lulu. "Did anyone ever tell you that you look like Edward Kingsley's daughter?"

"I've heard that," Lulu said, trying to be as casual as possible, while her heart thumped with alarm. She did not want to tangle with Jarinda, who was a shrewd politician and had a way of cutting other people down when necessary. Her father had always respected Jarinda, thought she had an impressive political future, and admired her savvy.

Bethany came to her rescue. "Meet my mother Jarinda Baxter-Welles and my stepfather, William Howland." Bethany hesitated. "And this is ..."

"Just call me Weezie," Lulu interceded, hoping Bethany and Jason understood.

Bethany's stepfather held out his hand. "Hello, Weezie. We appreciate your help in making this a memorable occasion." His fingers wrapped around her hand in a reassuring way.

"Glad to meet you. I understand you're a doctor, a G.P."

His broad smile transformed his brown features from ordinary to something special. His eyes shone with intelligence and a kindness not often seen. It touched Lulu, and she knew how much his patients must love him.

"Go ahead and enjoy yourselves," said Lulu. "Drinks are on the house, and we have appetizers set out for our guests. Ignore me as I go about my business."

"Get a picture of Bethany, William, and me over by the fireplace," said Jarinda. "I want it for PR purposes."

Bethany held onto Jason's arm. "Include Jason too, Mama."

Jarinda's narrowed lips told a tale of their own.

"I'll do different groupings," said Lulu, hoping to diffuse the tense moment.

"Of course," said William pleasantly, cocking an eyebrow at Jarinda.

"Oh, yes," Jarinda said, giving her a sheepish look.

"It isn't that Jason is white," said Bethany angrily. "It's just that my mother thinks I should marry someone she picked out. The son of a political friend—someone I would never even choose to date."

"Well, well," said William. "Let's get the party started. Right, Jason?"

Jason gave him a grateful smile. "Sounds good to me."

The two men wandered off, leaving Lulu with Bethany and Jarinda. Lulu stepped away and held onto her camera waiting for the moment she could put a positive spin on the tenseness between them. She was ready when Jarinda's arms came around her daughter and they hugged.

The men joined them with drinks, and as the four of them lifted their glasses, Lulu took several photos.

Having lived with a strong-willed politician herself, Lulu understood what Bethany must have been going through and was relieved to see that things between the four of them seemed better.

When they went into dinner, Lulu snapped a couple of discreet shots of them and quietly left.

She went into the kitchen to see what was going on and then, because it was a busy night in the kitchen with no opportunity to grab something for herself, she left to go home.

CHAPTER TWENTY-FOUR

The next morning the sun shone brightly as Lulu lay in bed mentally reviewing her plans for the day. One of the benefits of being involved with the inn was meeting a whole variety of people. Her father had given her a love of doing that. She couldn't wait to meet Bethany's father and his wife, and better yet, Stan and Caren Young, the couple who were to be best man and matron of honor—the two official witnesses to the wedding.

Another weekend wedding at the inn was taking a lot of Laurel's attention. Lulu was happy to fill in by helping to make certain everyone in Bethany and Jason's small wedding group was happy.

She got up and took Dolly outside. While her mother was staying in the house, Lulu didn't have to worry about feeding the dog or leaving her behind when she went to work. Later, Cami would drop Sophie off so the two dachshunds could play together.

Lulu hurried into the shower, then dressed for the day in a black skirt and white blouse in an attempt to be as unobtrusive as possible as she went about her work.

First on the schedule, some photos of Bethany and Jason with their friends having breakfast. Bethany had requested a small meal served poolside for the four of them.

When Lulu arrived at the inn, it was quiet. One of the perks of coming to the Chandler Hill Inn was fabulous room service and good sleeping weather. It made for some late mornings.

She went into the kitchen to check with Liz who usually

handled the early shift.

"How are you, Lulu? And how's that precious fur baby of yours? I swear Dolly is as cute as my little guy, Oscar."

Lulu laughed. After Cami received Sophie as a gift from Rafe, everyone at the inn had fallen in love with dachshunds. Now there were three in the "inn family".

"Are we all set for the Welles-Sands breakfast?" Lulu asked.

"Yes. Just waiting for them to arrive. Go check the table. I think it looks adorable. Very fitting for the couple."

Lulu grabbed a cup of coffee and wandered out to the pool. At the outer edges of the pool deck, a few tables had been set up for guests. In the far corner, away from the others, a table had been dressed. In the middle of the table covered with a pink-linen cloth, a single pink rose sat in a crystal vase. At each of the four place settings, a pink rose tied with a pink ribbon lay atop the white serving plate. Beside the plate, a white napkin had been folded into the shape of a flower. Simple but elegant, thought Lulu.

She'd just set aside her coffee cup when Bethany and Jason appeared with another couple. Interested as always in others, Lulu studied them. Stan Young was as tall and broad as Jason. Blue eyes sparkled in a face already reddened by being outdoors. Beside him, his wife, Caren, seemed petite. The round curve of her pregnant belly made her body appear thinner than it was. Her blond hair was pulled away from a face accented by an upturned nose and freckles.

Lulu thought the four of them together were adorable as they laughed and teased one another taking their seats. She took shots of them and then went over to introduce herself to the new couple.

"Hi, I'm ... Weezie, here to take photos for Bethany and Jason throughout your visit. Just ignore me. I'll try to stay out of your way."

Bethany said, "Thank you, Weezie. This is Caren Young, my best friend, and her husband, Stan."

"My best friend," said Jason. "They've agreed to be our only wedding attendants."

"We wouldn't miss it for the world." Caren smiled sweetly. "I'm just happy they didn't wait any longer. Our baby is due in another six weeks."

"I've already promised to babysit," said Bethany. "We can't wait for this little girl to arrive."

"You already know what sex it is?" Lulu said.

"Oh, yes," Caren admitted. "I'm a planner and wanted to have everything ready for the baby when she arrives."

"You wouldn't believe all the stuff that now fills our apartment," Stan added proudly.

Lulu forced a smile, but inside, pangs of disappointment pierced her, sharp reminders of what her existence might have been like for her. Earlier in her life she'd never given much thought to having a family of her own, but having come so close to it, she couldn't let the idea go.

"Well, I'll let you enjoy your breakfast for now," said Lulu. "When would you like me to return?"

"The wedding is at four, so I'd say come to my room sometime after three so you can take pictures of me getting ready," said Bethany. "As small as the wedding is, I want to have a few moments captured." She gave Jason as broad smile. "I don't intend to go through another wedding."

Jason's eyes lit with pleasure as he gazed at Bethany. "Me either."

Lulu gave them a little wave, and left.

The Barn was just opening when Lulu walked inside. She said hello to Gwen and went over to the book section and picked up a sweet storybook about a little bear being loved.

"Please put this on my account," Lulu told the clerk. "I'll pay extra to have it wrapped."

"Sure. Why don't you look around while I take care of it," the older woman said. "I'll make it very nice. Blue, pink, or green bow?"

"Pink, thank you. Perhaps you can arrange to have it delivered to Room 204. I'll write a note and give it to you."

In Gwen's office, Lulu wrote a short note on one of the special Chandler Hill Inn cards printed for such occasions, handed it to the clerk, and left, ready to face the day.

When she went back to the inn, a couple was just checking in. Realizing it must be Bethany's father and his wife, Lulu went over to them.

"You must be Mr. and Mrs. Welles. Welcome to the Chandler Hill Inn. I'm Weezie and will be taking candid shots of the wedding party throughout the day."

"Nice. I'm Chester Welles, and this is my wife, JoAnn."

They shook hands all around. As Chester registered at the desk, Lulu stood beside JoAnn, still stunned by his handsome looks. She turned to JoAnn, who was attractive in her own way, but no beauty.

"So how did the two of you meet?" Lulu asked, genuinely curious.

"We both work in the same law firm," JoAnn said. She gave Chester a proud smile. "He's brilliant at corporate law."

"Is that what you do?"

JoAnn shook her head. "I'm in family law. We happened to work on the same case. A very long, complicated one."

Chester returned to them and put a hand on JoAnn's shoulder. "She's my better half."

The look of adoration on JoAnn's face matched his own.

"Enjoy your time here. It's a beautiful day."

"Oh, yes. We will," said JoAnn with enough determination that Lulu got the impression that even though JoAnn looked a lot like Jarinda, she wouldn't let Jarinda walk all over her.

An interesting day ahead, thought Lulu.

With the morning free, Lulu headed back to The Barn. She wanted to check to see if some of the Christmas catalog gifts had arrived. They needed to be entered into the inventory and then shelved in a way that made it easy for the shipping staff to find. With online sales becoming the norm, their catalog business had grown. Lulu could foresee a time when they'd need to add to their shipping area, perhaps erect a separate building.

Gwen greeted her with a smile. "Wedding break?"

"Yes. Bethany is very particular about what photos she wants taken. I just met her father and stepmother, another interesting pair. Jason's parents will arrive a little later this morning. Even though I'm not required to take photos of them, I thought I'd go over to the inn at the arrival time."

"In the meantime, we're glad to have you here. I need you to look at something I want to show Cami. Come with me."

Gwen put an arm around Lulu's shoulder and led her over to a table on which a number of interesting items sat. She lifted up a small, white metal basket. "I thought we could use these to put in the rooms of wedding parties, filled with a few treats and information about bridal gifts here at The Barn. What do you think?"

Lulu smiled at her. "I think she'll like them. How much do they cost?"

"That's it. Unless you buy a thousand of them, they're on the expensive side."

"A thousand? That's putting trust in the future, but I don't see it as a problem. If you like, I can take one over and show it to Cami now."

"Would you? I can't leave here, but if she likes them, I need to put in an order right away."

Eager to help, Lulu picked up the basket and walked over to the inn. Instead of going through the front entrance, Lulu slipped through the garden entrance and knocked on Cami's office door.

"Come in!" Cami called.

"Good morning. I'm here to see you at Gwen's request," Lulu said brightly, and stopped at the sight of Cami's worried look. "What's wrong?"

"Jarinda Baxter-Welles knows who you are and wants me to set up a meeting with you."

Lulu felt as if her stomach had dropped to her shoes. "Why? I don't want anything to do with politics or publicity. That's why I'm here."

"I'm not sure what she wants, but if you're uncomfortable about being with her, I suggest you bow out of taking photographs of the group. I don't want you to get hurt."

Lulu plopped down in one of the two chairs facing Cami's desk. "You know, as much as I dislike being associated with my father, I am who I am, Cami. I can't change that. I know you've given me my nickname Weezie, and I love you for it."

"Then, let me go with you," Cami said.

Lulu shook her head. "No, I'll go alone."

"All right. I know how stubborn you can be," sighed Cami.

Instead of being offended, Lulu was delighted that they'd become true sisters and could speak frankly.

Lulu showed Cami the basket and got the approval for Gwen. Then, she called Jarinda's room. She picked up right away.

"Hello?"

"Ms. Baxter-Welles, this is Louise Kingsley. My sister told me you wanted to see me. May I ask what this is about?"

"I think it's best if we talk face-to-face. I have an idea that might help us both."

"All right, if you insist. Why don't we meet in the lobby? I'm free at the moment." Surely, Jarinda wouldn't make a scene in public.

"That will be fine," Jarinda said with a note of satisfaction. "Meet you there in a few minutes."

Lulu walked to the front windows of the lobby area and gazed out at the rolling hills she'd come to love so much. She was lost in thought when she heard someone call her name. She turned to face Jarinda, a strong woman with an imposing presence. Lulu suddenly felt uncertain.

They shook hands.

"I guess you're calling yourself Weezie now," said Jarinda, not unkindly.

Embarrassed, Lulu nodded. "Sometimes."

"Did you know I knew your father quite well?"

"He met you only a couple of times, but I knew he thought you were a shrewd politician."

"He was a forward thinker. He was interested in a program I encouraged for migrant workers. I plan to run for the California State Legislature and would like to have you on board to help promote that program and, of course, me. We're from different political parties and having you behind me would be a huge bonus—cooperation and all that, reaching across party lines."

Lulu stifled a sigh. "Thank you for thinking of me, but I have no interest in politics anymore. My heart isn't in it."

Jarinda studied her. "That bad, huh?"

Lulu looked down at the floor and then lifted her face. "Yes. No matter what you say, it's over for me."

"I'm disappointed." Jarinda rocked back on her heels. "Your father wasn't all bad, you know. But like some men, men in power especially, he made some bad choices."

Just then Chester Welles walked into the room.

"Don't we all?" muttered Jarinda and rose. "Hello, Chester. You made it for the wedding."

"Of course. She's my only daughter. JoAnn and I wouldn't miss it for the world. You and the Doc got here last night all right?"

"Yes, William and I had a lovely dinner with Bethany and Jason." The frost in her voice was noticeable.

"Is there anything you need from the staff?" Lulu said, eager to escape.

Jarinda and Chester shook their heads and went their separate ways.

Lulu let out a sigh of relief. *Poor Bethany,* she thought. *No wonder she wanted a small wedding.*

CHAPTER TWENTY-FIVE

As Lulu was preparing to leave, a couple arrived, looking bedraggled. She hurried over to them. "Welcome to the Chandler Hill Inn. May I help you?"

"Yes, please," answered the woman, wearing baggy jeans and a weary expression. Her gray hair was tied in a pony tail behind a face with no makeup. "I never thought we'd arrive. We're here for Jason Sands' wedding."

"Are you his parents?" Lulu asked, thinking the man with her looked a lot like Jason.

"Wilbur and Loretta Sands," he answered. A bear of a man, his deep voice rattled in his chest. Observing the size and strength of him, Lulu guessed he must have been a college football player like his son. Bald and overweight now, he looked haggard.

"Did you catch a flight from Montana?" Lulu asked.

"No, Wilbur insisted on driving. Said we'd save money that way," complained Loretta. "I tried to tell him it would be easier to fly, but you know how men are."

"We'll get you checked in and then hopefully you can have a restful afternoon." Lulu said with sympathy. She turned as Cami and Becca hurried toward them. "Here comes help now. I'll see you later."

As Cami approached, Lulu raised her eyebrows to warn her about the unhappy guests and after introducing Cami and Becca to the Sands, she quickly left.

Headed back to The Barn, Lulu made a quick stop at Chandler Hall to see how preparation for the other wedding was going. The wedding party of seventy-five had already gathered in the garden. A wedding brunch was to follow.

Walking into the building, Lulu caught her breath. Following the color scheme of rose and pink, glittering crystal goblets and vases of fresh rose lilies and pink hydrangeas enhanced the round tables of six covered in pink linen.

Laurel bustled by. "Don't miss the wedding. It's about to take place."

Lulu followed her out to the garden and stood off to one side. Cami had spent a lot of money on the landscaping, especially the garden, and it was lovely. The extended lawn area was discreetly divided into sections by lush plantings of shrubbery, low planting beds, and floral focus points, so weddings of various sizes had their own nooks. This wedding would be among the larger ones held at the inn and was taking place in the main garden.

White chair covers concealed the individual seats lined up in perfect rows on the grass. An aisle divided the seats into two sections and led to a simple altar of sorts—a plain, white wood table on which a brass cross now sat, flanked by two large, white candles in lovely, large, brass candle holders.

Lulu left before any of the wedding guests noticed her. She was in no mood to watch another couple who were madly in love make vows for their future together. Not when she didn't see that happening for her.

Back at The Barn, she worked on catalog material and waited for her afternoon photo shoot with Bethany and Caren.

Later, as she snapped photos of the two women giddy with joy over the upcoming wedding, her feelings changed. Bethany was a beautiful bride who'd chosen a simple, white, sleeveless dress that fell in soft folds to her ankles, suitable for a social affair and perfect for this small, woodsy wedding. Caren's peach-colored flowing dress couldn't hide the baby bump that protruded.

"God! I look like an over-ripe peach," she grumbled good-naturedly.

"No, you look adorable," protested Bethany. "I can't wait until Jason and I can start a family."

"Your mother thinks women should be more interested in doing things for other women to gain ground in business, doing whatever they want to do, not raising families."

"Don't remind me! I used to hear my parents fighting about it. My father wanted more children. He told her he'd worked his ass off to get through law school and provide for her. But she wouldn't listen. Now he has children with JoAnn and is very happy with her and my two half-brothers."

"Bet that pisses your mother off," said Caren.

Bethany grimaced. "If she didn't have William, I don't know what any of us would do. He's steady as a rock and sweet as can be. We all love him."

Listening to the women talk, Lulu snapped one photo after another and wondered how so many marriages could go wrong. Rafe and Lettie had never married, but their love was unending. That's what she wanted.

"How do I look?" Bethany said, turning to Lulu with a smile.

"Wow! I'm telling you the truth when I say you're gorgeous. You have such beautiful skin, and right now, your cheeks are glowing with happiness."

"Thanks," said Bethany. "I admit I'm a little nervous. Jason's mother doesn't like me all that much."

"They were a bit harried when they arrived," admitted Lulu.

"The good thing is it's a short ceremony with only one evening for all of us to celebrate, then everyone can go back to their own separate lives," said Bethany.

"Okay. Let's get this show on the road," said Caren.

Lulu raced ahead to take photographs of Bethany descending the stairs. Her father was waiting for her at the bottom of the stairway gazing up at her with such pride, Lulu stopped and lifted her camera.

"Are the others in the woods already?" Lulu asked him.

He nodded. "All set."

Lulu headed out the door and hurried to the edge of the landscaped area and into a wooded area that had been groomed and planted with flowers for such occasions as this.

When she stepped among the trees, Lulu felt as if she were entering a fairyland. Twinkling lights wound around the trunks of the smaller trees, and ferns and shade-loving flowers were carefully planted forming a colorful floral ring around a small, circular group of flagstones that created a stable place for people to stand.

Waiting for his bride, Jason was standing next to Stan beside a tall wooden table. The members of the wedding group formed a semi-circle along the edge of the flagstone.

Soft harp music played from speakers camouflaged among the foliage, filling the space with an ethereal sound. After taking a few photos of the setting, Lulu turned to take pictures of Caren, Bethany, and her father as they approached.

When she'd taken all the photos she wanted, Lulu stepped into the shadows and stood beside Laurel. Jason and Bethany had opted to have a simple ceremony with just the exchange of their vows—something else none of the parents liked.

Tears filled Lulu's eyes as she listened to their vows of love for one another. Spoken from the heart, their words were inspiring. She noticed Jarinda's eyes filling and observed Jason's mother dabbing at her eyes with a tissue. For the moment, Bethany and Jason's love had brought their families together.

After fulfilling her task of taking photos following the ceremony and throughout the special wedding dinner, Lulu left the inn and sat in her car, unwilling to go home.

She drove without purpose and then headed for Taunton Estates. The day's activities had sent her emotions in a spinning circle. Being in the space she thought of as the "moon room" in the house where she and Miguel had made love might, she hoped, settle her thoughts.

As she'd hoped, the driveway was empty of cars when she drove up to the house. The porch light was on, a round globe of light mimicking the moon above. In the main room downstairs, soft lighting shone a lemony yellow of welcome.

Lulu went to the front door and searched for the key she knew was hidden so workmen could come and go. She found it under the flowerpot she'd noticed earlier that week, picked it up, and unlocked the door.

Inside the entrance, she studied the furniture stacked in the living room. That area hadn't needed much work, but all around it, new construction had expanded and opened the space.

Awash in memory, she climbed the stairs to the second story. It was time to put things in perspective. She'd had one night of lovemaking, letting herself go in a way she'd never done before. And where had that gotten her? In trouble with a capital T.

She owed Miguel a face-to-face apology for judging him, and then, she told herself, she had to let the memories of them together go. They'd become and would remain friends. That's all. Because no matter how much she wished otherwise, he was the kind of man she didn't know if she could trust. Not when he was such a magnet for others.

Lulu entered the master suite and walked through it to get to the addition. The open space was just as she and Miguel had imagined. Easing herself down onto the floor, Lulu sat and gazed up at the moon above her, coating the earth below it with a silvery, shimmering glow.

As she often did, she wondered about the expanse of the universe. Studying the moon and the sparkling stars scattered around it, she felt small, insignificant, alone.

The sound of a car driving up to the house brought her to her feet. She ran to one of the front windows and looked out. The sight of Cami's car slowed her heartbeat. It would be good to talk to her, get her perspective on things.

She returned to the "moon room" and sat down. Cami would find her there.

At the sound of footsteps on the stairs, she called out, "Up here!"

A figure approached in the dark. A figure that was definitely not Cami.

Lulu scrambled to her feet. "Miguel? Oh, my God! What are you doing here?" Her voice was giddy with happiness.

Miguel stood in the doorway smiling at her.

"I could ask you the same." Miguel studied her, his dark eyes searching hers for what she didn't know.

"You're supposed to still be in Chile," she said nervously, suddenly fighting a new urge to run away. They'd talked about everything but what was still standing between them. Seeing him in person was a far cry from sending a safe email to him.

"Yes, but with all that's gone on with Rafe, I decided to surprise you both and shortened my visit." His gaze rested on her. "What are you doing here, Lulu?"

"I ... I came here to think about things." She couldn't take her eyes off him.

"Well, maybe this is a good time for us to talk," said Miguel. "We still have a lot to settle between us." He walked past her to stare out at the night.

Lulu fought for strength. "I'm sorry I judged you so harshly. I didn't mean to hurt you. I didn't think ..."

He turned to her and gave her a questioning look. "I think about you all the time. Why else would I be here?"

Tears stung her eyes. She wanted to say so much more, but she was afraid of revealing how much she liked him, how she'd come to treasure each message from him, how worried she was about something permanent happening between them.

He studied her carefully. "Are you trying to tell me something? Maybe that the night together was something you'll never forget? How much you really wanted our baby? That you can't wait to have others? Is that it?"

Lulu's knees grew weak. It was as if he'd read her mind.

His voice was soft, but his gaze was piercing, penetrating all her vulnerability, the fear that clutched the breath from her body. She was such a novice at loving relationships.

He continued to challenge her with a look that demanded an answer.

Feeling sick at the thought of making the same mistake as her mother had so many years ago, she blurted, "I ... I have to get out of here." If she stayed another minute, she'd break down completely from the uncertainty of his reaction.

As she hurried down the steps and out the front door, he called from behind her. "I know you have trouble trusting others, Lulu, but maybe it's time to trust yourself."

Her pulse pumping so hard she couldn't catch her breath, she ran to her car, got inside, started the engine, and tore out of the driveway.

In the rearview mirror, she could see Miguel standing in the driveway.

When she got home, her mother was watching television. She looked up. "How was your ..." her mother started to say and stopped. "Oh, dear! What's the matter?"

"Miguel's back," Lulu managed. She struggled to catch her breath and stop her tears.

She raced upstairs to her bedroom and slammed the door.

A short while later, Lulu heard the sound of a car and peered out the window. Miguel's truck was pulling to a stop in the driveway.

Shaking, she plunked down at the top of the stairs and waited.

The doorbell rang.

Dolly barked and raced to the door. Her mother followed.

"Hello, Miguel. What do you want?" Her mother's voice was cool.

"I need to talk to Lulu," came his reply.

"I'm sorry, I'm not sure what's going on, but I don't think she wants to speak with you. Haven't you hurt her enough?" Lulu was surprised by the anger in her mother's voice.

"Hurt her? No, I don't want to do that. Listen, it's important that we talk."

"Lulu came home upset because of you," her mother said sternly. "I think you should leave."

"Leave? Wait! You don't get it! We need to talk because I ... oh, hell! I *love* her!"

Her mother's gasp broke through the silence. "Oh, my! Yes, indeed, you do need to talk. Come inside. I'll take the dog for a walk and leave you two alone."

"Lulu?" her mother called to her. "Miguel's here. You'd better come on down."

CHAPTER TWENTY-SIX

Lulu heard the sound of the front door click shut after her mother left with Dolly. Gripping the handrail for support, she walked slowly down the stairs, one scary step after the other. Miguel was right. It was time to trust him, trust herself. Miguel was not her father or Will or the other people who'd hurt her. It would be, she realized, the biggest decision of her life.

Miguel stared up at her, shifting his feet back and forth, looking as nervous as she felt.

Her gaze never left him as she approached him. The wistfulness she saw in his expression touched her.

She stood in front of him, saying what she knew she must. "All those things you said to me back there? They're true. Every one of them."

"Oh, Lulu." He reached for her and drew her up against him. "I had to be sure."

In his arms, wrapped against his chest, a peace washed over her. She let her tears flow.

Rocking her gently, he whispered, "They were true for me too. I tried to tell myself we were just friends, but I couldn't forget that night with you." His voice caught. "Or the baby we made together."

"I wanted that baby so much," Lulu said, her words soft and true.

He lifted her chin and stared into her eyes with such love, her breath caught. She emitted a long, trembling sigh.

His lips came down on hers, searching for and finding what

she hadn't yet put into words.

When they broke apart, he cupped her face in his hands. "It's true, Lulu. I love you. I think I have from the moment Cami called you 'Weezie Lopez.' Other women might be interested, but you're the only woman I want in my life. It seems so right. You and me."

Lulu filled with joy. "Yes. Oh, yes."

His lips met hers, and she responded with her whole heart.

Their kiss told a story of its own, exposing their true feelings for each other, promising a happy future together. After they finally broke apart, Lulu gazed at Miguel in a daze, still lost in the sensual feelings he aroused within her. Her eyes filled. In so many ways, he was everything she'd ever wanted.

Giving her a steady look, he sighed. "I love you so much."

She smiled at the tenderness in his expression. Living with him might be full of challenges, but it would all be worth it, because in his arms, she felt at home at last.

FIVE YEARS LATER

Lulu sat on the stone bench next to Cami in the special grove of trees reserved for family. She studied the freshly turned earth where Rafe's ashes had been placed next to Lettie's. "He was a dear, dear man," she said, her heart aching with sadness. "I loved him so much."

"Me too," said Cami, dabbing at her eyes with a tissue. "He was a special person, loved and respected by all he knew. And he and Nonnee gave me a wonderful life." Her voice caught. "I'll always miss them."

Lulu wrapped her arm around Cami's shoulder. "You were so lucky to have such amazing people raise you."

"I hope my son will be as good a man as Rafe," Cami's voice hitched with pain.

"He's so adorable," said Lulu. At three and with his shiny black hair and dark eyes, little Rafe was the spitting image of his great-grandfather. "My two girls love that little boy."

"Chandler's very good with him," Cami said. The corners of her lips turned up. "She's very determined he listen to her."

A bubble of laughter rose from Lulu's throat. "Such a bossy four-year-old, she is."

Tears moistened Cami's eyes. "Whenever I was worried about being able to accomplish something, Nonnee would remind me that as a Chandler and a Lopez I could do anything I put my mind to."

"And you have so far," Lulu said. "Look at all you've done. The Chandler Hill Inn continues to win awards, as do the wines."

Cami arched her brows. "As long as my wines keep up with Taunton Estates wines and those of Lone Creek, I'm happy."

Lulu laughed. Competition among the three wineries was fierce, producing the best pinot noirs in the valley.

"Do you think Rafe is with Nonnee now?" Cami asked her softly.

Lulu nodded. "I'd like to think so."

Cami let out a sigh. "Me too. They shared such an incredible love."

Lulu patted her stomach, feeling life. "Chandler announced that she and Autumn want a baby sister. I haven't told Miguel yet, but I'm pretty sure this new baby is another girl." Still amazed at how her life had turned out, Lulu clucked her tongue. "After losing our first baby, we seem to be making up for lost time. Two babies, and now a third."

Cami's smile was warm. "If it's a girl, Miguel will love it. Little girls adore him."

Lulu laughed. She had no worries about other women grown or small in his life. Since they'd surprised everyone with their elopement, beating both Becca and Cami to the altar, Miguel proved to her everyday how much he loved her.

Lulu lifted her face to the gray sky. Contentment washed over her. Life was good. Her mother continued to do well, keeping busy with her activities in the valley and contributing to the care of the grandchildren who meant so much to her. Though Lulu knew she'd miss Rafe, she understood he wasn't unhappy at the end, that he'd waited long enough to be with his beloved Lettie, and she had to let him go to her.

Gazing at Cami, Lulu's heart welled with love. Life, like some thought, had turned out to be a bunch of circles. In this case, it had given her a new family, new friends, a new life.

A hawk circled above her, its wings spread wide, golden feathers against the gray. Watching it glide effortlessly above her, Lulu thought of the continuity of life and sent up a silent thank you for having known a man like Rafe. He'd given her a new faith in people and an abiding love for the family around her.

"I'm so glad you're here with me," said Cami. "Together, we'll make all we've been given even better, in memory of Nonnee and Rafe." Her smile was sweet. "After all, I consider you not only a Lopez but an honorary Chandler too."

So very grateful she'd found the sister she'd always wanted, Lulu hugged Cami. "Together we can do anything," Lulu said, believing it with her whole heart.

Thank you for reading *Home At Last*. If you enjoyed this book, please help other readers discover it by leaving a review on Amazon, Goodreads, or your favorite site. It's such a nice thing to do.

Enjoy an excerpt from my book *A Summer of Surprises*, a Seashell Cottage Book.

CHAPTER ONE

Jillian Conroy listened to her sister, Cristal's, voice on her cellphone and drew a deep breath. A call from her sister was always a surprise.

"So, start all over again, Cristal, and tell me exactly what it is you want me to do."

"It's easy, Jill. My friend, Hope Thomason, recently inherited the Seashell Cottage on the Gulf Coast of Florida, and she just needs someone to live at the cottage for the summer while we do our European tour, the one we've been talking about for years."

"That's it?" It didn't sound like something difficult. In fact, it sounded like a great way to escape the memories of the past. School would be out in another week, and she didn't have any exciting plans for her summer break from teaching. Maybe some extended time on the Gulf Coast would do her good. But every time she tried to do something for her sister, it cost her emotionally and often financially. A requested lunch date would end up with Jill paying for it. What was supposed to be a fun event of shopping turned into a nightmare when Cristal pouted that the dress Jill bought was the one Cristal wanted. Their relationship had always bordered on the toxic.

"There's one more thing. A friend of Hope's family, Greg

Campbell, is an older man who's agreed to do some work on the cottage. He's staying in one of the guest rooms for a few weeks until the work is done."

"An older man, you say?"

"Yes. He and Hope's father are friends. They're the same age."

Jill let out a sigh of relief. Too many friends had been pushing her to start dating again. She had no interest in doing so. Not after Jay's death two years ago.

"Think about it. I'll call you tonight for your answer." Cristal hung up before Jill could ask any more questions.

Clicking off the call, Jill sat in a chair and stared out the window of the kitchen inside the small bungalow she called home in Ellenton, a small town in upstate New York. She should've sold it months ago. The memories she held of her life in the house weren't pleasant. She'd thought by clearing Jay's things out of the house following his automobile accident, she'd be able to chase away the unhappiness she'd known with him. But now the space just seemed empty. And lonely.

Her thoughts settled on her sister. Three years older than she, Cristal was the beauty of the family. Their mother had declared to anyone who would listen that Cristal got her beautiful features, naturally blond hair, and bright blue eyes from a relative of hers, while Jillian looked like the Davis side of the family. The comparison was painful. Without the highlights she had to add every few months, Jillian's hair was a dishwater tan. Her hazel eyes held no trace of blue. Worst of all, Cristal's tall, willowy figure seemed to taunt Jill's shorter, curvy shape. It was a bad match-up all around. If it weren't so much like a well-known storybook scenario, it would be almost comical.

Restless, Jill got up and paced the kitchen. It wasn't their different looks that had made her relationship with Cristal so difficult. It was Cristal's tendency to manipulate others in order to get her own way. Jill knew how foolish it was to keep old hurts stored inside, but every once in a while, a hurt poked through the shell she kept around herself. How could she forget that Cristal stole her date in college, the one guy she'd dreamed would be hers forever? It was just one of the ways Cristal had hurt her through the years. A snort of disgust left Jill's mouth. She might not have even paid attention to Jay except Cristal thought he was a hottie. How was that for stupid rivalry?

Before she could go any deeper with that thought, the phone rang. Jill knew who it was before she even checked Caller ID. Her mother, Valerie Davis, had a nose for trouble. No doubt Cristal had phoned her for support.

"Hello, Mom," Jill said without enthusiasm.

"Hi, honey. Cristal called to tell me that she's arranged for you to have a very nice summer break. She's so thoughtful that way."

"She asked me to do her a favor so she and her friend can travel to Europe," Jill said calmly, still uncertain as to whether she should go ahead with the idea or even what it entailed.

"Well, if you don't do it, I'm sure they can find someone else to stay at the cottage. It sounds lovely. You should be grateful to Cristal for thinking of you," chided her mother. "A whole summer to relax."

It would be useless to argue. "Maybe you're right," said Jill. "I could use the break to get away." The idea suddenly appealed to her. This change in her normal routine might give her the opportunity to think things through, make some major decisions about her life, give her a fresh start. God knew she'd been in an emotional rut even before Jay had been killed.

"Splendid," her mother said with satisfaction. "I'm glad

you'll help your sister out. It would mean so much to her. She and Hope have been planning this summer tour for a long time, and poor Cristal has been working very hard."

"You mean as a hostess at the club in Miami?"

"Now, Jillian, she does the best she can, and with her looks, she doesn't need to spend her time teaching school."

"Oh? Because I teach school ..." Jill stopped herself. She didn't like the person she became when dealing with her family. Only her father had accepted her for who she was, and he'd died several years ago.

"I didn't mean that the way it sounded, Jillian," her mother said with a note of apology.

"Look, I have to go," Jill said. "I'll let you know what I decide."

"Please do. I care about both of you and hope that someday you girls will get along."

Jill sighed. "Goodbye, Mom." Though the day was ruined by the familiar routine with her mother, the idea of escaping to a place far away became tantalizing.

Later, while looking up information online about the Seashell Cottage, Jill filled with excitement. The pictures of it were lovely. It was not simply a cottage; it was a beautiful, three-bedroom, three-bath house that sat overlooking a wide, sandy beach. The house even had a screened-in pool.

Before she could change her mind or overwork the thought that something must be wrong if her sister was involved, Jill punched in Cristal's cell number and, when prompted, left a message.

"Hi, Cristal. Jill here. I've decided to stay at Seashell Cottage for the summer so you and Hope can travel. At the end of next week, when school is out, I'll drive down to Florida. I should be there by June 8th and can stay until late August. Let me know if those dates work with you and Hope."

Hating confrontation, she paused and took a deep breath. "And, Cristal, thanks for thinking of me."

That evening Cristal called. The noise of music and partying in the background made it difficult to hear, but the message did get through that Cristal was thrilled Jill would stay at the cottage. "You'll see. This summer is going to be good for you, Jilly. For both of us, really."

"I hope so," said Jill honestly. She was more than ready for a change.

Ten days later, Jill pulled up to the Seashell Cottage and felt tears of gratitude sting her eyes. It was beautiful. When she stepped out of her car, the salty air filled her nostrils. Without waiting to explore the house, Jill ran onto the beach holding her arms in the air as if to embrace this new existence. The sand, warm from the sun, caressed her skin through her open-toe sandals. She removed her shoes and tossed them into the air. It was going to be a carefree, barefoot summer.

Walking up to the water's edge, Jill stuck her foot into the lacy froth and sighed. The water was delightful. The cries of seagulls above her drew her gaze to the sky, and then she watched as a trio of pelicans flying in formation skimmed the surface of the water looking for food.

Jill clasped her hands together and let out a satisfied sigh. She'd been so right to come here. Already, she felt as if some of her old, silent secrets were itching to break free. This summer, she wasn't going to be Jay's widow, Cristal's younger sister, a kindergarten teacher, or a reliable volunteer at the library. She was going to find the person who hid inside her—the one that had been broken.

"Hello. You must be Jillian Conroy," said a deep voice behind her.

Jill whipped around to face a pleasant, red-cheeked, older man, wearing jeans and a gray T-shirt with "Smith's Hardware Store" printed across the chest. She smiled at him. "And you must be Greg Campbell, the handyman Hope hired for the summer."

"That I am," he said, returning her smile. "You're just in time. I've been here for a week and have left some things for you to do."

"Oh?" Jill managed to say while hiding her surprise. Cristal hadn't mentioned any tasks.

"Yep, the laundry is piled up, and I'm tired of fixing the same old meal night after night. I heard you were a great cook."

Jill gripped her fingers together and mentally watched her plans shatter and fall to the ground like pieces of broken shells. "And what else have you been told about me?"

"That you were excellent at taking care of people, that in exchange for being here, you're going to cook and clean for me and my nephew, Brody."

"Your nephew?"

"Yep. He's arriving tomorrow." He bobbed his head. "I'm happy to help you with your luggage."

"Thank you, that would be nice." Jill used years of training to maintain her composure when what she wanted to do was reach across space and shake Cristal silly. This set-up was so typical of her sister. The offer of a Florida vacation was a ruse. Apparently, she was to cook and clean for the work crew. She should've known better.

Once they got her bags settled in one of the bedrooms, Jill had a chance to look around. She realized though everything was attractive, the pictures shown online were outdated. The walls and wooden trim needed a fresh coat of paint, along with other refinishing touches throughout the interior. That was the reason, no doubt, Hope had hired Greg and his nephew for the summer. It was a wise time to do it. Jill guessed the cottage was booked for most of the rest of the year.

In the laundry room, a pile of dirty clothes sat on the floor near a front-load washing machine. Hiding her displeasure, Jill sorted through them and put a load of dark things into the machine, using the last of an almost-empty bottle of detergent. She drew a deep breath. A trip to the grocery store was in order. She wondered what other discoveries awaited her.

Sure enough, when she checked the refrigerator, she found a half-empty six-pack of coke, a hunk of cheese, and not much else. Her stomach rumbled. Even though she was tired from the drive, she gamely set about listing groceries she'd need to purchase. She'd passed a Publix supermarket not far from the cottage.

Greg had retreated to one of the bathrooms and was working on new grouting when Jill approached him.

"I'm going to the supermarket. Anything you need? Anything you're allergic to?"

Greg got to his feet and faced her. "No need for anything special for me, thanks. As I said, I'm glad you decided to take this job."

At his warm smile, Jill's irritation fled. Though Cristal had made it sound like a vacation, not a job, she wasn't about to blame him. He seemed like a nice man. "I'll do my best. I'm used to cooking for only myself."

"Not married?" Below a thatch of gray hair, Greg's blue-eyed gaze settled on her.

"Widowed. For two years."

"I'm sorry. Such a shame. My Annie's been gone for five years now. Life isn't the same without her. Brody, my nephew, is alone too. Divorced."

Jill simply nodded. If Jay were still alive, maybe she would've gathered her courage and she'd be divorced too.

On her way to the store, Jill called her sister.

Cristal answered with a cheery, "Hi, there! You in Florida?"

"Yes," Jill said carefully. "I had no idea I was hired to cook and clean for Greg Campbell. His nephew is going to be staying at the cottage too. Did you know that?"

"I did hear something about him coming, but I figured it was no big deal for you to take care of them. After all, you have to buy food and cook for yourself. How's the cottage? As pretty as the pictures?"

"Seashell Cottage is lovely. Right now, Greg is working on refreshing the interior and will be busy this summer doing other things. Still, it's a wonderful property, and the location is superb."

"That's all that matters. Enjoy. Hope and I are at the airport, ready to fly out. Can't wait!"

Hearing the click of the phone in her ear, Jill drew a deep, steadying breath. It wasn't worth being irritated. What was done, was done. She'd move forward and have the best summer ever. She'd loaded her iPad with lots of books and would enjoy a few weeks away from kids. She loved her young pupils, but a break from them sounded fabulous.

Back at the cottage, Greg eagerly helped her unload the groceries. "Looks like we're going to have some tasty meals," he said happily. "That's good because Brody just phoned. He and Kacy are coming in tonight instead of tomorrow. They should be here within a half hour."

Without crushing its contents in her hands, Jill carefully

set down the carton holding a dozen eggs "Who's Kacy?"

Greg gave her an apologetic look. "She's Brody's eight-year-old daughter. A bit of a handful, which is why Brody has her for the entire summer. His ex needs a break."

She heard a tinge of sarcasm in his voice and sank down onto the nearest kitchen chair. Her summer wasn't going to be anything like she'd envisioned. It had just gone from bad to worse.

Jill was in the kitchen browning onions, sausage, and hamburger for spaghetti sauce when she heard a vehicle pulling into the driveway. She removed the pan from the burner and went to check on the arrivals.

Following Greg out of the house, she watched with interest as a striking young man climbed out of a black truck, gave a wave, and went around the front to open the door for his daughter.

A pink-sneakered foot hung in the air before the girl jumped down onto the ground, landing with a thud. Dressed in a pink-flowered sundress, she reminded Jill of a little doll with her light-colored curls and bright-eyed, full-cheeked face.

"Here we are," said the man to his daughter. "It's going to be a great summer. I promise."

"Doughnuts every morning, like you said?" The little girl, who showed the physical signs of eating too many sweets, gave her father a sly smile.

He shrugged as he answered, "We'll discuss it. Now, let's go say hello. You remember Uncle Greg, don't you? And this is ..." He stopped talking as he met Jill's gaze.

She couldn't help staring at his coffee-colored hair, classic features, and the smile that crossed his face above a slight cleft in his strong chin. A shiver crossed Jill's shoulders as they continued to stare at one another. This man's green eyes drew her in as if they were old friends, not people meeting for the first time.

"Hello. I'm Jillian Conroy," she finally said, feeling a bit foolish for the length of time that'd had passed between them.

"I hate the name Jillian," Kacy announced, crossing her arms in front of her body and glancing from her father to Jill.

"That's rude, Kacy," admonished her father, giving her a warning look. He turned to Jill with a smile. "Hi, I'm Brody. Brody Campbell, and this is my daughter, Kacy. She's staying with me for the summer."

"So, I've been told," Jill answered calmly, watching Kacy grab hold of one of her father's hands with both of hers. Recognizing the girl's claim on her father, Jill gave her an encouraging smile. "Hi, Kacy. I think you're going to have fun here. Wait until you see the beach."

Kacy made a face at Jill as Brody turned to his uncle and clasped him in a bear hug. "Hi, Greg. Great to see you again. Glad we can work together here for the next couple of weeks. I think it'll be helpful for Kacy."

"No! I already hate it here," said Kacy, her lower lip protruding into a classic pout that she obviously knew very well.

"Aw, honey. We're going to try our best. Remember?" Brody said quietly.

Observing the interplay between the two of them, Jill clamped her teeth together. The summer was bound to be even worse than she'd initially thought. The idea of packing up and leaving was tempting, but she'd somehow make things work. This was her own fault. She should've known better than to trust her sister.

About the Author

Judith Keim enjoyed her childhood and young-adult years in Elmira, New York, and now makes her home in Boise, Idaho, with her husband and their two dachshunds, Winston and Wally, and other members of her family.

While growing up, she was drawn to the idea of writing stories from a young age. Books were always present, being read, ready to go back to the library, or about to be discovered. All in her family shared information from the books in general conversation, giving them a wealth of knowledge and vivid imaginations.

A hybrid author who both has a publisher and self-publishes, Ms. Keim writes heart-warming novels about women who face unexpected challenges, meet them with strength, and find love and happiness along the way. Her best-selling books are based, in part, on many of the places she's lived or visited and on the interesting people she's met, creating believable characters and realistic settings her many loyal readers love. Ms. Keim loves to hear from her readers and appreciates their enthusiasm for her stories.

"I hope you've enjoyed this book. If you have, please help other readers discover it by leaving a review on Amazon, Goodreads, or the site of your choice. And please check out my other books:

The Hartwell Women Series
The Beach House Hotel Series
The Fat Fridays Group
The Salty Key Inn Series
Seashell Cottage Books
Chandler Hill Inn Series
Desert Sage Inn Series

ALL THE BOOKS ARE NOW AVAILABLE IN AUDIO on Audible and iTunes! So fun to have these characters come alive!"

Ms. Keim can be reached at **www.judithkeim.com**

And to like her author page on Facebook and keep up with the news, go to: **https://bit.ly/3acs5Qc**

To receive notices about new books, follow her on Book Bub - **http://bit.ly/2pZBDXq**

And here's a link to where you can sign up for her periodic newsletter! **http://bit.ly/2OQsb7s**

She is also on Twitter @judithkeim, LinkedIn, and Goodreads. Come say hello!

Acknowledgements

Every book is a component of various exercises, different pieces of work, and a whole lot of cooperation between people to make it happen. The journey is challenging from the conception of an idea to the writing of it, the editing and proofing, the creation of a cover and the production of an audio book.

I'm so fortunate to have a supportive husband who has become an important part of the business both with the financials and as an editor, a content editor I love and totally trust, a book cover creator whose work I adore, and a wonderful narrator of my audio books who makes my characters come alive.

Thank you Peter, Lynn Mapp, Lou Harper, and Angela Dawe! I'm so grateful to each of you. Together, you are the perfect team!

www.ingramcontent.com/pod-product-compliance
Lightning Source LLC
Chambersburg PA
CBHW052038240626
47153CB00006B/2132